DEMON HEART

DORANNA DURGIN
JESSA SLADE
VIVI ANNA
ZOEY WILLIAMS
GEORGIA TRIBELL

MILLS & BOON

Published in Great Britain 2014
by Mills & Boon, an imprint of Harlequin (UK) Limited,
Eton House, 18-24 Paradise Road, Richmond, Surrey, TW9 1SR

DEMON HEART © 2014 Harlequin Books S.A.

Demon Touch © 2011 Doranna Durgin
Dark Hunter's Touch © 2012 Jessa Slade
Heart of the Hunter © 2011 Vivi Anna
The Demon's Forbidden Passion © 2013 Dana Hamilton
Demon Love © 2011 Georgia Tribell

ISBN: 978 0 263 91392 7

89-0414

Harlequin (UK) Limited's policy is to use papers that are natural, renewable and recyclable products and made from wood grown in sustainable forests. The logging and manufacturing processes conform to the legal environmental regulations of the country of origin.

Printed and bound
by CPI Group (UK) Ltd, Croydon, CR0 4YY

DEMON TOUCH

DORANNA DURGIN

Doranna Durgin spent her childhood filling notebooks first with stories and art, then with novels. After obtaining a degree in wildlife illustration and environmental education, she spent a number of years deep in the Appalachian Mountains. When she emerged, it was as a writer who found herself irrevocably tied to the natural world and its creatures—and with a new touchstone to the rugged spirit that helped settle the area, which she instills in her characters.

Dun Lady's Jess was Doranna's first published fantasy novel and she now has fifteen novels of eclectic genres on the shelves and more on the way. Most recently, she's leaped gleefully into the world of action-romance. When she's not writing, Doranna builds author websites, wanders around outside with a camera and works with horses and dogs—currently, she's teaching agility classes. There's a Lipizzan in her backyard, a mountain looming outside her office window, a pack of agility dogs romping in the house and a laptop sitting on her desk—and that's just the way she likes it. You can find a complete list of books at www.doranna.net along with scoops about new projects and lots of silly photos.

Chapter One

Sharp dark eyes, sharp jaw, black leather and habitual stubble, definite bad-boy attitude.

Deb had seen him in AutoStock before. She knew that face; she knew that confident walk. She knew how hard she had to pretend she hadn't noticed him at all.

Even though his visits to the modest little business had grown more frequent as Ohio bike-riding weather waxed along with spring, it was still difficult to keep her gaze from following him around the store. It didn't help that he sometimes hesitated and seemed as though he might make conversation—although in the end he always moved on. With confidence. With that free-striding walk.

Except today. Today he pushed through the door like anyone else: with a hesitation at the stiff resistance of it, moving without the pent-up energy that so often charac-terized his walk. He must have seen the momentary drop of her jaw; he gave her a rueful grin from behind the black eye, the split brow, and the artfully bruised face, even less shaved than usual. "That bad, huh?"

Surprise, and surprise again. That he'd responded with humor. That he'd noticed her at all, after so many absent nods. Maybe that's why she warmed to him in spite of herself—in spite of the bruises, the sharp jaw, and the sharp look in his eye.

"You should see the other guy?" she suggested, and then immediately regretted.

But he only gave a short laugh. "Yeah," he said. "You should see the other guys."

Guys. Plural.

Bad boys, bad boys, whatcha gonna do?

Run away, that's what.

But he'd already disappeared into the back of the store, returning shortly with a trickle battery charger tucked under his arm. Judging by the awkward way he handled it, she knew his torso—lean and fit beneath that black leather jacket—had fared no better than his face. He blew out a breath, every bit as rueful as the earlier smile, and swiped the heel of his hand across his brow in a gesture weary and resigned.

"I'm sorry," she said without thinking, flushing as he dug for his wallet. *Just take his money, foolish woman.* "I just meant…it looks like a tough day."

He made a noise she couldn't quite interpret—but his words were perfectly clear, and his tone flat—not the engaging response from a few moments earlier. "Nothing I didn't deserve."

She couldn't help it. She straightened, throwing her shoulders back. "No one *deserves* to get beat up."

He hesitated as he gave her a second look. Deb's face also bore a scar near her eyebrow and her once-straight nose was now just so slightly offset. Even though her jaw had clearly healed, it still didn't sit quite straight.

Mementos from another life. He said simply, "I started it."

Of course you did.

She made herself take the credit card he handed her, casually run the charge through, check the signature as she was supposed to, and return it. *Alex Donnally.*

She hadn't meant to pay attention.

But his fingers fumbled the card on return, folding over hers—not quite letting go. She looked away from the register and saw by his stiff posture and his slightly narrowed eyes that he was distracted. She followed his gaze to the small parking lot where a cop car sat.

She knew the cop—an experienced man who often used their lot as a turnaround in this small, off-the-interstate town—a town close enough to Columbus to offer city advantages and far enough from that same city to give a cow-and-corn feel to it.

She made her voice matter-of-fact as she handed him the receipt to sign. "He doesn't come inside very often." And then, as he dashed off a hard-penned scrawl, "What did you do?"

She'd surprised him again, it seemed. "Nothing," he told

her, but the smolder in his expression belied every word he said. "Do you think he'll believe that?"

"I doubt it," she heard herself saying. "*I* don't believe it."

Possibly the bravest words she'd ever said. Aside from three others she had once also said: *I'm leaving you.*

Although those words had just turned out to be stupid. She should have crept out in silence and saved her bones.

The second time, she'd been smarter. And he hadn't found her yet.

Yet.

But here and now, this man only looked at her as if he could see right through her unspoken turmoil and truly appreciate her honesty. As though in some strange way, it had touched him.

And then he winced and hitched over his side, one hand reaching inside his jacket...coming out with bloody fingers. He glanced out the storefront window, his gaze grim. The cop had opened the door of the patrol car to rest a foot on the pavement.

Deb discovered her copy of his receipt crumpled in her hand, her eyes riveted to the blood on his hand. She made a noise—even she wasn't sure if it came of fear or dismay.

He spared her a glance as he gathered up the trickle charger. "Will he walk around the store?"

She couldn't quite grasp the question.

"The cop," he repeated, his voice calm but insistent. "Will he come in and walk around the store?"

Her expression must have been enough of an answer; he cursed, low and short.

"You don't look very good," she told him, her voice distant to her own ears. He didn't, either—pale beneath his bruises, twitching visibly in reaction to some jerk of pain.

"I shouldn't have come out," he said, as honest as she'd been moments earlier. "Damned battery's going, and I'll melt the Magna's entire electrical system if I try to jump her. And I thought the worst—" He stopped, closed his eyes...forced a deep breath, pulling his shoulders back. "Was over." He caught her gaze and shrugged, quite matter-of-factly. "Wrong again."

"What will you—" she started, and looked out at the cop, who was pushing the patrol car door closed.

He didn't let her finish. "I'll be inconspicuous."

She couldn't help it. She snorted.

He grinned back. "Yeah. I know."

She handed him the receipt. Skin brushed skin—too hot, as though he burned with fever right through to his very fingers—and her gaze jerked up to his. She would have asked *are you all right* but her body exploded into sensation and the words never made it out. *His eyes, up far too close and personal; his breath on her skin. His groan in her ear, a possessively sensual sound that played out along every nerve ending she owned. His hand skimming along her body, her hands slipping under his shirt, finding a trail of crisp hair and tight, responsive skin.*

She gasped and jerked away from the counter, stumbling back. If there was any consolation at all, it came in the utter astonishment on his face, the way his hand had clenched convulsively around the receipt—the way he seemed, for that moment, to have stopped breathing altogether.

But that sharp, dark gaze had her pinned, and it looked just as it had looked in her mind an instant earlier.

If the cop hadn't been on his way—

Of all the unexpected things she'd said to him, the next came the least expected of all. "There's a break room," she said, pushing the words past a tight throat; they came out with a husky edge. "It's got a door out to the tires. And from there—"

He flashed a look at the cop, then back to her, understanding. *From there,* an exit out back. He stood, caught by the promise of her next words—caught, too, by whatever impossibility had just flashed between them.

She looked into his sharp, dark gaze, as if she *knew who and what he was.*

Chapter Two

D_{eb}.

That's what her shirt had said, clear and plain.

Her eyes had been a different story—shouting out mixed and shifting messages. Light brown eyes in a collection of interesting features—a nose with a bit of a bump, chin just a little bit square, and a sweet and cautious smile. But those light brown eyes had done their best to hide from him, as they always did—looking away when he came in, looking down, looking busy.

And then, finally, yesterday she'd been caught in conversation—and to judge by her expression, *caught* was the word for it.

Never mind what had happened next—the invading connection of the demon blade. *What the hell?* he thought, and not for the first time. *What the everlasting bloody hell?*

It had surprised him as much as her; it had snatched him up and very nearly carried him away. The feel of her, so very real; the sound of her, right there in his ear; the very *scent* of her—

Yeah, the ride home hadn't been a comfortable one.

Not that Alex could blame her for her reaction—not for her previous reticence or her response to that startling moment. Any wise woman would run from what the blade had made of him.

The blade sat in its favorite spot, its favorite form— the Sgian Dubh. Hidden not in his stocking like a proper Scottish knife, but tucked at the small of his back where it somehow never lost purchase. And while it could take any form it pleased, when it pleased, it usually stuck to the basics—the Sgian Dubh, a basket hilt-sword, a dirk...sometimes even a claymore, but only when it was showing off.

All Scottish. Alex had no idea why, not during the years since it had bonded to him, not through the times it had pushed him, prodded him, shoved him into danger...saved him from it. Just as he had no idea what had made the blade, or what had made it choose him.

He only knew for certain what it had done to him.

So did Deb at AutoStock, to judge by the look of her. And she had helped him in spite of it.

Yesterday morning, he'd pulled into this parking lot sicker than expected, full of the blade's healing burn and too broken to fake it as he'd planned. Today he parked with only a fading tingle along his bones, a lingering stiffness in his muscles. He dismounted from his bike and stretched, glancing into the store to find her watching him through that big plate-glass window.

She instantly looked away.

"Not this time," he murmured, holding his gaze on her until she looked up and found him again, and her eyes widened—understanding the message. *Yes, I'm here for you.*

He flipped open the Magna's saddlebag and removed the flowers he'd brought—spring snapdragons and daisies, with the tough winged stems and delicate flowers of sweet pea interspersed. Courtesy of his duplex neighbor, a young single mother who'd come to appreciate that the nighttime prowling that had once frightened her did in fact help keep her safe.

Deb looked at the flowers...looked back to his face... looked at the flowers...and yes, looked away again.

He opened the door with a much closer approximation of his usual manner than the day before—but didn't get any further.

The formerly neat store was a shambles, wiper fluid jugs scattered and broken across the floor, the rotating air freshener display tipped over and tiny lightbulbs scattered across the counter.

And Deb's reaction to his arrival—that was more than just dismay. Her clear olive complexion was pale, and her hair—normally pulled back in a tumble of a ponytail, the offside part dictated by a cowlick in that espresso-dark hair—disheveled.

Quietly, he set the flowers on the counter. "You okay?"

She said, "You need to leave now."

"Oh, no," he said, gently implacable. "I think here is exactly where I need to be."

Her words came of desperation—and he saw it then, that she feared what he would only escalate whatever had happened. "You don't understand—"

"More than you know." Even if the blade hadn't warned him—and whatever was happening, he suspected that was because she was here—safe—with him. And that the blade seemed, in fact, to have some sort of crush on her.

He had no doubt it was responsible, somehow, for what had passed between them. No matter that it had never done anything of the sort before—although since the night Alex had found the blade in his hand and in his mind, it had driven him. From place to place, from deep night action to roadside rescues—looking for harm and hate and sorrow, hunting bullies and bad guys and evil. A vigilante, the blade—and glorying in the blood it drank along the way.

Not a thing of goodness. Just a thing that had found a way to get what it wanted.

He pushed the flowers in her direction. "These are for you, by the way. Thank you."

Judging by the blush now on her high cheeks, her thoughts had matched his, going to that moment when the blade had connected them. Then her eyes widened and she spoke without thinking. "You don't mean—that is, you mean…the cop…"

He offered her the faintest of grins. "I mean the cop."

But she winced, then, as the sounds of a break room vending machine under attack reached the front of the store.

Ah.

He reached for the hilt of the Sgian Dubh. It turned warm in his grip, reshaping—flashing a glimmer of blue lightning even in daylight. Deb frowned slightly, clearly not sure if she'd seen what she thought she'd seen—and by the time Alex brought the thing down against his thigh, the blade had rearranged itself into a stout collapsible baton.

The blade's way of showing off. Not quite Scottish at that.

"Stay here," he told her, not heeding the harsh edge to his voice, or the note of command he had no right to give. He didn't care.

"You don't *understand*," she said, more fervently than before. She did an end-run around the stubby L-shape of it and put herself in his way. "You need to *go*. He's here because of—" And then she couldn't quite bring herself to say it.

He got it anyway. "Because of me." He shouldn't have been surprised—he was. He shouldn't have felt the fury of it, after the number of times he'd dealt with just this— he did. He shouldn't have felt the weight of it, adding to what already lived on his shoulders.

He did.

"You need to *go*." She lowered her voice—wincing as the vending machine crashed to the floor in the break room. "Someone saw you here the other day. He wanted the receipt from your purchase—the address."

Of course they did.

She said, her voice even lower, "He's just trying to in- timidate me. If you go, nothing will come of it."

"Because you don't intimidate easily," he said, filling in those blanks.

Something flashed in her eyes. "I intimidate at the drop of a hat," she told him, unexpectedly harsh. "But I'll get over it." Her gaze raked over him, growing more uncertain as it hesitated where his eyebrow had split, but now showed only a faint gap in the hair. "Don't even think about it. I saw what you looked like yesterday."

"I got over it," he said, deliberately echoing her words.

"If you go," she repeated desperately, "nothing will come of it."

Another vending machine crashed to the floor—the soda machine, to judge by the tremendous bounce and rattle of cans.

Deb flinched at the sound, and Alex's temper snapped. "Something has already *come of it,*" he growled at her, and the blade latched onto his intent, warming to his hand in its baton form...full of guile and thirst. Leaving her protest in his wake, he headed for the break room.

Deb should have stayed where she was. She should have called the cops, she should have called her manager from his lunch run. She should have done a lot of things.

She surely knew better than to follow on the heels on the man named Alex Donnally—a man with violence in his eye and violence written on his body—even if it had, astonishingly, somehow almost healed from the bruises and cuts she'd spotted yesterday.

She found Alex in the break room with the baton held

low, his shoulders filling the doorway. He didn't give the corn-fed tough guy in the room a chance to respond to his presence. He said, low and hard, "If you touch her, you're dead."

A derisive snort met his words, and a midwestern Ohio drawl. "Like the other night? When we took you down? We could have killed you then."

"If you could have, you would have," Alex said, no particular concern in his words. "I'm telling you this—you don't touch her. If you and your boys feel the need to teach me a lesson, you come to *me*."

"*This* is your lesson," the guy said, and kicked something inside the room—a chair, Deb thought, flinching back against the wall. It was easy to picture the scene—beefy ex-football player grown into a town tough, his light brown hair shorn close, his features crude, and his expression full of the bully. "You stay out of our business, or we'll get into yours."

"My business," Alex said, "is to stop your business. Or I can stop *you*. Either way."

Who were they? What business? Surely she hadn't ended up in the middle of a turf war...

Another snort from the bully. "We can take care of this right now."

"Your choice," Alex said, and he went into motion. The guy shouted; metal clattered to the floor. A chair, plastic and metal, bounced off the wall and rebounded into those on the floor, a clash and skitter that momentarily overrode the impact of flesh on flesh—swift, precise blows, the thwack of the baton—a cry of pain and a moment of cessation, with nothing but heavy breathing she somehow knew didn't come from Alex.

"The other night," Alex said, "you had some luck. It won't happen again. The other night, I didn't kill anyone. I wouldn't count on that happening again, either."

Just as she'd seen, barely hidden in him at all. Violence in his eye, violence written on his body.

Deb crept closer, getting an angle on the room as Alex shifted aside, leaving the tough guy a path to the back exit. Alex said, "I know you don't believe me yet. But you will." And then, so casually, he crouched beside a spatter of blood—a glimpse of the tough guy told that tale. Mouth bleeding, hairline streaming blood, one wrist clutched in the other hand.

Instead of a baton, Alex now held out a knife. A little hand knife, antler for the hilt and a shimmery temper line along the spine—the details more visible from here than they ought to be. And though the guy stiffened, Alex only laid the blade of the knife flat against the spattered blood, even as more of it trickled down the tough's face and soaked into his shirt.

Deb frowned, baffled.

But when Alex lifted the knife, the blood was gone.

Gone.

"It wants more," Alex said, his voice gone soft and deadly. "If you catch my drift. So you go back to your guys and decide if this is really something you want to do—or if maybe it's time to get out of the prescription street drug business."

The tough gathered himself. "That knife," he said, spitting blood in a defiant gesture, "won't stop a bullet."

"Not if there's anyone left who can still fire a gun," Alex agreed. He stood up—stood back, while the tough guy straightened and, glancing warily behind at every step, found the exit. Took it.

Alex tucked the knife away at the small of his back, leaving only a diminutive curve of antler above his waistband. He straightened the chairs, pushing them against the wall to make the toppled vending machines more accessible—paying no apparent attention to Deb as she stood outside the door, stiffly clenching her fists at her sides.

When he turned to her, it was with an expression both resigned and rueful. He didn't say anything, coming up to the door—just stood there, his gaze roaming her face—hesitating at the scar in her brow, the barely crooked path of her nose, the faint misalignment of her jaw that made her lower lip faintly more prominent than her upper.

She couldn't begin to hide her response to him...or her apprehension.

The look on his face said he knew what she'd seen, and how she'd reacted to it. He reached out, slowly enough to make it all right, resting his knuckles against her chin and his thumb against the soft fullness of her lower lip, there where the misalignment was just barely evident. "I understand," he told her—standing taller than she'd expected, leaning just close enough so she thought—her *body* thought—he might just kiss her. And her body, ever so slightly, shifted up to meet him.

But he only said it again—somehow both apology and promise. "I understand."

And his thumb trailed away, and his touch disappeared to leave her chin bereft, and he left.

Deb touched the tingling spot on her lip. For the first time in a long time, she understood nothing of herself at all.

On the checkout counter, she found a business card. Just a number. Not even a name. On the back, it said *If you need me.*

She intended no such thing.

Too late.

The next day, she came back from the stock room with a box of fancy new super-chamois to shelve, and she found a daisy on the counter.

Sharp dark eyes, sharp jaw and lean, mean bad-boy carriage...

She tried not to think of the memories that couldn't possibly be hers, the lingering sensations and the yearning for more.

The day after that, she found a small cluster of delicate purple-blue snapdragons sitting on a local newspaper. It lay folded to a police blotter page, which held a description of a bust from the day before. A big one for this family farm town: a local cluster of young men caught dealing prescription drugs to farm town high-schoolers. They'd been caught on an anonymous tip—almost as if they'd been set up, said an unnamed source from within the police station. Except for several of the toughest members, who had simply disappeared.

Deb pondered that for a few moments—and pondered the message. *You're safe.*

But...

Violence written in his eye; violence written on his body...

The sight of a knife that drank blood.

She shivered. And she didn't think those missing men would be found.

And then she touched the flower. Gently. Absorbing the contrasts of the man...trying to reconcile them.

As if her body didn't already know.

Except when she flipped the weekly paper out to lie flat, she forgot about the flower. She simply stared in dismay.

For there she was, in living black-and-white—a picture she hadn't even known had been taken. In it, her manager stood before the checkout counter with arms crossed in a proud defiance, the chaos of the vandalism scattered in the background...and Deb, perfectly placed amongst it, a slender figure in profile reaching to straighten a display.

She recalled the reporter's interest, coming in after the cops who'd taken the report had left. She'd still been dazed—and she'd had no idea the reporter had included her in the token defiant victim shots, small-town vandalism making the front page.

A day of violence. A day of flowers. A day of revelation and exposure.

Flowers on the first day. Flowers and news on the second.

And on the third, her ex-boyfriend found her.

Chapter Three

Alex woke with a start, rolling out of the old twin bed with a flip that landed him on all fours, the blade already in his hand—*ready—ready—*

Nothing.

Nothing except the deep burn of a blade-borne healing lingering in his chest, sending him into a hard spasm of coughing. "Son of a—" one last final cough, loosening up ribs that had tightened during sleep "—*bitch!*" and he glared at the blade, watching as it shimmered back to the Sgian Dubh. Subdued. Replete and smug with it.

It could afford to be. It had eaten well this past night.

Only then did he truly get his bearings. *On the floor of the sparsely furnished bedroom...second story of the small rental duplex...going on evening. The day after.*

They shouldn't have taken him lightly, that crude ring of small-town drug dealers. They shouldn't have preyed on young people. And once the blade had tracked them down and put him on target, they shouldn't have upped the ante.

Not that the first meeting had gone well. Not with that foolish teenager diving into the fray to make good with his dealers. Fighting *around* him had left Alex vulnerable— had gotten him hurt.

But even the blade had no taste for a confused teen not yet gone truly bad.

His cell phone burbled, startling him. It had been buried in his leather jacket—and now it had a message waiting.

He fumbled with the jacket, groaning with the stretch— a fresh burn seeping through his torso as the blade went to work. Turning the healing hard, because it knew as well as he did that the phone call was likely to put him back out on the street. And because sated, it had the power to do so—and it didn't mind hurting him.

It didn't mind it a bit.

Demon blade.

He stared stupidly at the unfamiliar phone number in his caller ID, then thumbed the button to reach his voice mail.

At the first breath, the first syllable, he recognized the voice.

Deb.

And she was scared.

"Please," she said. "You said…" She hesitated, then rushed onward as if realizing the voice mail would cut her off. "I need help. I really, really need help."

Behind the bakery, she said, and he thanked his luck that

there was only one bakery in this small town—because when he called back, she didn't pick up.

"I don't get it," he muttered—to the blade as much as anything else, a habit he'd picked up quickly enough. "We took care of the town idiots already."

He hadn't meant to move on them so fast. He'd have preferred to wear them down, disperse them...to stay away from the law, which was too often a temporary solution. But once they'd decided to threaten him through Deb...

How they'd known it would matter so much, he had no idea.

Unless it had been the simple, stunned and wistful look on his face as he'd grabbed up his bike, the cop evaded.

She'd done that to him, all right. Months of glimpses, months of shared awareness and pretending it didn't exist— because she'd so clearly been hurt. Because he wasn't good for her anyway.

And then came that one touch.

What could be...maybe *what should be*. Thanks to the blade.

He jammed his legs into pants, his feet into motorcycle harness boots—simple, black, plain supportive straps fanning out from a steel ring at the ankle. He stuffed his phone back into the jacket, and ran down the stairs as he shrugged the jacket on, still grabbing for the snap on his jeans.

The Magna waited, ready—always ready for speed, if not cornering—although upgraded shocks and brakes had stopped its squirming, and the blade-given night sight gave him all the advantage he needed. He pushed the bike hard in the abandoned night as the sound of her despair echoed in his mind. The realization, as she spoke, that she'd gotten only voice mail.

A block from the bakery, he eased in beside the curb, flipped down the kickstand of the light cruiser, and jammed his helmet over the handlebar.

The blade said nothing of danger, and Alex made it to the tiny employee parking spot behind the bakery in silence. He could have found her then, but he gave her the control—standing quietly; waiting.

After a moment, he heard her voice—uncertain, wary... the fear trickling through. "Alex?"

The basement stairwell. He didn't shift to look at her—gave her that illusion of invisibility—for a bit longer. "Yup," he said.

"Get over here," she told him, the desperation clear in her voice now. "He'll see you."

"There's no one here." But he moved quietly toward her, taking the three steps down to where she huddled against the brick wall and painted metal handrail. Her light coat wasn't nearly enough for this brisk spring night; he pulled his jacket off and draped it over her shoulders, settling in beside her to take her cold hands between his own.

The blade would keep him warm, if it came to that. Begrudgingly, and not without its price, but it would keep him warm enough to fight. Its images of *could* and *should* teased at him, pulling his mind to touch and glory. He took a breath and pulled it back.

"It's 4:00 a.m.," he said, gently chafing her hands. She

didn't even seem to notice; she looked shell-shocked. "What happened?"

"My picture," she said. "I didn't realize—"

high flush over a round breast

"He—" She faltered, but pushed forward with determination, curling her hands into fists within his grasp. "Found me. He found me. From the paper. I didn't even finish closing the store. I just—"

gasping breath and grasping hands

She made a strangled noise. "I ran. I called Jeff to get the store and then I—"

body arched and smooth and full of curves

She sucked in a breath. "But I couldn't lose him. He just kept—"

a desperate touch, an aching cry

Alex found his hands closing around hers, his body tightening, his breath hard to catch in a way that never happened in a fight. "Stop that, dammit," he told the blade. "I can't think when you do that."

Of course she recoiled. *"Me?"* she said. "You're the one who—"

"You can hear that?" He couldn't hide his startled response—too far off-balance to hide anything right now. But he looked again and saw the brightness of her eye, the blush on her cheek…that she no longer shivered at all.

And he counted himself lucky that she couldn't see him with anywhere near the same clarity.

She said, *"Of course* I—what are you even doing? Don't

you even think for a moment—" and started to pull her hands away.

He didn't let her. He gentled his touch—not so needy—and he shoved the ongoing whisper of the blade to the back of his mind, letting his body burn with it—mingled pain and pleasure, thanks to blade's displeasure. "It's not me," he said. "I'm not—" But he stopped, because how did a man say *I'm not the one shoving myself inside your head with images of what I'd like to do to you and with you and the sooner the better...*

He tried again. "It's complicated. Let's figure out what I can do for you and—" No, too much double entendre under the circumstances. "I mean, let's get you warm and—" Damn, like that was any better. He drew breath to try again, and suddenly realized she'd ducked her head, that her hands quivered slightly in his. "Are you *laughing* at me?"

From the sound of her voice it was clear enough, even if she hadn't said the words. "Oh, yes. *Yes.* What else can I possibly do?"

"Great," he said. "All part of the service."

She snickered out loud. *"Service,"* she repeated. "Oh my God, suddenly I'm twelve again."

In that moment, he lost a little bit of his heart to her. Cold and frightened and hiding in the dark, handling an inner landscape she couldn't begin to understand...bouncing back to laugh at them both.

Shaky as it was.

He gave her hands a light squeeze and backed off, barely

encasing them with the warmth he had to share. "Start again," he told her. "Your boyfriend found you."

"Ex," she interrupted, her vehemence startling. "*Ex-*boyfriend."

The tone of her voice brought things together for him. "He did this to you. It wasn't a car accident, it wasn't some childhood thing."

"He changed my face," she said, bitter agreement.

"You ran from him," he guessed. "You've been hiding. And now he's found you."

She sighed, a weary sound—shifting the coat around her shoulders, relaxing slightly beneath it. "I don't know if he wants to teach me a lesson or whether he wants to drag me home. It adds up to the same thing: *No.* And *don't* even talk to me about restraining orders or police or—"

"Didn't even cross my mind."

She looked at him through the darkness—what she'd be able to see of him, probably nothing more than the vague pale shape of his face, his clothes blending into the night. "No," she said. "I don't suppose it would." And then, after a moment during which he digested what this was supposed to mean, she said, "Thank you for the flowers."

That warmed him, too—in an entirely different way. Sweet and slow, and entirely his emotion. "You're welcome."

"They weren't necessary. It wasn't your fault."

He laughed, keeping it low. "Damned straight they were necessary. Did you think that was just apology? All the months I've been coming in there and seeing you, seeing you seeing me, trying to respect that you obviously didn't want to talk to me? Did you think I was going to pass up the chance?"

Her mouth dropped open—she probably didn't realize he could see her so clearly, or she wouldn't have stared so openly, or bitten her lip, or let the truth of his words show through.

sweet smile gone sultry, lips kiss-swollen, hands closing around him with greedy familiarity

Alex made a strangled noise, exasperation and clenching need.

Deb broke free from the blade's invasion with a gasp. "What *is* that?" she asked, startled into blunt demand. "Don't you dare say it's complicated!"

Alex groaned again, biting off those very words and struggling for new ones. "It's what is," he said. "It's what will be. It's what *should*."

She narrowed her eyes at him, not knowing he could see that, too. "Does that line work for you?"

As if he could help himself. Or stop himself from lowering his voice to the rasp that waited to say, "You tell me."

She closed her eyes, turning her face away—and she swallowed hard, her hands tightening ever so slightly on his. She was well aware when he slipped a hand from hers—she tipped her head ever so slightly to meet his fingers as he touched her lower lip, caressed it—slid his hand across her cheek to cup the side of her head.

She knew it when he moved in to kiss her—with such

care, such restraint—hunting the slightest sign that she wasn't sure, that she didn't want.

Maybe she sensed that care. "Yes," she whispered, not opening her eyes.

Yes.

And there, in the darkness of the bakery basement stairs, he kissed her, and he kissed her well. He kissed her hard and gentle and sweet and long, and he damned near kissed himself senseless. Her hands curled into his shirt, around his sides—a plucking demand for more.

Which, in the darkness of the bakery basement stairs, neither of them would get. He pulled away, lingering for one more barest touch of a kiss, and he leaned his forehead on hers. "You tell *me.*"

This time, she didn't hesitate. This time, there was a faint, confusing touch of misery in her voice. "Yes," she said. "Since the first time I saw you. It's why I had to hide so hard."

"From me?" He frowned. "You've always been safe from me. You always will be."

She laughed shortly. "From *me.*" She stroked his face, fingers brushing stubble. "From mistakes I can't afford to make again."

His hand closed over hers, no longer quite as gentle— the meaning clear, the implications acknowledged. That he, too, would be a mistake. He slowly pulled his hand away. "Deb," he said. "Deb…"

"Marchand."

"Deb Marchand. What do you want from me, Deb? *If you need me*, I said. I meant it."

"I don't—" She stopped in confusion, and pulled his jacket more tightly around herself.

"Do you want me to get you out of here? Do you want me to take you somewhere? Do you want me to walk away? Whatever it is…just ask."

When she still hesitated, he said, "I can make sure he doesn't bother you again."

She stiffened at that. "You wouldn't—"

"Not like that." He wouldn't—but the blade might take advantage of the situation. Hard to explain in a dark stairwell.

She let it go, accepting the reassurance. "For starters? I want to get warm, and I want some rest. I want to feel safe while I figure out how to leave town." Her voice took on a defiant note, as if she was prepared for him to say she couldn't do any of these things.

What he did was stand, and hold out his hand, and pull her to her feet. "Then you will."

And she came with him.

Too good to be real.

Alex's warm hands…his warm jacket. His response to her phone call; his response to her kiss.

A man with so much heart, and yet so much violence.

In her experience, the two didn't go together. And the violence ended up directed her way.

"Okay?" he asked, and his voice still held the rugged note it had taken after that kiss.

Okay. After bolting from the store as she saw her former boyfriend's car slide into the parking lot—a predator, just like Gary Hines himself: gleaming, sporty, a growl in the engine and street car attitude in the details. The same car, nearly a year later. No doubt with the same handgun in the glove box.

She'd so hoped he'd moved on to someone new—that he'd dismissed her from his life—found someone new to woo, so charming, before he slowly tightened around her with control and temper. But in that first flush of fear upon seeing him, she realized how futile a hope it had been.

There was no way he'd simply let go of her defiance. If nothing else, he'd need to teach her one last lesson, leaving her bloodied and broken—putting himself back in control.

Maybe even leaving her dead. In her heart, she believed it of him.

Especially since he'd brought a friend.

So she'd run. It was a small town, and she'd planned for this; she'd known where to duck aside, and which sharp turns gave her the most cover on the way through the complex little warren of alleys. He'd followed her for a while—giving her just a glimpse or two of his black gimme cap and linebacker's shoulders. Right up until she'd hurried through the little grocery store on the corner, ditching out through the employee-only exit and doubling around to the bakery.

There, she'd lost him. But her panic still hit a high note, her plan to return to her car completely thwarted.

The bakery had put in a privacy fence since she'd mapped out this route.

A hurried scramble over a stack of pallets had given her the view...and the bad news. She'd have no better luck risking a dash to the Madame Psychic store lot to her right, or the tiny leather goods shop to the left. They'd all added fences, separating themselves from the residential yards backed up against their lots.

And so she'd waited to be discovered. Not daring to call for help as dusk turned to full dark, and not daring to leave on her own. Not daring to believe that Gary wouldn't, having come this close to her, somehow already be at her little rented trailer, waiting for her.

It had taken her hours before she realized she had Alex's business card tucked in her jeans back pocket; it had taken another hour to get up the nerve to use it, reading it by the light of the cell phone display. She'd called twice with no answer, and finally, finally, left a message.

Okay, he asked? She was nowhere close to being okay. But she said, "The sooner, the better."

"My bike is nearby," he told her as he headed out into the pitch darkness, sure-footed at that.

She immediately balked, unable to see anything more than the indistinct shape of his face—and then, after he turned away, not even that.

He came back to her with more patience than she'd expected. "Hey," he said. "Don't worry about it. I can see fine." He pulled her hand around his back to rest on his opposite hip, gently draping an arm over her shoulder. "Trust me."

She didn't voice that bitter little laugh—*trust*—and she didn't voice the relief of sliding up against him, feeling from his confident movement that he did, indeed, know just where he was going; feeling the warmth and strength of him.

Feeling his shirt wet beneath her hand. "What—?" she said, and started to pull away.

He held her close. "I cut myself shaving. It's nothing."

"I can't trust you," she said, finding that she had grown stronger in this past year after all, "if you lie to me."

He laughed under his breath, guiding her confidently into the alley and nudging a bottle out of her path with his foot along the way. "Damn, I like you. How about this— it'll wait until we get somewhere else. By which time it's likely to be nothing."

She scowled into the darkness. "It is just not right that I think you mean it. Not when you make no more sense than *that*."

"I know." His voice held both humor and apology. "Here, there's a pothole. We're almost—"

Halogen headlights snapped on from the facing alley across the street, blue-white and blinding. Alex cursed.

And then the engine gunned, and she realized what he'd understood immediately—that the headlights were no co-incidence. Nor was the familiar engine with its growl of power and anger.

When the tires squealed, she froze—understanding the threat. *Gary*. He must have known she was back in one of these alleys—he must have seen the fences. And rather than risk losing her as he searched the wrong back lot, he'd simply waited for her to emerge.

The patience of a predator.

I should have known.

It was her last coherent thought, as the car surged forward, headlights bouncing. Alex grabbed the hand from his hip, yanking her behind and to his right—a quick and startling surge of strength against which she had no resistance even as his left hand, limned a stark shadow against the light, dipped into his pocket and out again. She had the impression of movement, a whipping blow...he shoved her hard against the side of the leather shop and threw himself on top of her, grinding her into brick. The air left her lungs; her ribs creaked. Glass shattered, scattering around their feet—air blew past in a rush of hot engine and burning rubber, and she never even heard the brakes before the car slammed into the privacy fence.

Alex's weight disappeared from her back; he flipped her around to face him, and even in the darkness she could perceive the intensity of his expression. *"Deb,"* he said. "Are you—"

"Okay," she said, even if it was on a gasp of breath.

He transferred that gaze to the end of the alley, where the glow from the car taillights revealed everything she feared she'd see.

The violence. The willingness.

Even now, he turned to go for them, and somehow—
somehow—

No. That was *not* a sword in his hand.

It was *not*.

She found her tongue. She didn't try to talk him out of it—didn't try to tell him what to do. She simply blurted the truth. "There were two of them!"

And if she'd been thinking about the odds of two against one when she knew Gary would have that handgun, she understood instantly from the look he gave her that he cared more about the fact that one of them might reach her while he was busy with the other.

He slipped his hand around her waist and pulled her to his side—and suddenly she was running through darkness, clinging to him...trusting him.

Behind them, Gary's car spun its wheels, fighting the wreckage that enclosed the hood—pulling what remained of the fence down behind him.

They're coming! she wanted to say, and couldn't find the breath. Alex barely slowed to lift her to the bike, his left hand free once more—and she'd barely settled into the cruiser's shaped passenger seat when he mounted the bike in front of her, turned to jam a helmet into her hands, and fired up the engine.

She'd barely plonked the helmet on—too large at that, and half covering her eyes—when he accelerated away from the curb. With completely unabashed terror, she flung her arms around him, waiting for his headlamp to come on…and realizing that in spite of the moonless night, he wasn't going to use it.

By the time Gary backed his car out of the alley, they'd spun out into the darkness, finding an alley of their own. A dodge, a weave, a wild clutch around his waist, and his route spat them out on an abandoned street, where Alex accelerated into the night.

And, as an afterthought, finally flipped on the head-lamp.

Chapter Four

Alex took a circuitous route to the duplex—an older home right on the outer edges of town, bridging the gap between open rows of newly planted corn and the town proper. He let the bike coast to a stop and halted it with a final whispering touch of the brakes, propping his leg out to stabilize it as the other foot reached to toe down the kickstand. The light bypass sat firmly in the default *on* position, making the bike perfectly legal again.

She didn't release her death grip around his ribs.

Not that he minded. Her cheek between his shoulders, her body pressed up against his back, her thighs clamped around his hips—

sweaty, gasping, crying out

She jerked against him, and instantly pushed herself away.

"Sorry," he murmured.

She sounded infinitely weary. "What did I say about lying?"

"Ah," he said. "Right. Got me. Not totally sorry." But he added, in the silence that followed, "Not sorry for *me*. I'm sorry you don't feel the same."

"Bad boys," she muttered, somewhat nonsensically. The bike shifted slightly as her foot sought the ground. "Maybe it's me I don't trust, then."

"Maybe you should start," he suggested. He stood, and managed to disengage from the bike even as she did, catching her elbow while she found her feet.

"Where are we?" she said, looking at the wide, well-lit front porch somewhat askance. "Besides *not a hotel*."

"You said you wanted to feel safe," he told her. "This is where I can make that happen."

"This is your place?" she asked, and that disbelieving tone returned to her voice. The wary one. "I don't really think—"

screams and splashing blood and breaking bone

She sucked in a gasp and held it there. He let her get her balance, supporting her elbow, until she said, "What—?"

He didn't answer right away, absorbing the blade's message. When he spoke, he couldn't hide the new tension in his voice. "It's from the blade," he said. "It's *what is*. It's what *will be*—what *could be*." In her silence, he added, "It was meant to be a warning. A kindness, I would say. It's hard to tell."

"The blade," she said flatly.

"My knife. You've seen it. You have some idea of what it is. What it does."

"Your truths," she said, with no little asperity, "are missing pieces."

No doubt about that.

"Safety," he said, and nodded at the porch—one double door plain, the other decorated with a child-made welcome sign and sporting a pink girl's bike with streamers and training wheels. Flower boxes overflowed with blooms—snapdragons and sweet peas and daisies. "A hot shower. Rest. And then I'll take you wherever you want to go."

"I've never seen the Grand Canyon," she muttered.

"Then we'll go," he said.

Maybe it was the utter simplicity of it. Maybe she'd simply gone as far as she could this night. Maybe she understood the blade's warning.

Maybe it was, in some neonatal fashion, trust.

Except there, on the porch, with the squeaky screen door propped open and his key on the lock, she hesitated again.

He couldn't entirely blame her. He knew who he was—what he was. What he'd become, these past few years. And it was those past few years that gave him some true sense of what she'd likely been through.

The beatings he'd stopped. The killings he'd thwarted. The men—and occasional women—who had died at his hand, determined to turn their violence upon him when he protected their victims.

That's when the blade was the happiest.

a shattered windshield, a gun grabbed from the glove box, a confusing juxtaposition of faces old and new, all sneering...all full of disdain and victory.

The boyfriend was looking for her. For him.

He was looking *hard*.

He wasn't here. He wasn't anywhere near. But all the same, best not to be out on the porch.

Alex slid a hand to the small of his back, moving slowly as she stiffened—even more slowly as he brought out the compact Sgian Dubh—and held it out to her.

She returned him a look of utter disbelief.

"It's a Sgian Dubh," he told her. "It's at rest."

"Skain Du," she repeated, still in utter disbelief. "And what makes you think I want to touch it?"

He laughed, short as it was. "Good point," he said. "But you're safe from it. And it changes which one of us is armed."

She narrowed her eyes, there in the light where she could see him perfectly well. "What did you do in the alley?"

"Baton," he said simply. "Broke the windshield. I doubt he even saw that fence."

"Baton." She looked at the blade. "Show me."

He shook his head. "It's dozing," he said. "Better not to wake it, don't you think?"

She made a little huff of noise. "Tell me, then."

"Inside," he suggested, and presented the blade to her again, even as he couldn't believe he was doing it at all. It had tried to kill him once, on the day it had become his. Now it had entwined itself around his soul, becoming pushier as the days and weeks and finally years passed by.

It would not be pleased to be in her hands. He had no doubt it would make him pay.

But then, he paid for its presence on a daily basis.

She slapped her hand on his, picking up the blade—pushing past him to enter the house. He locked the door behind them. "I know he's looking, but he won't find you here."

"But tomorrow…how can I be safe if you're at work?"

He latched the door chain. "This *is* my work," he told her. It didn't trouble him to relieve loan sharks, drug dealers, and thieves of their money. "The blade and I."

But when he turned back to her, he found her a lot closer than he'd expected.

He found her drowning in his leather jacket, swamped by fear…and the spear of a blade pointed right at his belly. Touching it.

He sucked back that vulnerable flesh. "Hey, now—"

"Turn around," she commanded him, and her eyes had gone hard. For a moment, he thought the blade had gone to her after all. For a moment, he thought he'd done utterly the wrong thing. And if so, best not to resist at all.

But when he turned, feeling the prick of the blade up against his spine, it was her other hand that went to work—fumbling at his shirt, yanking it up. He knew what she was staring at. He knew, too, that it was mostly healed by now. The unnatural burn of it had faded; the blood was dry. So was his voice. "I was sleeping it off when you called."

"Sleeping it off," she repeated flatly.

He turned again, this time ignoring the press of steel against his belly. If the blade wanted to cut him, it would have done so by now. That edge sliced skin without so much as a whisper of effort. "Deb Marchand," he said. "This is the life I lead. It's what the blade wants."

"How can a blade *want?*" she asked, her voice hardly more than a whisper. "And how can you *know* when it does?"

"How can a blade reach into the now and the future and show us what should be?" he countered, reaching to touch her lip with his thumb. In spite of knowing who he was and what he was, and how much collateral damage he'd already left strewn in his wake.

"What could be," she said sharply, not missing a beat.

"Deb," he said simply, and slid his hand around behind her head to bring her in for a kiss. And while again he waited for the resistance, the denial...all he found was a hint of hesitation.

When she leaned in, he stopped thinking at all. He damned sure stopped waiting. He cupped her head in his hands and angled his mouth over hers, and all his careful intent turned instantly to need. Too deep for lust, too complete for infatuation. Months of watching and waiting, stoked by circumstances and the hot presence of the blade she held between them.

But far too soon, a phone buzzed—the sound of a no-ring vibration.

The significance of it filtered slowly into his mind, and his mind slowly overcame his body, and he ruefully stepped away while Deb struggled to reach her messenger bag and finally shrugged away the jacket to disentangle herself; Alex caught it before it fell past her shoulders, dropping it over the coat tree beside the door.

Deb pulled the phone out after it had stopped its fuss, and hesitated over it. "It's the middle of the night."

"Closer to morning," Alex agreed. He wrapped his hand around hers over the phone, holding it there when she might have put it away. "It's either a lot of nothing, or it's a lot of something."

"I don't…" she said, and shook her head. "I don't really want to know." But she thumbed the number to her voice mail, and tapped in a quick code number before putting the phone back to her ear.

And then she went utterly pale; for an instant, he thought she would throw the phone.

With his hand still wrapped around hers, he hit the speaker toggle and the button that allowed him to replay the message.

"Did you think I wouldn't find you, babe? That boss of yours was really accommodating. I think he might have warned you if I hadn't given him other things to take care of, but don't worry. He'll heal. You, now—you're a different story. Because you know what? You really shouldn't have hooked up with a guy who's already pissed off some important people."

She gave him a sharp glance; he kept his attention on the phone as ex-boyfriend Gary offered his parting shot. "You're not invisible any longer, and neither is he. See you soon."

She grabbed the phone back, stabbing at the buttons.

"Delete your ass," she muttered, and jammed the phone back in her bag. Then she said, "I need to borrow some money. I need to get out of here."

"Hey," he said, startled—stepping back to spread his arms as he might meet a potential adversary on the street. *Peace.*

"You heard him." Her voice rose into the sharp range. "I've got to get out of here."

"Safe," he reminded her.

"Nowhere's safe! He's hurt my boss, he's got my number—you can be damned sure he knows where I live! He knows *you*. Somehow he knows *you*."

"It's a one-bar town," he said. "It doesn't matter. I'm off the grid." He gestured at the house around them. "I pay for this place with cash, the utilities go through the landlord…even if they had my name, which they don't, they couldn't find me."

"I'm not taking any chances. You said you'd make sure I was safe. *Did you mean it?*"

Oof. Direct hit. "I meant it," he told her. "If you want to go, I'll take you. Right now. But there's safe, and there's *safe*. This guy's already just blown through an order of protection, right?"

She watched him with widened eyes, startled out of her rising panic. "How did you—"

"Know the type," he said. "The law's not going to stop him. He's already gone for your boss. So now he's got to keep looking. It's more than a matter of pride—you deserve it, for causing him so much trouble. You've earned it."

She sucked in a breath. "How *dare*—" and then she stopped, briefly covering her face with her hands. "No, no, I get it. That's him. That's what he's saying. And you're right. He is."

"So you keep running," he said, "which isn't safe. It just feels safe for a little while. Or you take a stand, and then you *are* safe."

"Oh," she said bitterly. "You say that as if it's just so easy. Don't you get it? *Nothing stops him*."

He gave her his darkest smile. "I will."

Chapter Five

Deb stood in shock, absorbing Alex's words—and fighting the impulse to grab his jacket and race out to the bike and *run*.

Even if she had no idea how to start the bike.

He spoke into her silence. He stood there in this mundane kitchen of pale yellows and little flowered curtains and cracking linoleum floor, with no apparent awareness of just how he filled it or how he *smoldered* while he was at it. "You need food," he said. "You need rest. And then we'll decide how to deal with this guy."

"But *why?*" she blurted, so suddenly at a complete loss—so suddenly immersed in the surreal nature of it all. Nothing seemed familiar; nothing even seemed *real*. "Don't even tell me it's because it's your fault he found me. It's not enough."

He gestured at her hand, where she still clenched, all unaware, the small knife. She lifted it; looked at it. A thing of beauty, it was, finely crafted antler handle, a gleaming blade with a dagger point, one edge sharp all the way to the hilt and the other fading into a spine with alternating grooves. A visible temper line marked the metal, reflecting faint layers of glimmer and darkness.

"Deb," he said, "this is what I am. This blade and I…" He shook his head. "I used to work iron—specialized welding for gates and furniture. Creative stuff." He shook his head, the smile wry. "And then this fellow came by and asked me to destroy this blade. I wasn't into it, you know?"

"It…" She looked at it again, turning it in the light—seeing the beauty and quality of it. "You were a maker."

Relief showed in his eyes, that she understood. "I don't know how I didn't see it in him, but…he tried to kill me with the thing, and I took it from him. Don't even remember how it happened, but there he was, dead. And then suddenly…well, the blade feeds. It *drinks*—flesh, blood…all of it. So suddenly he wasn't there at all."

A gleaming clean floor, where there had been blood.

She took a step back, staring aghast at the blade in her hand. The shaky note found its way right back into her voice. "What *is* it?"

He took a breath, watching that distance appear between them. *"Demon blade,"* he said, sounding resigned. "That's what it tells me. It *wants*. It feeds. And it finds people in trouble." He shook his head, then drove home the final truth. "It doesn't care about them so much as it uses them—an excuse to do what it wants, in the name of doing good. But Deb…" He took another breath, a deep one, his eyes closed, his jaw tense. "*I* care. And I care about you."

Temper flared. "You don't even know me!"

passion and need and curling warmth

It struck him as well as it did her—she saw it in his widening eyes, the body that stiffened as though taking a blow. But he managed a rueful grin in response to her assertion. "You don't think so? I've seen you in that store for months now. I know your smile, I know your eyes when you're lost in thought. I know you keep a mitten box for the kids in winter and that you help the stray cats in the parking lot. I know you make up discounts on the spot for those who need them."

Her jaw didn't drop, but her mind stuttered to a brief, astonished stop—the clash of what he'd just said with her reaction to what *was*. The *no this isn't happening* and *there's no such thing as a demon blade* and memory flashes of Alex holding weapons that came from thin air when all he ever seemed to *have* was this knife.

All of that didn't seem to matter as much as what she'd seen over these past months. "Oh, yeah?" she said. "Well, you're the one who helps people change headlights in the parking lot and who closes car doors for the little old men who probably shouldn't be driving. You're the one who admired that kid's junker…you're the one who always says hello to the dogs at the car windows."

His expression shifted—surprise, a little embarrassment…a faint sign of hope. He spread his arms—a gesture of surrender, a gesture of peace…an invitation. "Deb," he said, *"you're* the one holding the blade."

It stopped her short—all the unspokens in those words. *Trust me, as I'm trusting you. Believe in me.*

She swayed, the lure of him hit so strongly—sensations whispering through her body, that hint of what could be, *should* be.

"Deb," he said, ragged—standing there with the effort of restraint written all over his body—muscles tense, shoulders tense, a hard swallow in his throat. But giving her that first move.

One step, then two—and then the final distance, closed all at once. She lifted her face to meet him, her hands already pulling at his shirt; his touch drifted along her shoulders, skimming with restraint—down her arms even as their mouths met in a hard and seeking kiss. She gasped with surprise as that gentleness turned demanding, hands closing around her waist and lifting her right off her feet.

Her legs wrapped around his hips. She cried out as he met her with a shift, a jerk of response, and let herself fall briefly back against his grip—arching into him, hearing his grunt of surprise—secure there, leaning back against his supporting hands. He brought her back up and she wrapped her arms around his neck, tightening her legs around him.

He groaned and cupped one hand behind her head, angling his mouth over hers to gain better access. Her hair came loose from its ponytail and he threaded his fingers through the hair at her nape and—

Trapped. It didn't matter that she knew why. *Gary's hands in her hair, controlling her, forcing her, kissing her hard enough to bruise and bloody—then flinging her aside.*

She found her feet on the floor, her body ready to bolt, her mind already there.

And Alex, startled and wanting and yet...waiting. Standing, instead, with understanding in those sharp dark eyes. Standing, simply, with his hands out to his sides—that same gesture. Peace. Surrender.

An invitation to what could be...*what should be*.

Alex closed his eyes and thought about the panic he'd seen in Deb and marveled at the strength she'd shown her attempts to fight it. To come back to him.

It was the hardest thing in the world, to take a step back. To stay just out of her reach, his hands where they were, his body aching for the touch of her. To hope she would take that next step toward him.

She did. And by the third step she understood, and by the time they reached the narrow stairs, she no longer waited—she crowded him, her hands touching his chest, slipping in under his shirt, gliding along his flanks, his torso, skimming the waist of his jeans.

And so he led her, without once touching her. All the way up the stairs, down the short hall to the sparsely appointed bedroom and its twin bed. There, beside the bed, he stopped—hands so pointedly held in neutral, a little shrug in his shoulders. *It's up to you.*

As words unspoken, they came through loudly enough.

She pushed him back on the bed; he let himself fall there. And made himself watch instead of bouncing right back up when her hands went to the hem of her shirt, stripping it off in one smooth motion. Her fingers hesitated at the snap of her jeans; she eyed him, assessing him—and then smoothly stepped free.

Alex swallowed hard; he shifted, seeking ease and only making it worse—and knowing she had to feel safe. Without taking his gaze from her, he raised his arms—up over his head, as if at gunpoint—*might as well be*—and took firm hold of the bed frame.

Her eyes widened slightly; her breath caught. She understood the offering perfectly. *It's up to you.*

She smiled—slowly, a curve of that beautiful mouth from sweet to something else altogether. Alex felt it right down to his toes—which she exposed in short order, pulling off his boots and letting them clunk to the floor, running her fingernails up the seam of his jeans so he closed his eyes, stiffening against the pressure—forgetting to breathe while he was at it.

But he didn't move his hands, and when he opened his eyes and found her watching, he understood the test. He caught her gaze…said nothing. Meant everything. *Bring it on.*

Her hands found his waistband, played with it—dipping fingers beneath, caressing the snap, caressing him through the tough material and letting her fingers scratch the texture of it along the way. She touched herself, an absent trail of fingers down her neck, between her breasts, fingers spread across her stomach—her skin flushing, her attention completely on him.

Bring it on. Had he thought that? The more fool, he.

A sudden motion and she straddled him. When he sucked in a breath and lifted his hips to reach her, she gave him a sharp look and, reassured, returned her attention to his chest—pushing his shirt up to examine his ribs, finding the small raised tattoo over his heart that had come with the blade...bending down to lick it while her hair brushed his chest.

He squirmed. He by golly squirmed, and he made a noise he hadn't heard from his own lips before, and he thought, dimly and suddenly, that it wasn't going to be the first of those. Not as he squelched another impulse to reach for her, wrapping his hands around the plain bars of the headboard, pressing his head back into that flat pillow...just *feeling*. Hands and light fingernails and lips and tongue, as if she had to acquaint herself with every part of his body—following the contours of his chest, scraping lightly against the hair concentrated there and arrowing down his abdomen, and then following that, too. And all the while moving against him, taking pleasure from him, a silent and thorough conquering of his body—and hers. For when he opened his eyes, he found the flush gone high on her cheeks, her eyes gone bright and dreamy, and her mouth...

Bring it on. Oh, definitely a fool. She bent to lick a nipple; he sucked in a breath. She breathed over his ribs; he bit his lip. She slipped her hand down to find a spot beside his hip bone that he hadn't known existed and *ah!*—that noise again, and louder this time…a pleading note to it. She tugged his jeans down, followed with his briefs, and lavished such intimate attention on him that he gasped and clenched the headboard bars and turned his head to the side, and he made that noise again…and again…and again. Lost in it, lifting his hips to seek her touch when it eased, legs starting to quiver and sweat gathering along his neck and temple.

When she disappeared altogether, he blinked hard, struggling for focus. He found her stripping what little remained of her clothes—and while he sought composure, she dug his wallet from his jeans and riffled through it to find the emergency condom.

This so totally counted as an emergency.

And then she glanced at his hands—reassuring herself… reminding him. When she settled over his thighs again, the warmth of her, the softness of her…it nearly undid him. She made a soothing noise—an understanding noise. A confident noise. But no, of course she couldn't just apply the damned thing. She had to play with him, she had to explore the feeling of their skin on skin—touching him, moving against him…her own breath coming short until he did more than squirm—he arched for her, he thrust for her, he closed his eyes and gripped the bed and cried out for her.

Please—

He felt her shift, felt her hands on him, knew it was coming—and yet the sudden soft enclosing warmth wrenched another cry from him, and another, and then suddenly it was no longer her and him, it was them, and it was her soft cries mingling with his harsher voice, and it was her, gasping the words—the demand. *Hold me!*

In an instant, he released the bed and found her hips. He slammed them together, fully and completely, and again, and she made a surprised sound, a sharp sound, a sudden, "Oh!" and *"Oh!"* and louder, rising with it—and then a cry he only heard half of because she closed down around him, stiffened and quivering, and that unfamiliar sound burst anew from his throat as he lost himself to her.

Lost.

And maybe just a little bit found.

Chapter Six

Deb fell asleep draped over his chest.

Not for long, and not deeply. Just the perfect doze, flirting with complete sleep while perfectly aware of where she was. How she felt. Who she was with.

When she lifted her head, his hand shifted down her back—as dozy as she, and just maybe as dazed.

His image from moments earlier lingered luxuriously in her mind's eye—Alex, giving her the moment, giving her the control. The obvious strength it had taken from him. The trust he'd given her—and how it had played out through his body. The extremes to which he'd allowed her to take him.

I know you, he'd told her. In some ways, maybe not at all. In others…clearly so.

And maybe, if she had to admit it, she knew him, too.

So here she was with him, in spite of knowing who he was and what he was.

Maybe because of it.

Beneath her, he made a mindless noise of contentment, his hand curving over her butt cheek. She brushed the hair from her eyes, and hunted for a clock on the basic little bedside table. The glowing numbers confirmed her sense of early morning.

She also found the knife. Tidy, smug, and sitting beside the clock.

He responded to her noise of surprise, turning his head…grunting an acknowledgment from his place of contentment. "It does that," he said, and ran his hand over her hip. How convenient for him that he was still inside her, shifting to life again. "I shouldn't have left it downstairs. It's probably cranky."

"It saw this," she realized. "Everything we…" She couldn't quite finish it.

His eyes opened from their half-mast sleepiness. "Actually," he said, "I believe it showed us things that haven't yet happened. But we can fix that." He, too, glanced at the clock, and quite obviously made up his mind, reaching up to tuck her hair behind her ear. "We," he said, "will fix it all."

For the moment, she let herself believe it. And she let him touch her, stroke her, and worship her into a state of intense satisfaction, not the least of which was his deep groan and gasp of release, lingering in her mind to send her back to sleep.

When she woke again, this time from the most profound of sleeps, the day had grown into sunshine and a brisk wind moving leafy shadows against the window. She wore one of his T-shirts; sometime during the morning, he'd climbed back into his jeans. Not, she thought, through any need to put distance between them. More like habit. Not willing to have the day sneak up on him and leave him unprepared for—

He grunted, a surprised sound—jerking in his sleep. His hand closed on air, grasping nothing. His nostrils flared; his mouth twitched. He made a sound of distress and she'd had enough.

"Hey," she said, nudging him. "Shh. It's just a dream—"

He shot awake, his eyes gone wild and big, his breathing a gasp.

"A dream," she repeated.

"No," he said, and suddenly his expression reminded her of only days earlier, when he'd come in on the vandal at the store—when he'd realized the guy was still there. Sharp and fierce, a predator come alert. "The blade—"

"What *could be*," she whispered, and shrunk back into herself. "Gary?"

His gaze shot to hers with an involuntary abruptness that told her she'd guessed right. "Something's changed." He rolled out of bed even as he reached for the blade— she saw it, whether he meant her to or not, that he didn't grasp it so much as it moved to his hand. "Get dressed," he said, all business—if only he hadn't glanced her way, let the worry of it show. Let the caring sneak out.

She scrambled for her pants. "What?" she said. "What

did it show you?" Surreal to be saying those words out loud, as if that was the way the world worked.

"Here," he said. "It happens here. I don't know how he found us—but it doesn't matter. We won't be here." He slipped the knife in at the small of his back, and it sheathed itself on the way; his boots were a matter of *jam and stomp* over bare feet. "Ready?"

Ready? She laughed, short and dark. "I thought I was supposed to stop running."

He turned on her from the doorway, caught her eye— stalked right up to her. He didn't take her upper arms like she thought he might—that same restraint he'd shown the night before. Leaving her that space. But he might as well have, the way his voice hit her, his gaze hit her. "Do you trust me?"

It startled her. "I—"

"Do you trust me?"

She thought she'd never seen anyone as frightening as he was in that moment.

But she thought again how he'd given himself to her, how he'd made himself completely vulnerable to her touch and her whim and her need—and some scared little piece of herself crumbled away. This man, she trusted. Not in spite of who he was...

Because of who he was.

She stood on her tiptoes and quietly, gently, kissed him—right on that hard, grim mouth. It didn't yield to her; she didn't expect it. Not with the moment before them. But when she settled back to her heels, his expression had softened. He took a deep breath. "We choose the moment to meet him," he said. "It isn't now." He leaned down, took her mouth in a sudden, unexpectedly sweet kiss. He disengaged with a smile crooking his mouth, his face still so very close to hers. "It's not running. It's repositioning."

"I'll remember that," she said, and her voice barely made it to the surface.

She followed him down the stairs at a jog. He grabbed his jacket; she grabbed her messenger bag, and shoved her feet in the shoes she'd snagged on the way down. He stopped just long enough to rifle the cupboard for some sort of toaster pastries, ripping them from their individual wrappers and pushing one at her even as he bit off a huge chunk. At her hesitation, he said, "We haven't eaten. We haven't had enough sleep. These'll help for a while." He grabbed a quart of juice from the fridge, shook it up... drained half of it from the bottle and handed it over, too. "Fortified," he offered, so deadpan she almost didn't get the absurdity of the situation—almost didn't laugh out loud.

But she did, and he grinned back, a fierce and ready grin, and then he left her to check what was happening outside the front door

Deb finished her pastry, took her last gulp of juice, and wiped her mouth with the back of her hand. "Ready for repositioning, sir!"

He cast a startled look over his shoulder at the double entendre, quickly turned narrow-eyed and meaningful. "Don't tempt me."

She joined him at the door, peering out into that tree-

lined street—great overarching maples, straighter ash...
shadows and dappled silent and silence, even the dog
hushed for now. He nodded and they moved out quickly,
heading for the Magna at a jog. She stepped off the curb
to settle into place as though she and the bike were of
long acquaintance, finding the foot pegs and wrapping
her knees around his hips, so comfortably familiar after
this past night.

By then he had passed back the helmet, hit the ignition,
thumbed the starter, and shifted the bike from the kickstand. He glanced over his shoulder; she answered him
with a squeeze of her hands at his waist, settling in against
the square padded back rest.

She thought she'd remembered the bike's profound acceleration capabilities from the night before.

She was wrong.

She clamped her hands tight; she clamped her legs tight.
Then she panicked and thought it was the wrong thing to do
to a man controlling this beast, and she tried clutching the
coat instead, and then she realized he'd done fine with her
the night before and knew well how to handle the bike—

And only then did she feel the sudden striking heat of
the demon blade between them—feeling his reaction, his
tension, realizing how his posture had changed—that he
was looking—

She almost didn't hear the shot.

He jerked, a blow she felt through her own body. The
bike wobbled. It straightened, barely...heading for the
side of the road, hardly slowing. No curb there, just right

onto the grass, bogging down just enough so when the tire slammed the edge of a massive maple, it didn't crumple or shatter or flip.

Deb flipped right off the back, skidding across the grass...rolling to a stop. "Alex!"

She thought she'd screamed it, but even as she regained her sense of up and down, finding the bike and finding him half-pinned beneath it, she could do nothing but stare stupidly at him, air whooping back into her lungs only after an agonizing delay. "Alex," she said, and it came out as a croak.

How still he was, how crumpled...his arms flung out in rag-doll fashion, his body twisted around his trapped leg.

So fast. It had happened so fast.

She barely registered the crunch of tires at the edge of the lawn, or the slam of a car door. Only belatedly did she hear the footsteps coming up close.

"Stupid bitch."

She closed her eyes, acknowledging the defeat—her fingers digging into the sod as if it could anchor her there forever.

"You are *done* screwing with my life."

The irony of that forced a cough of a laugh from her.

He toed her with his booted foot. "I bet you thought you were safe. But you made a helluva mistake." He grabbed her by fisting the coat between her shoulders and hauled her to her feet; the coat cut cruelly under her arms. She wasn't solid enough to stand; he let her hang there, jerking the motorcycle helmet from her head and throwing it aside.

"It turns out that particular bastard already made himself some enemies." He nodded at the man beside him. "And you know the great thing about a one-bar town? You find all the right people there."

The man scowling at her looked not much different from the one who'd trashed the store. White, beefy, light brown hair shorn tight, T-shirt stretching over beefy muscle. "You talk too much," he said shortly, his gaze flickering to Gary. "Get her out of here. I'll take care of him."

Gary grabbed Deb's hair, threading his fingers through at the nape...twisting. She cried out as her head cranked back—a sharp and painful angle. But still she tried to see the tree, the motorcycle...*Alex.*

"What's going on out there? I'm calling the police!" an elderly voice cried out; a door slammed.

The local guy hesitated—frustrated, cursing.

"Screw Donnally," said Gary. "Hell, he's probably dead already. And I have what he wants, so if he's alive...let him have nightmares about what I'm doing to her. You can pick him off whenever you want to."

A glance in the direction of the voice and slammed door, and the local guy made up his mind. "Let's get the hell out of here."

Alex—!

Alex clawed his way out of darkness and pain, the knife hot at his back, the fiery burn of a hasty healing turned to a coal in his side, a warm flow of blood turning clammy cold on his shirt. The Magna bore down on his leg, pinning it with a certainty.

Shot. He'd been shot. And if he'd been shot, that meant—

He forced his eyes open, lifted his head…found what he most feared to find.

Deb, tears streaming down her cheeks, bloody nose and cheek and fat lip. Not so far from him, but completely, undeniably out of reach.

And in the hands of the man who had once thought to control her, and who'd come back to claim her. The wrenching angle of her head, the twisted nature of her arms…said it all. The anguished and silent word forming on her lips. *Alex—*

Beside that, the presence of the only remaining local drug dealer was inconsequential—except that it told him everything.

Not surprising that these two had found each other in this small town…or that they had acted on their coinciding needs.

But if it hadn't been for the blade—for Alex and his blade-driven crusade—Deb would still be safe. Hidden away at her job at the car parts store, living her new life.

Instead of turning into collateral damage.

Hell, no!

He reached for the blade.

Didn't matter that it was a small thing; it threw well and deep. Didn't matter the awkward position; he'd thrown from worse. If he threw with heart, he'd hit the target, no matter the sneer on the man's face at the sight of the small Sgian Dubh.

Gary's sneer turned to uncertainty as the dealer pulled a Glock from his waistband. "Don't tie me to this, man— not right out in the open."

"Not leaving him alive," the dealer said. "Go, then."

Gary didn't need to be told twice.

Neither did Alex.

The dealer stepped aside, raising his gun in a parodied gangsta grip. Gary jerked Deb around, giving the dealer one last annoyed look—and startling back as Deb came alive.

"I won't!" she cried, struggling in his hold. "Alex! Alex, no, don't—*Alex!*"

Gary backhanded her. He probably expected her to crumple, as she likely had so many times before.

"No!" she shrieked, kicking out at him, flailing at his face with clawed hands. "I'm—done—running!"

Gary twisted Deb's hair back, so cruelly—taking her down to her knees. Leaving himself fully exposed.

Hell, yes!

Alex took the moment.

So did the dealer.

The blade flew true.

So did the bullet.

Gary went down, astonishment etching into his final expression, the blade thrusting deep in a suddenly elongated spear still flashing stark white lightning with the change.

Alex jerked with the impact of the bullet, a deep wrong-

ness flaring in his chest. There was no burn of the blade…
no healing. Only the sudden awareness that he could no
longer catch his already labored breath, that the back of his
throat filled with salt and copper. Through the struggle to
focus, he found Deb fallen but free, flipping her disheveled hair back to find herself next to not Gary's body, but
the melting remnants of it…and then only a small blade
alone, lying naked in the clean grass.

The dealer didn't even look back at her—hadn't yet realized that Gary no longer existed in any sense. He stepped
close to Alex, his lip curled—the gun raising again, far too
point-blank to do anything but finish a job well-started.

Alex spat blood, sucked in the next harsh breath, and
glared back.

Deb made an atavistic noise, the snarl of a warrior. She
snatched up the knife and skidded it across the lawn, slick
metal on short grass—it found his hand, as it always did,
a gleaming flash of changing metal—ultra light, ultra balanced, whippy and extended.

Alex slashed the baton across the dealer's shins; brought
it back as the man fell, hands outstretched and a curse on
his lips.

When it came down again, it was sharp glimmering
blade, preternaturally sharp metal that didn't so much as
hesitate before cleaving flesh and striking ground.

"Alex!" Tear-streaked and bloodied, Deb flung herself
across the lawn, never quite making it to her feet before she
reached him—clutching his shoulders, jerking the leather

jacket back to find round holes and welling blood—touching his face, kissing his brow.

Alex coughed, a deep and tearing sound, full of froth and copper. He fell back against her lap and the sky turned gray and then dark, and her tears fell on his face.

But the blade rested in his hand, and it sang softly of *sweet lingering kiss and summer night and touching hands,* and he smiled as that darkness fell.

Chapter Seven

"They can't stop talking about how well you healed." Deb set a lunch tray beside Alex's bed, balancing it on two stacked, packed boxes neatly labeled in her hand: *Knick-knacks. Donation.*

She'd been clearing out what she'd made of her life here.

"Would have been faster on my own from the start," Alex said, eyeing the sandwich. He was hungry. Always hungry, since he'd come home from the hospital and the blade had begun the healing in earnest, able to work unfettered without raising questions.

There were plenty of those questions already left unanswered. A random drive-by shooting with two abandoned vehicles parked nearby, the owners of which weren't to be found...the cops weren't quite buying it. But with no evidence besides the disgruntled word of an elderly man who'd never done more than shout out the door at an unseen ruckus, they'd finally left it alone.

"Grand Canyon for me," she said, spreading a napkin in his lap—so very familiar with his body, so very much at home as she sat on the bed beside him. "And then Albuquerque for you. But still no particular reason for heading that way?"

"Second thoughts?" he asked, suddenly not hungry at all.

Not that he'd blame her. It was the blade, nudging him toward the southwest…tugging him. More than just the usual. But she'd been ready to leave Ohio behind—ready to run toward something now that she no longer had anything to run *from*.

Ready to start something new…in Albuquerque.

"Mmm," she said, and shook her head. "Not in the least." Her own bruises were long healed, her hair clipped back at the sides and swinging free, her expression relaxed. "I seem to recall seeing one or two *could be, should be's* that we haven't actually experienced yet. That knife of yours might not make the future, but it's damned good at nudging it around."

"Blade," he murmured, a glance at the bedside table where it lay, unprepossessing and silent. "Demon blade."

She frowned, a slight gathering between her brows. "You should have thrown that *blade* at the dealer, not at Gary."

He wasn't surprised at her words. He suspected it lay behind many of the small and thoughtful frowns he'd intercepted since the ambulance had deposited him in E.R. and the doctors had begun to speculate why he wasn't already dead. "Then Gary would still have had you, and I couldn't have stopped him."

"But you could have died! *Should* have died!"

Memories mixed with the lingering touch of the blade in his mind. *On the motorcycle, Deb wrapped around him, the quiet rural street unfolding before him, the blade's sudden warning...*

Could have been. *Deb, her neck broken, hanging limp from Gary's grip. Alex, simply broken.* Would have been. *Death clutching them, the dealer with a newly acquired blade in his hand...*

"There are worse things than *could have died*. Being in this world without you...that's one of them."

"Couldn't...shouldn't...*wouldn't*," she said, and wrapped herself around him.

* * * * *

DARK HUNTER'S TOUCH

JESSA SLADE

Jessa Slade always knew she wanted to be a writer. Her very early works include "MY POMES," a grade-school poetry chapbook rampant with unicorns and misspellings and a torrid tween cowboy romance which her editor/mother asked her to revise and resubmit, changing the "lovers" to "soul mates."

She lives in the Pacific Northwest where the potential for up to a hundred and twenty days in a row of measurable precipitation keeps her at her computer. Like many writers, she lives in her head, so appreciates interaction with people whose dialogue she doesn't have to make up and revise for clarity.

Prologue

The old Lord of the Hunt had finally unleashed his passions, and the *phaedrealii*—the court of the steel-born fey—ran black with blood.

The Hunter whelp, who was still very much leashed and would be until he had full control of his magics, crawled between the thin, grubby bodies of his young brethren, chained near him. They should have snapped and growled at him for such impunity, and he would have growled and snapped back.

Now, a few groaned, but most of them lay silent and unmoving.

The steel-spiked collar dragged at his neck, but the deadweight of his half-severed wing was heavier, though he tried to ignore the twisted burden.

The agony and dread were heaviest though he tried not to feel that either.

He edged toward the full-fledged Hunter, fallen just

moments ago, minus his head, hands still raised defensively. The Hunter had not believed he would be slain by his lord and master. Biting back a whimper that would mean his own death, the whelp avoided the head with its open-mouthed expression of shock.

The old Lord paced. The blood of his rampage was invisible on his widespread ebony wings, but the rusty-sweet scent swirled around him. The violent agitation in every boot step thudded through the ground and made the whelp quake as if his bones were cracking inside him from the tightly bound terror.

"You have brought this upon us, Queen of the Steel-Born, Queen of Lies!" The cry shivered the very walls. Mad he might be, but the Dark Lord of the Wild Hunt had magics to rival the Queen herself.

And now he had turned his might against the *phaed-realii*.

Too late, the whelp understood why the courtiers who had passed through the compound had circumspectly sought the Hunters' assurances that their Lord was not suffering from the Undoing. An Undone *phae* let his sentiments run amok, a lack of restraint forbidden since the Queen had ascended to the Steel Throne centuries ago. The Hunters had scoffed at the courtiers' fretting. No *phae* had come Undone since the Hunt began enforcing the Queen's edict upon pain of death.

But death had come for the Hunters instead, and the whelp knew the unabated gush of blood over his shoulder meant he was on the same path.

He froze as the old Lord swept past. His seeping blood

crystallized in jet-black beads from the force of the ancient Hunter's wrath when the *phae* bellowed, "Ankha, you vicious bitch. *You* were my Undoing! Do you hear me?"

"Lord Hunter, every being in the *phaedrealii*, and the sunlit world too, has heard you."

At the soft rejoinder, the old Lord turned to face his Queen. His fuming breath frosted the suddenly icy air.

The whelp shivered helplessly and reached for the ring clenched on the dead Hunter's hand. The steel band froze his skin as he tugged, but the pain of his ripping fingertips was nothing compared to his wing, and the amber stone nestled in the metal was still faintly warm. He clenched it in his palm and dragged his hand to his chest. The stone— the likes of which would have been his one day had he become a Hunter full fledged—returned him a small measure of strength.

The Queen glided forward. With her white gown and her hair in a white corona, she glowed softly in the whelp's fading vision. Her voice was softer yet, so the whelp doubted any of the *phae* courtiers gathering in the shadows heard her, aside from himself and the old Lord. "I will not let you do this, Lord Hunter."

"Call me by my name, my Queen."

"I told you I would not. This is why."

The old Lord's face twisted. "Lies. All lies."

"And the blood?" She lifted the hem of her pure white skirts—spattered now with black and crimson—to point the toe of her gore-stained slipper. "Also a lie?"

The tangled lines of his face deepened. "The price of true passion. Mine and yours, the *phae*'s…"

"The first never was, and the last cannot be."

"Without the Hunters to enforce your ruthless edict, it *will* be."

"No," the whelp whispered. Not that anyone heard him. But the Queen also said, "No."

She raised her hands, and the glow around her edges expanded like crystals of hoarfrost. Behind her, the gathered courtiers exhaled as she drew her power through them.

But the old Lord also raised his hand. Though the triangular glass sword clutched in his grasp did not gleam through the blood, its bone handle was as white as the madman's knuckles. It sang the hunger of the Undoing, and the song was sharp as steel, sweet as blood, bright as starlight in the deepest veil of night.

The whelp ducked his head down into his shoulders to block the seductive sound. The motion wrenched his wing into fresh agony, and he cried out just as the old Lord charged the Queen.

The whelp smashed the amber stone against his spiked collar. Light, shining like the sun he had heard stories of, burst asunder.

He cowered, as the old Lord whirled back with a surprised shout....

The Queen only smiled and loosed her power at the Lord's back in a boom of thunder....

Half blinded, half deafened, half dead, the whelp drifted for a heartbeat....

Until a gentle touch on his cheek roused him.

"Here now, you mustn't cry."

He cracked open his swollen eyes. At first he thought

the Queen, white and beautiful, had deigned to speak to a Hunter's whelp. But no, it was just a silly little *sylfana*, younger and smaller than him. Her short white wing buds, not yet unfurled, stuck out awkwardly from her shoulders, bared by her palest pink shift. Even at the peak of their power, *sylfana* could barely fly. They mostly danced and sang and flitted around the court, their laughter as shiny and empty as mirrored bells. When she came into her knack, she would be nothing but a reflection of the idle whims and pleasures of the *phaedrealii*.

But at least her wing wasn't hacked half through by the Lord Hunter's bespelled sword.

"I wasn't crying," he croaked.

She wrinkled her nose, easing the strain the Queen's draw of power had left on her heart-shaped face, and held up her finger. A droplet sparkled. "I won't let them see."

He looked away from the startling blue clarity of her too-knowing gaze.

Behind her, *phae* were milling through the destruction. Some of the courtiers had swooned, drained by the Queen's demand. No one attended the black-winged corpses though. Even in death, most *phae* avoided Hunters.

Except this silly *sylfana* who knelt at his side. Between her bare toes, the end of his leash lay coiled in the dirt and blood. How had she struck the chain? Every other link was pure iron, sapping his *phae* magics until he was strong enough to control himself. A *sylfana* should have fled, shrieking, from the metal ore.

Reluctantly, the whelp's gaze slid back to her. "Where are my brothers?"

"Five are dead, two stayed hidden and won't come out, and three are wounded, though none as badly as you." She curled her hand into her lap, her fingertip still glistening with his tear.

He closed his eyes. When the patrolling Hunters returned, they would choose a new Lord Hunter from their ranks and deal with the dead. And then they would deal with him.

A wingless Hunter could not hunt. A Hunter who could not hunt was…nothing.

"You were so brave," she murmured. "No one else stood up to him."

"I could not even stand." And now he would never fly….

"To fly? Is that what you want?"

Had he let the wistful words escape him aloud? He opened his eyes to glare his fury at her. "I am Hunterborn. A Hunter needs his wings to find what he hunts."

She stared back at him, idly winding a lock of her hair around her finger. The shining strands held all the colors of the amber he had smashed: copper, gold, and bronze. "Do you know what a *sylfana* does?"

"I know you'll never reach even the lowest clouds," he snapped.

"We have the power of wishes."

The whelp sneered as he had seen the older Hunters do when they complained about the *sylfana* who served a parallel court function to the Hunt, acting as the Queen's lures. Where Hunters were the bullet, the *sylfana* were the hook, wielding temptation and enticement in place of violence, equally merciless but masked in pleasures, the precise nature of which remained frustratingly unspoken around the whelps.

But for the first time, the whelp understood the anger—and the longing—in his older brothers' voices. He leaned away from the *sylfana*. "I don't need your wishes."

"It is not my wish." She reached around herself to poise her tear-dampened fingertip over the bud of her wing where the first scalloped edge was just appearing. "It's yours."

He shifted. "You can't do that. It's magic."

"Of course it's magic. We are *phae*." She touched the tight furling of white. When she lifted her finger, the tiny scales glittered alongside the salt of his tear.

He watched, warily, as she stretched her hand toward his shoulder where the joint of his wing had been so horribly slashed. He stiffened. "I don't think—"

"It's just a wish. Are you scared?"

He was. "No."

"I am. Just a little." She smiled at him, and he knew he would never forget the light in her blue eyes. "Ready?"

He wasn't. "Yes."

She closed her eyes and exhaled. The sweet scent of her breath and *phae* magic banished the stink of blood, and he found himself leaning toward her. She touched him.

The fire went through him in a ferocious blaze, a thousand times worse than the prismatic sword's edge or the Queen's thunder. He screamed but could not pull away.

"Hush. It won't always feel like this."

But it would. He knew he would always feel like this.

Chapter One

She wanted to feel it all. Her body burned. Sweat slicked down her skin, a sensuous tickle, and her chest heaved with each pounding stroke. When she gasped, the taste of salt prickled on her tongue.

Imogene *needed* her sunlit runs. With her body, mind, and senses so immersed in the moment, she might camouflage her presence from the Wild Hunt. The inexorable path of the sun, immune to any magics, helped keep her on *her* path, pretending to be a true inhabitant of this earthly realm—but for how long?

She wanted to run forever. That's how long the Queen's *phaedrealii* Hunters would search for her: forever. Creatures who stood with only one foot in the world's time had that advantage. Though the *phae* could be blithe and capricious, once Hunters were loosed upon the object of their hunger, they would never falter. The black dogs and their dark masters were so dangerous that the Queen herself chained them when they prowled her inner court.

The sun fell into the streaked clouds over the Pacific Ocean like a fading ember. Its glow burned a red hole through the veil of the blue-gray sky, and the reflection in the water rippled with secrets. A chilly breeze breathed out from the pine forest rising from the rocky headlands beyond the dunes. Imogene slowed to a jog and flapped her oversized T-shirt to let the breeze tickle her belly.

A creep of awareness between her shoulder blades made her glance back.

Down the beach, a dark silhouette closed the distance, tall and menacing. Her heartbeat ramped up again and all her muscles tensed. For a confused moment, a swirl like black wings spread above the figure, and even the ceaseless churn of the ocean seemed to hush.

Then the sun flared out behind the clouds one last time, and Imogene recognized him: just a fellow jogger she had passed many times over the month since she had moved to the Oregon coast. He waved at her again—not wings, just a regular old human arm—and she chided herself for seeing monsters in every shadow.

Still wary, she let him catch up. All the other times, they had waved but never spoken.

"Hey, I think you dropped this." Still a dozen strides away, he tossed something toward her.

Reflexively, she caught the chain that spiraled through the air. The metal tingled in her hand: steel. From a bezel at the bottom dangled an odd, blue stone—partly clouded but transparent in places with occlusions that caught and scattered the low slanting light. The pendant gleamed like a sky changing from the clear blue of day to the darker blue of evening, a sight she had longed for when she'd been trapped in the halls of the *phaedrealii*.

With regret, she shook her head. "Beautiful, but it's not mine." She held the necklace out to him, looking up.

And her breath, which she had finally caught, escaped her again.

They had always passed each other at a distance—part of her promise to herself to stay far away from humans on *this* trip through the sunlit realm. She had noticed only that he was dark haired; had a smooth, gliding stride that ate up the beach miles; and didn't usually bother with shirts despite the chill.

Shirts were overrated anyway—especially if they committed the crime of covering such a perfectly sculpted chest. The hard planes of his pectorals blurred beneath just enough dark curls to declare the undeniable presence of testosterone, and the narrowing arrow of hair over his abdomen commanded her attention down toward testosterone central.

She jerked her gaze up before she could wonder if the ripstop nylon fly of his shorts was rippling from the breeze...or from something else.

Judging by the sly smile playing around his lips, she knew he hadn't missed her once-over, but the confident tilt of his head said he thought he could take it. No doubt he got plenty of once-overs, not to mention twice-and third-overs. Even the haughty courtiers of the *phaedrealii* who objected most vociferously to the idea that there might be any shared blood between humans and *phae* would be willing to claim this one as kissing cousin.

The wicked edge of male beauty had carved jaw and cheekbones in bold relief from his deep-set dark eyes. Salt spray and sweat had frozen his dark hair in untamed tousles. Only the fullness of his lower lip seemed out of place, as if some all-powerful fairy godmother had decided this chiseled work of unassailable masculinity needed a touch of bruised tenderness and had taken a soft bite of his mouth before breathing him into life.

Imogene caressed the smooth, blue stone—still holding his body heat from his pocket—and imagined running her finger over that lip. Desire pooled low in her belly, warm and glowing as the stone. She curled her hand into a fist and crimped the chain in her grip. The slide of metal links through her fingers, each coiling into the next, echoed through her body. Her skin tingled again, not from the touch of steel, but as she pictured his big hands on her.

His jet eyes glittered. "Are you sure it isn't yours? You seem like you want it."

She wanted something anyway. For a heartbeat, she reveled in the sensations cascading through her. These were feelings the *phae* could never understand and would never allow. She would be able to summon this fantasy for months, forgetting the cold, remote, untouchable glory of the *phae* in this sizzling—if only imaginary—craving.

The Wild Hunt would never suspect such delicious longing in a princess of the *phaedrealii*. A breeze whisked past her, carrying the tang of ocean along with a hint of the man—a musk that fit perfectly with the salt and pine and coming night.

"I can't take it." She couldn't keep the deep sigh out of her voice. "It's not mine."

He made no move to retrieve the necklace, only crossed his arms over that incredible chest. A silvery ring gleamed on his forefinger. "Well, it would look right on you."

Yes, *he* would look gorgeous on her, she thought wryly. But she would never entangle a human in the dangers that followed her. She had gotten tougher since she left the hollow illusions of the court, but even a month of determined running instead of careless dancing would not put her beyond the reach of the Queen's Hunters.

"Someone else must have lost it," she insisted.

"Tell you what. You keep it, and I'll let you know if that someone comes looking."

She cocked her head. "And how will you let me know?"

"I guess you'll have to give me your name and phone number."

She shook her head. "I'm not in the habit of giving those to strangers." Names had power…phone numbers, not so much, but she didn't own a phone anyway. The *phae* often amused themselves with human toys, but she wanted only the brazen sensations of the earthly world.

"We're jogging partners, not strangers."

She wrinkled her nose. "Partners? More like two ships in the night. And the morning."

"But this time we didn't pass each other. My name is Vaile, and you're the first thing I see before coffee. There. Not strangers anymore." He smiled in a way that she thought was probably intended to make him look harmless. Instead, she was reminded of the smug wolf in Grandma's bed.

Despite her own best intentions, she smiled back. After all, she should know how to handle fairy tales. Besides, the *phae* knew the real story of that particular *volken*; Grandma hadn't at all minded being eaten.

"You can call me Mo. And I can't accept gifts with strings attached." She waggled the necklace so the chain swung.

"Mo? Really?" Vaile held up one hand. "Okay, fine. No phone number. I see you all the time anyway, and I don't think that necklace belongs to anyone else. High tide washed it up just to match your eyes. Pretty blue with a touch of heavy metal."

She slanted a glance at him. "Wow. There's a line. Too bad I'm not a fish."

His smile widened, and his dark eyes sparked at her with amusement—and a deeper, simmering heat. "So you won't bite?"

Her gaze locked on his lips and she sighed to herself. "Sorry, no."

Since her running shorts didn't have pockets, she slipped the necklace over her head. The pendant nestled between her breasts, warm through her thin T-shirt. While they were talking, the sky out to sea had gentled to seashell pastels. But the shadows under the trees had crept farther over the dunes, emboldened by the close of day. Rising above the spires of the inland pines, a slim crescent of moon failed to hold back the darkness.

Imogene restrained a shiver. "I have to go."

Vaile's expression tightened. For a moment, his features were as still and hard as the rock cliffs, and then he nodded. "I'll see you around then. Maybe I can get the ocean to find me a few strands of amber beads to match your hair, too."

She shook her head but didn't say anything. She couldn't very well tell him that her freedom—and his life—depended on them moving in opposite directions. Her midnight fantasies might keep her grounded in the human realm, but they could never be more substantial than fairy dust in morning's light.

She turned reluctantly to go, indulging one last look at Vaile over her shoulder.

He opened his mouth—that fine, fine mouth—as if he wanted to call her back. But whatever words he might have spoken were lost in a sudden clarion call, bright and sharp as a blade slicing through the night.

Vaile glanced back just as down the beach, from the deep shadows under the pines, the Wild Hunt burst forth.

For an instant, her heart flew at the sound of that silver-bell note, her blood sang with the wind of their coming, her pulse pounded with the beat of cloven hooves over sand.

Riding to the fore, the horned Lord of the Hunt lifted his bugle. At the klaxon, three streaks of mottled silver and black leaped ahead—the dogs, almost as tall as the Lord's stag. The first hound lifted his middle head and cried fury. Eight other hounds' tongues answered.

"What the hell?" Vaile stood facing the onslaught, hands on hips.

Jolted from her reverie, Imogene grabbed his elbow and whirled him around. "Run!" She took two steps, realized he wasn't behind her. "Follow me or die."

He glanced once more over his shoulder, and then he was pounding the sand beside her. Cold both from fear and the rising wind, still she felt the hot bulk of him as he ran.

Though slowed by the soft dunes higher up the beach, the Hunt was angling toward them.

"They're driving us toward the cliff," Vaile panted. "We'll be cut off."

Earlier, she had jogged around the headland through shallow water where a small river cut through the cliff rocks. At high tide like now, she would normally hike up into the trees to catch the road back rather than risk a scramble over the loose stone on the high cliff. But if they headed inland or tried to descend toward the mouth of the river, the Hunt would capture them.

Anyway, she would be captured. With the three-headed dogs on their scent, Vaile wouldn't be so lucky.

"You're faster than me," she gasped back. "Run ahead, toward the ocean. The Hunters won't cross the moving water of the river."

"Won't leave you." His voice was grim despite the wheeze.

"I'll lose them in the trees." Not likely, but at least he would have a chance.

"Won't leave you," he repeated.

They were closing fast on the cliff edge, chunks of rock under the sand threatening to break an ankle. The Hunt was closer yet behind them, and the breath of the hounds was an icy dread on their heels. The enraged baying eclipsed the twilight, rising to a hyena pack's gibbering cackle and promising doom.

Still, Vaile didn't veer off. The rock, brittle and gray, broke under their pounding feet. The scrabble of long claws hissed behind them.

Imogene sucked in a huge breath, the mist of fresh river water on her tongue.

She slowed by one step, letting Vaile draw just a heart-beat ahead. He must have sensed her hesitation because he looked back for her. The black edge of the cliff made a broken line against the evening sky just a stride beyond.

She lunged at him and caught him around the shoulders. Salt and heat exploded between them at the contact. The force of her blow knocked them in an arc over the edge.

Below, the little river glimmered moon-silver. The breeze skirled around them, as if desperately wanting to hold them aloft.

The three hounds skittered to a halt at the edge of the cliff with a howled chorus of rage. When she dropped her glamour and the illusion of humanity fell away, their nine-part harmony of preternatural wrath spiraled to the stars.

She held Vaile close and spread her wings.

Chapter Two

It had been a very long time since he'd fallen so hard for a girl.

And from his precarious position dangling two stories above rock and sand and river, Vaile thought it just might get harder yet.

"Don't squirm," his flight attendant warned. "I'm trying not to drop you."

"That's comforting."

They came in low and fast, skimming the river. Then his trailing legs caught a dune, and they went rolling in a ball of sand, seawater and swearing.

He staggered to his feet, instantly whirling to face the cliff they had descended so fantastically. The three misshapen dogs paced the rim, drawing back only to make room for the horned rider who stared down.

Vaile gave him a vigorous middle finger.

"Don't mock them." Imogene climbed to her feet a few steps away.

"Why? Will they do something worse than push us over a cliff?"

"Technically, they didn't push us. I did."

"Ah. True. But since you were trying to save my life, I forgive you."

She stared at him. "You're taking this awfully in stride for someone who just flew off a cliff."

"I have a long stride," he reminded her. "Plus, I have more pressing issues, such as the impressive amount of sand in my shorts."

Her gaze flicked downward. "Oh. That's all just sand?"

For a moment, he thought his cheeks actually heated. But it must have been road rash from the tumble.

She glanced away, brushing at herself. Along with the sand, she brushed off her T-shirt—all the way off. The cotton had shredded under the burst of her wings, and the sorry remains fluttered down around her sneakers.

Judging from the prickling heat that flushed through him, he had road rash all over.

She definitely blushed, raising one hand to shield her breasts. She had beautiful breasts, which he judged would fit neatly in his palm. The blue stone glowed dark against her pale skin. He wanted to lace his fingers through hers and spread her arms to expose her to the light of the moon, to demand she forget such modest notions after she'd so boldly defied their pursuers and gravity itself.

His blood pulsed in a hot tide through his limbs, roused

by her moon-white curves. A gentleman would avert his gaze; he decided not overtly salivating was concession enough. "Lingerie commercials aside, I suppose you can't wear a bra over wings."

"It does tend to ruffle feathers." The silvery white wings that cascaded from her shoulders to midway down her thighs weren't truly feathered, more like shimmering metallic leaves or the scales of a magnified butterfly wing.

"I can't believe you managed to glide us down on those."

"I'm stronger than I look."

"I am starting to see that," he murmured. The note of surprise in his voice should have gotten him a raised eyebrow at least, but she was obviously considering more immediate problems.

She stared up the empty cliff. "We have to find a place to hide. They'll go upstream until they can cross at the culvert, and then they will be after us again."

"Where can we go?"

She directed her clear blue gaze to him. "Don't you want to know what they are or what they want?"

"They are bad news. They want you. I am in their way." He ticked off the points on his fingers. "I was focusing on the important stuff."

She pursed her lips. "You were focusing on my breasts."

"Important stuff," he reiterated. He flashed her a lazy smile.

Another blow from the horn—farther away, but still too close—shivered each grain of sand and droplet of water so that the beach scintillated with uncanny brilliance. The otherworldly beauty froze his smile in place.

"The Hunters are coming fast," she whispered. She stepped closer to him. He breathed the scent of her, wild and heady, like a rare flower that shouldn't exist trapped here between bare rock and vast ocean.

"There is no place to hide." He didn't bother whispering.

"In plain sight." She took another step closer. Even streaked with sand, with her red-gold hair roughed into standing waves and her wings tucked demurely behind her, she shone almost too pure for his gaze.

His hands twitched, reaching out to her of their own accord—wanting.

She gazed up at him with glimmering gemstone eyes. "Do you trust me?"

How could she ask that, when he was the one with his hands settling at the tender junction of her neck and shoulders, just above her bare breasts and her delicate wings? He brushed his thumb along the line of her jaw and felt her tremble.

Afraid, was she? Of the Hunters following? Of him or of herself?

"I just jumped off a cliff with you," he reminded her in a ragged voice. "And I didn't scream at all."

"Then kiss me."

His stroking thumb stilled. "Kiss you? Here? Now?" Even with those furious Hunters on their path, his heart had not hammered as painfully as it did now. "But—"

"Kiss me." Her voice quivered then smoothed, like

bright quartz pebbles turning over in a gentle wave. Helplessly, his body swayed toward her, drawn by the undertow. "Kiss me as if there is no room even for moonlight between us, as if we have only one breath to share. Kiss me now."

Before she finished speaking, his lowered his mouth over her parted lips and did as she commanded.

Ah, sweet good night! She was *more* than he had dreamed. Every time they had passed, with every fleeting glance, she had thrown one more loop of mystery around him. Now he had her in his arms, and he would finally have his answers.

She tasted of forbidden yearnings, of sunlight that made the shadows deeper. He curled his fingers in the fall of her hair, and the silky caress over the backs of his knuckles set his every nerve ablaze.

He drew her close against his body until the pendant ground into his breastbone. The twinge distracted him, and he tried to gentle his grasp. It was too much too soon. But she gripped his biceps and drew herself up to her tiptoes, surfing his chest like a perfect breaking swell.

Her tongue teased his. Yeah, something was definitely swelling.... He returned the favor, tracing the slick inner curve of her out-thrust lip. He nipped gently, and her grip tightened on his arms.

She pulled back just a bit. Her eyes, searching his, were wide enough to catch a last spear of moonlight just before the clouds closed entirely.

He stroked one finger down her exposed spine. Beneath his calloused palm, the trailing edge of her wing was softer than velvet. He rubbed the scalloped bottom, amazed how the tissue-thin substance flexed with curious strength against his gentle tug, as if at the memory of a restless wind. The sensation delighted him on some deep level. The feeling was obviously mutual because she closed her eyes and swayed into him.

He caressed her wing again in one long, slow sweep from shoulder blade to backside. His fingers were faintly slicked with a silvery powder that smelled like sex; as if she wasn't irresistible enough, her wings cast off an aphrodisiac.

He closed his eyes briefly, struggling to find his control even though the musk of arousal was pushing him toward an edge with a sharper drop than the other cliff she'd pushed them over. "Do you want me to stop?"

She shuddered. No, the movement wasn't hers. The sand beneath their feet quaked. Their pursuers were coming closer.

"Don't stop!" A chill mist rose around them, and her cry twisted in a desperate plume.

He gathered her closer. His shoulders stiffened as if he could warn off all that threatened her with his possessive stance. Even as he claimed her for himself, he understood why the Hunters would never stop searching; with the silver glow of her spirit and the sky-blue sparkle of her eyes, she was too precious to lose.

The pounding of hoofbeats echoed in his ears, along with the sound of hungry hounds panting....

Or maybe that was just him.

He flattened one hand against her back to brace her and then bent her gently to trail his lips down her neck. The slender arch of her throat trembled under his mouth with the resonance of her breathy moan. He inhaled the earthy perfume of salt and damp sand and rousing flesh. His own shaky exhale unfurled like dragon smoke across her skin.

The mist had thickened and coiled in sinister figures, half seen and menacing...ravenous and seeking.

Well, they could back the hell off; he already had her.

The pendant had slipped off center and the V of the chain arrowed over her left breast. He framed the lower curve of her breast between his thumb and forefinger and plumped the flesh until the blue stone shifted over the darkening skin of her nipple. She moaned again as he pressed his lips to the center of the V, just off the upper swell of her breast where her heartbeat matched itself to his.

"I refuse to scream 'Mo' when I come," he whispered. "Give me your real name,"

She shook her head fretfully. "Who said you are going to come? And my name doesn't matter."

"It does to me." He looked at her. The cold nipped at the moisture of her skin, dampening his lips.

"Imogene," she gasped. "Just don't stop."

He dipped his head again and laughed against her flesh. His lower lip brushed over the steel and closed on her puckered flesh. He traced his tongue in a slow circle around her nipple, drawing the peaked pebble deeper into his mouth.

She moaned and threaded her fingers through his hair, holding him close.

Around them, the shadows shifted in vain, as if casting around for something gone missing. Vaile closed his eyes and ignored the cold darkness that pulsed around them in favor of the vibrant warmth beneath his hands.

His body shifted in response to each minute motion of hers, like a dance. She tilted her shoulder, and he suckled at her other breast. She angled one foot back to take his weight, and he nudged his knee between her legs. The wispy fabric of her shorts slipped over his thigh, less obtrusive than even the sheerest bedsheets. He might as well be naked for all the modesty his own shorts offered.

As if she'd read his thoughts—certainly she could not mistake his interest—her hands slipped along his shoulders and down his arms to settle just above his hip bones. Another scant inch and she could slip down his waistband.

Instead, she pushed him back. "Vaile." Her voice was hoarse. "They're gone. You can stop now."

He kept his feet planted in the sand. "I'm not sure I can."

"You will. You are not like them."

The words doused his ardor like a sneaker wave. He straightened and let the leverage of her hands set him back a step.

As if the same invisible wave had cleared the shadows, the moon was back. The clouds had parted. The coiling mist was nowhere to be seen. "You are too cruel."

"I used to be, but I am trying to change that." She lowered her head. The moonlight glimmered on her wings as she pulled the forward segments around her ribs to hide herself. The short drape left her shoulders bare and a deep exposed V from neck to navel. The blue stone dangled like a hypnotist's charm in the shadow between her breasts.

He dragged his gaze away and ran his fingers through his hair. The harsh rake didn't erase the sensation of her hands clutching his head as she arched beneath his mouth.

"Damn," he muttered.

"You're safe now. They are too arrogant to double back; they will never believe they overlooked us."

"They were right on top of us." Almost as close as he'd been on her. "A kiss made us invisible?" Of course, it had been more than a kiss.

"They weren't looking for two enraptured lovers on the beach. They are hunting a rebellious *sylfana*." She clutched the folds of her wings tighter without looking up. "A *sylfana* is a heartless, useless *phae* princess, cold as ice over stone, inhuman, unfeeling."

He reached out to touch her averted face and tipped her chin up to meet her gaze. "But you hid us—which was quite useful, I think—and they didn't see, so you must have felt something."

Her eyes caught the moonlight. "I could not lie about that."

"From the stories I remember, fairies lie all the time."

"Not when you get ahold of them. Skin to skin, they must tell the truth—if you can find the skin—the truth—under their glamour. But then you can never let them go."

"I'm not holding you now," he pointed out.

"No." Regret throbbed in her voice. "Which is why I have to go. The Hunters might not return tonight, but tomorrow when the sun sets, they will come again and try to catch my scent." Slowly, she reached up to touch his jaw, echoing his caress. "I might not be able to protect you again."

"Since when is protection in the job description of fairy princesses?"

"It isn't." Her hand slipped down his chest to rest above his heart. "Usually *sylfana* lead men out of the sunlit realm and into our Queen's court of illusions where you are summarily devoured, in more ways than one. But I will not do that—will not *be* that—anymore."

"Brave of you to fight them."

She gave a harsh laugh and fisted her hand on his chest. "Brave? Not me."

"Then if the Hunters come back, I will just have to kiss you again." Frustration made the promise sound vaguely threatening.

But she shook her head. "Not *if* they come back…*when*. They are relentless. I will never truly escape them. And they mustn't find you with me. It is too dangerous."

"Maybe I am dangerous too."

A wobbling smile tilted her lips. "I will keep that in mind."

"At least let me walk you home. If you're wrong and they do come back, I—" he swallowed hard "—suppose I can sacrifice my virtue for you."

This time, she laughed softly. The sound lifted his heart in ways her wings hadn't. "My noble knight. Where is your shining armor?"

Fifty pounds of steel would be no protection from her smile. "Must have left it in my other pants pocket. Which way are we going?"

She studied him pensively, and for a moment, the breath caught in his throat. His skin tightened, as if she was looking through his nakedness. Then she nodded. "Just for tonight."

And he told himself one night was all that he wanted.

Chapter Three

Imogene guided Vaile by the faint, tricky light of the will-o'-the-wisps that winked and teased amid the towering trees. When they had crossed into the primeval forest, he had laced his fingers through hers and stayed close at her side.

The forest rose, cathedral silent, on all sides. Once upon a time, she had played like this with her *sylfana* sisters, leading human males astray with sparkling lights and lilting voices in the darkness. It had all been mere mischief, a fleeting entertainment, hardly worth the remembering. Except now she knew sometimes the bewitched and bewildered humans never found their way out again.

The ring on Vaile's forefinger was a thick band in her grasp. The touch of the steel made her shiver a little—just enough to remind her that she was not and could never be human.

How many bones moldered unfound because of her? The

thought wrenched a shuddering breath from her belly. Not that the exact number mattered. When the Hunters found her, she would pay for her desires just as the human men had: with her life.

Vaile squeezed her hand. The warmth of his fingers seemed to trickle through her veins. "Are we getting close? You must be tired, and my shoes are soaked."

She knew her *phae* vision was sharper than his, making the shadowy forest less daunting, but his concern for her made her feel delicate and cherished—like a true princess must feel. "Almost there. I came to this place because of all the rain. Water runs everywhere here."

"And you said the Hunters won't cross moving water."

She nodded. "That is why I took a cabin surrounded by streams." She tugged him onward. "There. See the bridge? That's the only way onto my island. At least I'll have some warning when they come."

Where the rickety bridge and stream had carved out an opening in the forest canopy, a blooming cherry tree struggled to make a place for itself between the dark pines. At the bridge, he tugged her to a halt on the mossy wooden planks. "And what will you do with that warning?"

He pitched the question as if merely curious, but she heard the anger in the rumble underneath. "I can't hope to stop them forever, but I will not let them take me back."

"What are you saying?"

She set her jaw. "I can't explain the *phaedrealii* to you."

He gripped her arms and stared his command into her eyes. "Nothing is worth killing yourself."

"Exactly."

"Right." He blinked and released her. "Well, that was easier than I thought it would be."

She rubbed her arms where the hot echo of his grasp was fading. "I mean *nothing* is exactly why I'd…why I won't go back. The court life of a *sylfana* is nothing but a timeless, thoughtless mist of idle pleasures."

Vaile's lips twisted. "Sorry to sound dim, but I'm not seeing the downside of eternal beauty and bliss."

She didn't return the wry smile. "Our life span runs centuries longer than humans', but we aren't immortal. It just *seems* like forever."

"Right. Now I see how suicide is your only other option."

She squared her shoulders, though her conviction wasn't quite strong enough to tighten her wings. "Many humans are driven mad by a single night in our presence. And I think even my own people have not entirely escaped that fate. Your poets call us merciless. Your church calls us devils. Your adults call us bedtime stories. I just wanted to live for a little while. Simply…*live*."

"And fairy princesses aren't allowed to live?"

"They won't let me have what they are too afraid to want for themselves. Even those of us who walk in your world for a while always return to the court. In the end, we lock ourselves away from what we most desire."

"Maybe they have a reason to be afraid."

She stared at him, trying to see past the rigid lines of his expression. But she'd never been strong enough to break anyone else's illusions. "A man who dives off cliffs with strange fairies doesn't know the meaning of fear."

"Oh, I have fears." He stepped closer to her, so close that a kiss was almost fated.

She tilted her face up. "I can't imagine."

"I was afraid I would never have the nerve to catch you on that beach. I was afraid I'd spend the rest of my life with the image of you running away from me." In the murk, his pupils were blown wide, like a night-stalking predator, but his smile—the quirk of that soft, full lip—was a temptation she couldn't resist. "And right now, I'm afraid you're not going to ask me in."

So close he stood and yet he didn't touch her, but the memory of his kiss, of his hands roaming her skin and her wings, clouded her mind like the Lord Hunter's confusing mist. She had no doubt Vaile's mouth could lead her astray.

And maybe this time, she deserved it.

She wavered toward him. The cherry tree shivered in the breeze, and pale blossoms drifted around them. The will-o'-the-wisps danced between, illuminating the petals.

Vaile's lips—which she was watching very closely—quirked. "See? Even the tree gives its blessing."

"That was just me." He wasn't even touching her, but she felt compelled to tell him. "The *phae* are mostly illusions and lies, but we all have one gift, a knack, that is real and true. Mine is an affinity for breezes. They bring me sweet scents and little presents, like the cherry blossoms. Nothing powerful. The *sylfana* rarely are." She closed her eyes. "Your knack seems to be making me babble."

"Like the brook under the bridge," he agreed.

"Sorry." She bit her lip.

"Don't be. I want to know more about you."

"We don't share, usually. According to your fairy tales, we won't say our names—and we are private about that, because words have power—but it is our knack that reveals our true selves. Telling our knack is more intimate than…" This time she managed to stop herself before she said something embarrassing.

But the breeze fluttered around his shorts again. He glanced down. "The wind brings you *little* presents, huh? Should I be offended?"

"I couldn't say. I would need to find out, first, which parts are real…" She clamped her hand over her mouth. "Babbling," she muttered behind her palm.

One more half step brought him closer still, so that the circling breeze carried the fall of cherry blossoms in a helix around them both.

He tilted his head in the opposite direction of his crooked smile, giving him a charming-bordering-on-roguish air. "Your cheeks blush petal-pink. What other parts of you do that?" He reached out to pluck a blossom from the swirling air and tucked it behind her ear. "I suppose I'll need to find what is real and true myself."

She took his hand and led him through the fall of petals. "Then come in."

She let him use the cramped shower in the minuscule bathroom. After ducking under the low lintel of the front door, he'd taken one look around the A-frame cottage's tiny confines and asked, "Do the seven dwarfs live here too?"

Outside the bathroom door, she left him her baggiest pair of boy's jeans—and her silly *sylfana* sisters thought diaphanous gowns of spider silk were comfortable—before she stepped out onto the back patio with its ancient wooden picnic table to shake the last of the sand from her wings. One whisper to the night breeze carried the dust away. Thanks to her knack, this fairy princess didn't need showers.

What a pity.

While she nibbled on a piece of a chocolate bar, she imagined the water coursing down the hard planes of Vaile's chest, feathering rivulets through the rings of his hair like the streams coursed through the dark woods. Down the water would go, around the pillar of his... In the cottage, the pipes groaned before she could.

By the time he stepped out to join her, she had her breath under control.

Until he crossed under the dim patio light...then her breath was gone again. Oh, such a human pleasure!

What were lazy sags of denim on her was skintight midnight-blue over his lean hips. She swallowed past the lump in her throat. He had pulled the zipper barely to half mast, and the shadow behind the fly teased her with sights unseen.

She dragged her gaze up. When she had grabbed herself an open back halter dress, she hadn't found anything that would fit him—not that he had seemed ill at ease with his state of undress out on the beach. Now the crisscross straps that normally felt so free and left her wings exposed seemed a strangling confinement.

He halted beside her on the edge of the pavers where the pine duff softened the stone. He hadn't put his shoes back on, but he didn't seem bothered by the damp night on his bare toes. Instead, he gestured at the pale will-o'-the-wisps that danced among the closest pines.

"I thought maybe you would hide your wings and weird lights again," he said. "Try to make me think I imagined it all."

"You'll forget soon enough. Humans can't sustain the memory of us without our presence. Yet another symptom of our nothingness." Which was worse? Being nothing, or being forgotten by him? She tilted her face toward the drifting sparkles that were only a shade lighter than her moon-green dress. "Besides, the wisps go where they please. Even our Queen with all her power can't command them."

"They follow you everywhere, though. I saw them trailing after you on our beach runs." He snorted. "I thought I was hyperventilating."

She slanted a glance at him. "Do you often breathe heavy?"

He grinned. "Only when watching you."

The heat in her cheeks felt nice in the cool air. "The wisps actually gave me the idea to run away. They would dance in on my breezes. And then dance out again. As far as the *phae* are concerned, I am not much more significant than they are. I thought if they could just float off so could I."

"You aren't insignificant. You aren't nothing."

She shook her head, surprised at the intensity in his voice.

He was silent a moment, seeming to gather himself. "What will you do next?"

"Run again. They haven't caught me yet." This time, the thought of escape didn't ratchet up her heartbeat with the thrill of fooling the Hunters. Instead, a twinge, sharp as a runner's cramp, made her cover her heart with her hand. The blue stone pressed against the pulse of her wrist.

"Not tonight anyway."

A grim note in his voice made her stiffen.

"You can't run tonight," he clarified. "They are out there, looking, and this is as good a place as any to hide. Now, are you going to share that chocolate?" When she passed him the gold foil-wrapped bar, he broke off a square. "Ah, the good stuff."

He creased the foil carefully over the remaining bar and then licked a chocolate sliver off his fingertip, as if even that tiny taste was a treat to be savored. The steel band of his ring glinted, but the view of his tongue roused a damp heat between her legs and banished her moment of disquiet. A man who knew chocolate was a man to be treasured.

She cleared her suddenly tight throat as he handed her back the bar. "Dark, seventy percent, shade-grown, single origin. You need only one piece. Not that the *phae* understand that. They prefer multi-night feasts with dozens of courses. The napkins alone would cover the beach in both directions."

"That must be something to see."

The intensity of his gaze over the chocolate made her think of the Hunters' hounds eyeing one of those courses. She laid the bar on the picnic table; if she put it in her pocket, the chocolate would melt in an instant from the heat of her flushed skin.

Her wings flexed forward, curving around her to hide her hands—a silly, nervous gesture. She smoothed back the edges self-consciously. "That is pretty much all you get...what you see. Most of the banquets are illusion. You can have endless courses when the food never fills your belly. The wine is water, and silty at that, or so you notice when you wake the next day with mud under your tongue. The napkins are only dead leaves."

"Then why not just be happy with a piece of real chocolate? The good stuff, of course."

"The *phae* would laugh at you for even suggesting it. Our Queen comes to power based on the force of her illusions. She keeps the throne by her ability to hold the entire court under her spell." She shrugged. "Besides, everything—even good chocolate—gets old after a century or so."

He was silent a moment, letting the chocolate melt in his mouth. Finally he said, "Not everything."

He took her in his arms, a slow embrace she could have fended off—if she wanted to.

"Tonight," he murmured. "Tonight you can stop running."

His kiss was even slower than his embrace. She tasted the chocolate first, of course: sweet complexity with a touch of bitterness. The night breeze flirted with the hem of her short dress, shifting over her thighs. His mouth slanted across hers, that full lower lip a soft and generous gift she accepted with delight.

His earthy desire wrapped around her, almost tighter than her own wings and so intense the Hunters' dogs would be hard pressed to find even a whiff of *phae* beneath his excitement...or her own.

Her pounding heart left no room for illusion. She wanted this. Wanted Vaile. She wanted him not just for the protection his touch offered but for the warmth that blazed from him, the life she could pretend to live as long as the night lasted.

"Come inside," she whispered against his lips.

"Gladly."

She led him to her room. The wisps outside the window provided the only illumination, dancing like silver and gold raindrops over the old glass.

He drew her close to kiss her again and then cast a dubious glance over his shoulder. "Will that bed hold us?"

"Side by side maybe."

"Well, I don't want you any farther away than that." He stroked his hands down her arms, and his fingertips grazed the forward edges of her wings.

She closed her eyes and sighed.

"You like when I touch them?" His voice dropped with another stroke of his hand down her wings, more lingering this time.

"I...I didn't realize how much." She stretched against the broad expanse of his chest. "No one else has touched me like this."

"Silly fairies. Why not?"

"I don't know." She fanned her fingers over his collarbone not to push him away but to steady herself. "The *phae* are afraid to touch, I think. It can be overwhelming, this feeling..."

"What feeling? This?" He ducked his head, and his tongue teased the pulse in the hollow of her throat.

"*Any* feeling," she gasped. When he raised his head, she said more steadily, "The *phae* have always lived under the strict rule of our Queen. For all the wildness of the *phaedrealii* court, she allows no true freedoms. Feelings are too..."

His dark eyes glinted, reflecting the wisps outside. "*Unruly?*"

"Very."

"And you want to be unruly too."

She smiled. "That wasn't my intent. I've always been a proper *sylfana*. But now that you bring it up..."

"Oh, it is up all right." He bent and lifted her, as easily as one of the hounds might snap a wayward wisp from the air. She shivered a little but not in delight this time. Why had that comparison come to her mind? Maybe because he was strong like the hounds, and lean, so the flex of his muscles played under her palm, denying any chance to pretend she might escape. Not that she wanted to escape him, though.

He laid her down on the bed beneath curls of ivy that decorated the headboard. Smoothing her wings as he pulled his arm out from under her, he stared into her eyes. "If you tell me to go, I will."

She shook her head and reached for him.

But he resisted her tug on his bare shoulders. He wrapped his fingers around her wrists, gently pinning her to the mattress. "I want to hear you say it. And remember, I'm holding you, so I will know if you lie."

"Stay," she whispered.

The darkness of him loomed over her like night. But instead of extinguishing the glow in her core, his nearness only stoked the blaze higher, a bonfire of desire that sparked all the brighter for the shadows around them.

She arched her hips toward him, echoing her words with the curve of her spine. He growled low in his throat and released her wrists, freeing his hands to unknot the halter from behind her neck.

He anchored his arm under the small of her back, holding her in the arch while he danced his tongue from one nipple to the other.

She gave him a breathy laugh and laced her fingers through his dark hair. "That tickles."

"You wanted to feel." He traced a slow circle around her areola with his lips, still a tease but hard enough to make her gasp, as if he was drawing the air from her body.

"And I want to feel you *here*." He settled square between her thighs.

She sighed and corkscrewed into his embrace, entwining arms and wingtips around him. She felt him all right, his heat and the friction of his skin. This was a physical enchantment not even the most powerful *phae* could conjure.

With the halter top undone, she easily shimmied the dress down to her knees and kicked the crumpled fabric aside.

"No panties," he noted with an approving leer.

"Bras get in the way of wings, underwear gets in the way of—" he smiled slowly "flying."

He stilled, and his arm behind her tightened. "You think I can make you fly?"

"I know you can." While he was distracted, she tucked one hand between them and eased the zipper on his jeans all the way down.

With each tick of zipper teeth, he pushed harder toward her. "Imogene…" On the last tug, he hissed out a breath as she took the hard length of his erection in a gentle grip. He bucked against her hand. "Imogene, wait. I didn't think…"

"Then I won't think either." She stroked him once, delighting in the velvety slide of his erection, holding him fast though his body trembled over hers. "Don't worry. Human and *phae* might share common ancestry long ago, but this encounter won't have any consequences, for either of us unless I wish it." And even if she might wish it otherwise, their time together would be as fleeting as the moon's path across the sky.

"But…"

She captured his mouth with her own, tangled tongue to tongue to draw him back to her own earthly spell. He came willingly.

With fumbling hands, he shucked the denim. Each awkward bump of his hips against her center sent another crest of excitement through her. The cool skin of his flanks, the hot press of his erection left her senses reeling.

But when his hands settled on either side of her, pressing the mattress down, she had to open her eyes, to see him naked.

All that running had given him a Hunter's body, lean and strong. She could spend hours—the kind of enchanted hours that passed as centuries—tracing each line of muscle, each ridge where his pulse throbbed. But she didn't have that kind of time.

Only the wisps against the window lighted the side of his face. Their dreamy illumination caught and refracted in his eyes and gleamed back at her like a promise. His skin held darker shadows that lured her closer.

When she reached for him though, he caught both her wrists in one hand to still her. "Let me see you," he murmured.

She squirmed a little under his intense regard. "There's not that much to see. The *phae* may be physically more diverse than humans, but we were all drawn from essentially the same well."

"I want to see *you*," he emphasized. "To be sure…"

"This is what I want." She spread her wings to either

side, making a lure of her own, an irresistible soft landing. "I want you."

Supporting himself on one arm, he cupped her jaw and leaned in for a long, lingering kiss.

"I want that," she whispered against his mouth. "And more."

With a sudden flex of her wings, she rolled them.

He caught the edge of the mattress before they fell. "There's more where that came from. Much more." With both his hands free, he roamed her body, reshaping her flesh with each stroke of his fingers, each lap of his tongue.

And somehow, through her skin, he loosened her spirit too, made her soar where her wings had never taken her, urging her toward an elemental release unlike any of the magics she'd known.

She gasped, her whole body flush with sensation. Her breasts plumped for his caress, and her nipples drew almost painfully erect. The tingling that rang like silent bells through her depths echoed the ache until her hidden folds wept for his attention.

But when she looked down, his face was as severe and remote as that brief moment on the beach when he had frightened her. He was holding something back. But why?

She touched the chiseled edge of his cheekbone. "Don't worry," she whispered. "No consequences, remember? The perfect one-night stand."

"What if *I* wanted more?"

When she tried to draw back, he tangled his fist in the pendant. The chain tightened at the back of her neck, not biting—not yet—but a tightening snare. "I don't have anything more. I *am* nothing more. Just a dream, gone with the morning light."

His jaw clenched, the muscle flexing against her palm. "That sounds like something a fairy would say as a tease."

"It is not a tease. It's only the truth. See? I'm touching you." She eased down against his chest, loosening the pendant's restriction. The brush of her thighs over his didn't smooth his expression, though. If anything, he clenched harder, all over.

She brushed her cleft down that most rigid of muscles at his center. The jerk of his hips was a truth too, despite the furious set of his mouth. She dipped her head and nibbled at his lower lip. "We have to take what we can, while we can."

"Definitely spoken like a fairy. *La bella dame sans merci.*"

A cold draft of disquiet swept through her. From the chill of his words, he seemed almost too familiar with the transgressions of her kin, and the haunting words of Keats's poem felt uncomfortably close to the truth. "I didn't mean—"

"You did mean it. You were touching me, remember?" In one powerful heave, he flipped them again so he was on top, pinning her with his knees between her thighs. "Take it then. Take what you want."

"Vaile..." Despite her weak protest, she wound her legs behind him. The nudge of his erection made the trailing edges of her wings curl inward as every part of her body made a welcoming nest for him.

His hand worked between them to part her folds, slick with wanting him. The play of his touch made her arch and gasp, and still he held back, making her want and want and want until she thought she would unravel.

She clutched at his biceps, her knees drawn high, while he slid first one finger then two inside her. She writhed against him, a cry caught between her teeth. This is what it must be to come Undone.

He tilted his head back, the pulse of anger in his throat lost beneath the maddening acceleration of his heartbeat. She felt the tidal pull of his blood, his desire, and still he held himself apart while the whirlpool in her belly and thighs circled ever closer to the verge. Unwilling to go alone—not tonight—she pulled herself up with her hands anchored on the bunched muscles in his shoulders and ducked to bite his nipple. The thud of his heart almost deafened her, and he gasped out her name as he buried himself in one thrust.

Chapter Four

Vaile froze as all breath left him, as if he had just fallen off a cliff after a heart-shredding run.

Oh wait, he *had* done that. This was definitely better.

Imogene gazed at him. He stared back, dazzled. The illusion that had hidden her wings earlier in the evening had dampened her otherworldly beauty. Not that she'd been hideous in her human camouflage but since she'd dropped her disguising veil, the pale glow of her skin and the dark red-gold of her hair shimmered—untouchable, and yet here, within his grasp.

She tightened around him in delicious torment. "Now who is without mercy? Don't you dare stop." She set her teeth over his other nipple, and he shuddered at the cascade of sensation that threatened to... No. How could she be a threat? So delicate, never mind the heft of her wings and her bold resistance to those who pursued her.

She cupped his ass, and the tickle of her wings across

his backside made him jerk again. She smiled up at him with wicked delight. "I said don't stop."

"Never," he gritted out.

She was so hot and close around him, pulling him in with such ease he decided he had better rethink that threat—if he had the ability to think, which he didn't, not with his flesh so perfectly bound within her, the aphrodisiac scent of her wings an invisible cloud around them until he was almost dizzy with need.

A grind of his hips, slow and certain, made her gasp and loosen her grasp, letting him ease back and into her again as a protest rose on her lips and deep in his bones. He wanted to be here, wanted to give her what she wanted, wanted her to feel all of him.

Again, he eased back and in, setting up a rhythm that she followed with every clench of her hidden muscles, as powerful as her other secret strengths. A tease, a promise, a threat...it all swirled in his head, washing away reality.

There was magic in the world, and by rights he should be terrified to realize how it had captured him—how *she* had captured him with a nip, a tickle, a smile.

And the lush, swelling *feeling* she demanded of him.

Because, damn, he felt it too. How could he not? No wonder the others wanted her, why they wouldn't let her go. They knew, as he now knew, the passion in her was something to be coveted, stolen if necessary.

He raised her hips to his, tilting her to reach deeply, fully. The slick dampness of their coupling glistened where his cock met her smooth mound, gleaming in the wisp light. Underneath his knees, the bed groaned, and Imogene echoed it with a moan of her own. The sound quickened his pulse, and he quickened his rhythm, like they had sprinted together with the hounds of hell behind them, toward that cliff's edge.

This time, he would push them over. This time he would carry her as she fell.

He felt her muscles tightening with anticipation, tempting him to lose control, to forget everything except the lust exploding in his veins, but he powered through every stroke—deeper, fuller—counting the wisps beyond the window to stop himself from coming.

Her breath rattled in sensual pants, singing along his nerves until he was breathing with her, each thrust moving them closer, closer...

Despite his best intentions to linger, the force of her climax seized them both. She jackknifed against him, clasping him tight with arms, wings, the vibrating flesh inside her that contracted around him with a power that made his eyes roll back in his head. Helplessly, his body followed her lead. His cock spasmed in violent bursts. Every spurt rocked him against her, and she called his name in time, more breathless with each gasp.

A last shudder racked him as his limbs collapsed, and he slumped over her, chest heaving. If he'd been thrown down a cliff, rolled across a sand dune and tossed into the ocean, he would not have been left more wrecked.

Arms trembling with a mortifying weakness, he managed to prop himself to one side of her. Their legs sprawled entangled, her wing limp across their thighs.

She stared up. "Oh. Oh my."

The wonder in her voice made him grin. He settled one hand on the soft curve of her backside. Her skin quivered in aftershock. "Did you feel that?"

She rolled her head across the mattress to meet his gaze. "You know I did. Don't get cocky."

He lifted one eyebrow and flexed inside her.

She giggled. Then she put her hand over her mouth, but her eyes twinkled at him. Slowly, she lowered her hand. "Very well then. You may get cocky. Again." She was obviously trying for a tone of royal indifference, but her lowered hand kept lowering, sweeping down the length of him, which made sure that no part of him was going lower.

Thinking of going down was giving him ideas, and he flexed again. Her smile faded and she half closed her eyes, a sultry look.

"We have the night, you said," he reminded her.

"Every minute. I did not forget."

"I won't either. I'll count each second."

"So few." Her whisper tingled on his skin.

"Enough."

When she might have objected, he kissed her, drawing her in, losing himself.

It was still dark when they finally fell, side by side, sated.

She splayed across his chest, stroking circles over his skin. With one limp flap of her wing, she covered them both.

As her breath evened, she laughed softly. "Phew. Good thing I've been running."

"Good thing I run faster." He tightened his arm over her shoulder.

She snuggled down to bump the crown of her head under his chin, her head resting over his heart. "Good thing I got caught."

Her sigh was warm down his bare chest. But something inside him went cold.

"Not caught," he protested. "Merely…where you belong."

She nudged him again. "You think I belong here, hmm? That is what the *phae* say too. I am a wanted *sylfana*. Lucky me."

When he swallowed, the weight of her—which had seemed so negligible before—pressed hard on his chest. "You are lucky to be wanted."

She tilted her head back and captured his gaze before he could look away. "Wanted by you?"

"Obviously."

"That makes me feel…" She pecked a kiss on his jawline. "Happy."

"Happy." It came out as a growl.

"The court is a place of violent expression, from riotous glee to bleak agony, but never just happy. That is too much of a real emotion. I am beyond happy to feel happy."

He pulled her higher on his chest, never mind the weight that now seemed to push every breath from him. "Then I am…happy too."

She grinned at him, a slow dawning smile that lightened her blue eyes. "I can tell."

With a louder growl, he rolled her and slipped into her ready warmth.

She held him close, never looking away, so that he wondered who exactly was caught.

He took his time, measuring each stroke to the depths of her sighs. Her orgasm was slow and languorous, and she stretched full-length against him, her wings spread wide to either side in a shimmering background.

And still she looked at him, so he felt as if he were falling. Unable to bear such intimacy—even with his body buried in hers—he dipped his head to kiss the arch of her neck. The steel chain he had given her was cool against his lips.

"Come with me." Her murmur vibrated her throat against his tongue.

"I will." And he did, in one wild tumble like a bird on the wing pierced through the heart.

It was a long time, if not quite an eternity, until he caught his breath. So much for all the early morning and late night running.

But finally he pushed himself up off her and looked down. "This is how I will imagine you."

She had been smiling—a satisfied, sleepy smile that made him want to summon another hundred Hunters just so he could fend them off by kissing her again—but at his words, a faint shadow crossed her eyes. "You will forget."

"Never."

"Then maybe I will, with the *phaedrealii* walls around me. When I fade back into the nothing again."

"No. You aren't like that."

"You don't understand." The edge of her wing curled to cover her. "I was exactly that."

Careful not to fall off the narrow bed, he rolled to one side and pulled her close. "That is why you ran away."

She nodded against his chest. "At first, when she took power after the Iron Wars, the Queen would send *phae* out here just to watch. She has always been curious about humans—many of the *phae* are—and since you purified your iron into steel, we can walk more freely in the sunlit realm. Sometimes humans would follow us back to the *phaedrealii.*"

He kissed her crown. "I'd follow you anywhere."

She twisted her head to frown up at him. "Don't say that. You must never enter the court, or you might never leave."

"Maybe I wouldn't mind—" he kept his gaze fixed on hers "—if you were there."

She bit her lip, hard enough to leave crescents like tiny, blood-red moons. "That would make it worse." Her eyes glimmered. "If you are feeling something... The Queen uses emotion to enhance her power. The rush of anger that speeds the tongue. The lightness of laughter that makes the heart seem to float. The swell of desire that makes the world narrow and deepen. These are magics she wants to take for her own. But she wants more, more than the *phae* can give."

He reached up to smooth his thumb over Imogene's lip. "How bad could it be?"

"Bad." She let out an unsteady breath. "Not long before I ran away, I was summoned to the Queen's chambers. When I arrived, her chancellor made me wait in the corner, because she had a man—a human man—in her bed. He was one who had followed a *phae*—followed *me*—from the world back to court."

Vaile lifted one eyebrow. "I've read the story of Tam Lin. Fairy queens seem prone to such behavior."

"And fairy princesses too?" She echoed his raised brow. "Yes, some *phae* take human lovers, but this man wasn't just enthralled. He was...empty. The Queen had taken everything from him."

"She killed him." Vaile kept his voice matter-of-fact.

Imogene shook her head. "All that remained was a husk, but he lived, if you want to call it that. She was still working with her glass knives and burning steel when I arrived, and she spoke aloud as she took the man apart. She was saying, *And this is his heart, which we will call love, because we save the cock for other uses.*"

Vaile's arm tightened around her. "What sort of dissection is that?"

"The chancellor keeps a dozen stolen smart phones, and he was so thrilled to show me pictures of what they had done to enhance the Queen's power. They had taken the man's spleen to render down for anger, a lung for laughter, his leg for fear because the chancellor said cowards run." She tucked herself tighter against him. "That is when I knew I would run. I looked into the man's eye—they had plucked out one, and all I can think is the eyes are the window to the soul, and they took his soul—and I saw he knew what he had lost. That man was losing himself, as the *phae* have already lost themselves. As I will lose myself again and become the nothing I feared."

"Imogene—"

She surged up to kiss him, hard. "When you say my name, I think maybe it is possible I could be more, with you. But I won't risk you." She kissed him again.

When she lifted her head, he smoothed back her hair. "Skin to skin, we can't lie, you said. I see there is something more in you. You have something they don't. You feel something they can't. Or won't. That is why they want you back."

"That is why I am doomed." She tried for a wry smile and failed.

"Imogene…"

"You made me happy. You don't have to save me too." She stroked her fingertip across his lower lip when he would have argued more. "Till tomorrow."

She opened her wings over them, and a delicate swirl of her aphrodisiac drifted around them. He closed his eyes at the rush of pleasure, not just at her touch but at her happiness…

And he awoke to a tickle against his lashes, light as a fairy's kiss. He smiled slowly and opened his eyes.

Above him, the morning sky gleamed pale gray between the coils of ivy that framed his resting place. The soft mist sifting down between the leaves—too fine to register on his skin, just heavy enough to remind him of fairies and kissing—had wakened him.

Where was the damn roof?

And where was Imogene?

Vaile prowled the boundary of the tiny island. Shallow creeks encircled the area, just as she had said, but the cottage where they had spent the night was mostly a crumbled ruin. The hole over the bed that had let in the rain was one of many, and the bed itself was a pile of pine boughs and damned ivy.

All an illusion—and not one she had cast since she said she wasn't that powerful. No, he had seen only what he wanted to see.

He cursed low under his breath, little more than a growl. What else had been a lie? Her story of running away from her heartless brethren, of wanting only to *feel*? What about her breathless cry as he had sunk into her?

He scratched at a tender spot on his shoulder. It was probably just a rash from the pine needles. Maybe she had never dug her nails into him while she whispered his name.

A glint of gold lured him to the picnic table where they had stood, watching the wisps. Time and rot had eaten through the boards of the tabletop to reveal the cracked concrete patio slab underneath.

At least the chocolate had been real.

He devoured the rest of the bar and crushed the foil into

the pocket of his jeans—her jeans. The scent of her was also real, lingering deep in his skin, rare and precious.

A faint imprint of slender bare feet led through the moss across the bridge. The cherry blossoms lay undisturbed—pink and still in the spiral where they had fallen when their sustaining breeze vanished. There, the footprints disappeared.

Imogene had disappeared.

He spun the ring on his forefinger. Set in the brushed steel band, the blue stone he had kept turned toward his palm looked dull under the sullen sky. He breathed in the fragrance of her again, his pulse accelerating at the memories, false though they might be.

From the depths of the rare blue amber, a cat's eye gleam sent a ray of light across the smooth surface. He pointed, aligning his fingertip with the arrowing glint of light. That way.

He spread his wings, black as his mood, and launched into the mist.

Chapter Five

Imogene ran.

This time, there would be no escape.

She had gone south along the coast, as quickly as she could, hoping the salty air and flowing water would disguise her scent and her tracks. When her thighs started to seize from the running, she flew, though using her *phae* magics would draw the Hunters' attention. Not that flying gave her much advantage in speed or distance, *sylfana* wings were meant for coy fluttering, not fleeing.

But she had to get far away—not to save herself. The Hunt was too close this time to lie, even to herself, about having a chance to evade the hounds.

She had to lead them as far as she could from Vaile.

The memory of his fingers trailing down her wings made her falter, and she landed with a harsh sob in a spray of sand at the edge of the high-water mark. Thankfully, much of the Oregon coast was still wild, and with night coming, the span of beach was empty except for one strutting gull. The bird gave her a sideways glance of professional disdain at her fumbled landing and launched himself inland.

She sank to a crouch, one leg folded under her in the wet sand. She hugged her other knee so the pendant pressed into her breastbone. The muscles in her thighs and wings quivered from exertion. The sensation was nowhere near as pleasant as the night before when Vaile's touch had inspired shivers of desire. She drew the hot memory around her to ward off the chill since her halter dress wasn't much protection from the settling mist.

She needed just another moment to remember the tilt of his smile and how it had lifted her heart like a perfect breeze angled beneath her wings. Another moment, and then she would force herself to rise and run.

But she didn't rise, because more than his touch she longed for the piercing intensity of his gaze, how he had looked past the illusions and gave her what she so wanted: a chance to feel.

Her throat ached from the wheezing gasps. No wonder more than one of her *sylfana* sisters had kept their human lovers entranced, never to find their way back to the world. No wonder the Queen was stealing and binding the power of emotion. More than the endless running, more than the strain of flight, Imogene was crippled by the truth that she would never again feel this way.

She stifled the sobs. *Phae* tears were too dangerous to shed in the sunlit world. Any magical thing might fall—

poison, evil dreams, a river to drown a village. More reasons the *phaedrealii* existed under prohibitions against
the Undoing.

Not that she would have to feel anything much longer...

While she mourned, the mist had grown heavy and
pressed too close to be natural. She lifted her face, and
the droplets beaded on her lashes.

Through the swirling veil, the three hounds paced.
Under heavy studded steel collars, their nine heads hung
low, blunt muzzles fixed on her scent, panting up geysers
of sand. At least she had led them a merry chase—merry
for them anyway.

She pushed herself upright, grabbing the pendant as it
swung drunkenly, and locked her wobbling knees. Mere
exhaustion... She was too numb to feel fear.

The center hound lifted its middle head, and the red-
yellow glint of its eye pierced the mist.

But the hounds didn't lunge toward her as she expected.
Without a sound, they fanned out to surround her. As they
prowled in shrinking circles, their claws left tracks filling
with water like fatal wounds in the sand; they could have
her in pieces in less than a heartbeat.

Equally silent, another dark shape coalesced through the
mist. Black wings arced sharply above the figure, nothing
like the languid drape of her wings.

It was a Hunter, a being as remorseless as the *sylfana*
were silly. Facing him now, she wondered why she had
ever thought she had a chance, even in the good old days
when she was still lying to herself.

This made her stolen time with Vaile even more wondrous. She lifted her chin as she waited for the Hunter's inevitable command to attack.

He halted, still wreathed in the mist. One of the hounds raised its head and whined, eager for her blood, no doubt. The Hunter snapped his finger and pointed. The hound half closed its red-yellow eyes in appeasement, and all three slunk back to his side.

She locked her gaze on the Hunter's finger. A stone gleamed in his ring. Hunters usually armed themselves with amber in flaming colors like the hound's eyes. The fossilized tree resin held magics perfectly suspended, much as it encased insects, leaves and small stones. But this amber ring was blue.

Blue, like the pendant around her neck.

Her fist clenched around the stone, driving the edge of the steel bezel into her flesh. Though the iron was too refined to hurt her, still her heart constricted painfully. "Vaile. If that is your name. I have never heard of blue amber."

"Imogene. And yes, that is my name, though I give it as rarely as one finds blue amber." He stepped out of the fog he had woven to disguise himself from her.

Actually, part of that fog—the seductive lie that pure sensation would save her—she had held together herself. Her own fault. But it shredded now on the sharp talons that topped his wings and the cold, cruel winds of reality.

All that time she had been fighting against the *phaedrealii*'s love of delusion she had never wanted it so badly as this moment. She would just have to reweave it herself, out of the tattered threads of her pride.

Lies and pride offered thin coverage at the moment, though, so she drew the edges of her aching wings around her as she tilted her chin imperiously. "One night. That is all we were supposed to have together. That night is long past."

"It wasn't enough."

The low pitch of his voice reverberated through her, finding a yearning echo in places deep within her core.

"It was more than you deserved," she said. "Even skin to skin, you lied."

As she yanked the chain over her head, she swallowed against the hurt that cracked her voice. That was not a truth she would give him.

"I didn't lie to you. You didn't ask me anything."

As if that made her feel less the fool... "You should have just let the hounds shred me yesterday when they caught us on the beach."

"No."

Without the softening human glamour he had worn, his skin shone like the backlit razor edge of an obsidian blade, highlighted against the velvety black of his wings and the darkly mellow gleam of his leather jeans. The steel-studded collar around his neck glinted like bared teeth. But his naked chest was the same, a broad expanse of flight-honed muscle where she had rested her head last night.

She squelched the memory and lifted her lip in a sneer.

"I know the Lord Hunter keeps all his killers on a short leash. Did you need a night with a *sylfana* so badly?"

His bare shoulders squared against the arc of wings as he met her gaze without flinching. "No. I wanted you."

The answer silenced her for a heartbeat. "Why?"

He shrugged, and his wings dipped in an almost bashful movement. "This."

At first, she didn't understand what he was showing her. Then he reached up to spread his long fingers in a V on both sides of a raised scar at the joint where his wing met his shoulder. Though the edges had knit well, the wound must have been horrific. In fact, his wing must have been nearly severed...

"You," she whispered. "The Hunter whelp."

"I did not even have a name then." His finger slid over the knot of scarring. "You told me I wouldn't feel it forever. You were wrong. I still feel it. But it reminds me of what I wished for, what I wanted most."

"To fly."

"No, I wanted you," he repeated. "Apparently it was you who decided to fly away."

Her throat tightened. "Not soon enough, not far enough."

"After I became a Hunter fully fledged, I saw you at one of those never-ending feasts. The wisps danced around you, and the breeze tugged your hair into loops around your shoulders. You just stood there, but every part of you yearned for flight."

That could have been any one of hundreds of nights. "The Queen's illusions are much too strong for me to see through, but her court always stinks of ashes when I face into the wind."

"I never noticed anything except you. I wanted to make you dance."

Imogene narrowed her eyes. "You are probably a *phae* strong enough to force me to burn through my slippers."

"No. I meant…" The hesitation went on long enough for even a long-lived *phae* to get impatient. "I wanted you to want to dance. With me."

She wished she had seen him on that night, just another one of the Queen's Hunters, keeping watch from the shadows—for trouble both beyond and within the *phaedrealii*. They could have indulged in one of the court's meaningless liaisons and parted ways without this pain. "You felt that longing? Then don't you see that the Lord Hunter was right? The *phae* should be free to want, to desire, to feel. It is a magic within us, and we have no right to steal it from others."

He loosed a rough laugh. "You say the Lord Hunter was right? He killed my brothers, almost killed me. Wanting you as I did—until you filled all my senses and every path I took on the hunt brought me back to you—only proves the Queen was right to outlaw the Undoing."

She shook her head with bitter resignation. "So you told the Queen you would hunt me down, show me the error of my ways."

"I told them I could bring you back alive."

"I won't go back. Especially not with you. You are everything I finally left behind. Cold and unfeeling."

His eyes darkened as he stepped into her space. The arc of his wings made his looming mass even more imposing. "Not cold at least," he growled. "Didn't I prove that last night?"

Rage at the reminder—and the sudden, fierce longing it roused in her that made her whole body clench with need—conjured one last burst of strength in her, and she hurled the necklace at him. The breeze spun up in answering agitation and flung an arc of sand with the chain. Vaile lifted one arm to shield his eyes.

She whirled and ran.

The hounds howled in delight at the renewal of the chase. Their claws hissed in the sand behind her.

With their hot breath on her heels, she took a half-dozen steps and launched herself out of the Hunter's mist into the crystalline night sky.

A *sylfana*'s wings might not be made for high-speed chases, but desperate fury pumped fresh power past her aches. The breeze that had shed its sand belled under her wings, urging her upward. She thrust herself higher with each stroke and swirl.

The woeful howl of the hounds, deprived of their prey, echoed in the air, but a darker pressure threatened her from behind.

Without looking back, she darted sideways. She tucked her shoulder and angled her wing to catch the wind. The force tumbled her end over end, and she jolted onto the new trajectory like a butterfly catching erratic breezes.

Vaile overshot her like a black rocket—a cursing rocket.

The downdraft from his heavy wing beat almost sucked the air out from under her, but she caught the rising edge of the vortex in his wake and flitted away, out over the waves.

She would not lie to herself. She could tease the Hunter only so long; his strength and stamina completely eclipsed hers. He could fly circles around her—literally. Even now, he was looping around in pursuit, and though she might dodge him with a butterfly's whimsy, he would double back again and again. But she would not walk meekly back into her prison. He would have to drag her back. And he would have to catch her first.

He dove. She dodged. They had skipped the winged *phae*'s aerial foreplay in their first encounter, and now the dance was a deadly game with only one winner. Another lunge and evasion, but this time she lost altitude. The spray from the waves tickled her legs and added damp weight to her wings. Another reckless midair tumble edged her farther out to sea.

Too far.

Her heart crashed in her chest, louder than the waves breaking on the shore that now seemed frighteningly far away.

"Imogene, come back. Imogene!"

When she had thought he was human, she told him that the *phae* believed names had power, but only now did she appreciate how that string of syllables that defined her could lift her—as when he had shouted her name on the verge of his release—or tear her apart as it did now. How she longed for her *phae* lies.

He overflew her, and she darted to evade him, but her wings were tiring. Her bones burned with exhaustion, and the fitful wind of her knack whistled a weak apology past her ears. She faltered, and her wingtip grazed the water.

She gasped as she cartwheeled through the air. Her fingers touched the water. She closed her eyes to wait for the chill kiss of the ocean. This was not such an unexpected way to die—in the embrace of the ocean as cold, relentless and unchanging as the *phaedrealii* itself, but oh no, she had never meant to bring Vaile down with her....

A heavy weight slammed between her helplessly spreading wings, and her eyes snapped open at the impact as Vaile, clamping his arm around her belly, tried to lift them from the fatal plunge.

The trailing edges of his wings hit the water with a vicious slap, and water sprayed up around them. He strained against gravity and the weight of water, as if by the magic of his ferocious will alone he could power them skyward.

His leathery wings snapped out to full extension, shedding droplets in a shimmering arch that caught the moonlight. For a heartbeat, they hung together, suspended in the monochrome rainbow of night-dark ocean, pale foam and silvery droplets. Then one more powerful downward thrust rocked her head back against his shoulder, and they shot free, high above the waves.

She had never commanded such power on the wing, and the wild thrill of it made her pulse sing in her veins.

Or maybe that was Vaile's arm, locked tight under her breasts.

"Drop me," she hissed. "Leave me to drown."

"Let you escape, you mean? After all I did to hunt you down? That's *my* knack, you know. I always find what I want."

"Your prey."

"You."

Why would he tell her his knack? Maybe he thought telling her would keep her from running again. As if she would ever have another chance. Back in the *phaedrealii*, her desires would wither, like her rarely used wings. Returning to a *sylfana*'s carefree, thoughtless existence, she would forget everything she had felt. She would even forget how badly she had wanted to feel at all. Nor would she be bothered by the cruelty of Vaile's betrayal—cold comfort at that. "Just tear off my wings, and drop me in the ocean."

His breath was a warm sigh in her ear, and his bare chest almost scorched the damp folds of her wings trapped between their bodies. "Imogene—"

"Whatever you do to me, it will be no worse than what the Queen has in mind."

He tightened his grasp. "Even she is not so…well, she is that cruel, and you said you have seen worse from her, but you haven't done anything that unforgivable. Yet."

"I led that man not to his death but to the loss of everything that made him who he was, from his delights to his fears. I gave him to the Queen, and she took all that from him. And worst of all? I told myself that I was running away to make his sacrifice meaningful, to make sure that even though he had been used up, I would never again be used to ensnare another man. But the truth is, when I saw those treasures of his emotions, I wanted to feel them too. Like our Queen, I wanted to take that passion, all of it, and that is why I will never forgive myself."

The wind of their flight nudged tears from her eyes—just salty water. There was no magic of emotion in them.

Although the tears seemed to sap Vaile's power—because he dove toward the shore—he backwinged abruptly, in one leathery sweep, to land them with a knee-jarring thud. He kept a grip on her arm as he circled around in front of her. It wouldn't take but a moment for the hounds to catch up. For that moment, though, they were alone.

But his expression wasn't horrified. He looked pissed, his eyes sparking with the same light as the angry hounds. "What you saw the Queen do to enhance her power is terrible, no doubt. But the illusions of the *phaedrealii* must remain intact. If all the Hunters had been killed the night the old Lord came Undone and if all the *phae* were loosed of the Queen's restraints, do you think they would stay behind the walls of the court? No, they would take to the sunlit world with their havoc. We save two realms by holding ourselves apart."

"At what cost?"

"It could be worse. It has been worse, though not since the Iron Wars. But now that I've found you, that is over. The *phaedrealii* will take you back like nothing ever happened."

"Exactly," Imogene whispered. "Like nothing."

He growled, making her heart race faster than when the hounds were on her heels. "You. Aren't. Nothing."

"But I will be, once I'm back there."

"At least you'll be alive."

She had come alive, one night in his arms. "Never again."

His jaw worked, but he didn't answer. He tightened his grip so she had no chance to flee as he reached into his back pocket and withdrew a narrow steel vial. The steel held just enough carbon to contain but not destroy the *phae* magic inside.

If only humans realized how much protection they had lost against the *phae*, purifying all their iron into steel. But then again, if they did know, she—silly little *sylfana* that she was—would never have been able to cross into their world. The steel-born *phae* would no longer be kept at bay with the old charms.

But now Vaile was conjuring the way back. He uncorked the vial and sprinkled the contents in a circle around their feet. The dust drifted into the sand, and the spores sprouted with preternatural speed to mark the shifting boundary between realms. Button-sized caps spread like little golden wings, and Imogene couldn't help but breathe the whiff of honey that floated through the widening gateway.

The fragrance was another lie; there was nothing sweet about the *phaedrealii*. If a human stepped into the circle before the gate magic dissipated, he would awaken to find himself trapped in a realm that would probably destroy him, his mind and soul if not his body.

And if a human ate the sprouted spores… The phrase "magic mushroom" was more appropriate than mortals knew.

She closed her eyes as the gate magic encircled her, and she slipped into the dream.

Or, considering the darkly menacing *phae* Hunter behind her, into her nightmare…

Chapter Six

Vaile hadn't caught even the briefest glimpse of Imogene in…forever. In the sunlit world, only a couple of weeks had passed. But in the *phaedrealii* court, the separation stretched like an eternity. That one night of fierce sensation had obviously skewed his perceptions.

The Lord Hunter—one of the Hunters who had been away when the old Lord had come Undone—had kept him busy since his return. His brethren's eyes were on him, watchful and wondering why he had taken a full cycle of the moon to find a missing *sylfana*. Since he couldn't admit he had found her on the very first day and then proceeded to run after her every day thereafter, on foot, without actually catching her, he bit his tongue and took the hounds' dung tasks the Lord Hunter slung at him. He had to be the unflinching Hunter; if they thought he was losing his edge, they would turn on him quicker than the hounds. And then they would turn their vicious attention to Imogene.

But a dozen more *phae* repatriations—most of them straightforward, though three had been lethal—couldn't keep his mind off one sweet *sylfana*. In fact, the captures had only made him think harder.

Just as his brethren were watching him, he was listening to them. The Hunters were being called on more and more often to find wandering *phae*. The mood of the *phaedrealii*, always mercurial and secretive, was changing, and the power of the Queen's illusions—though holding for the moment—seemed to be thinning. He might not have even noticed the pattern except that Imogene had forced him to open his eyes. What if the *phaedrealii* deserters had wanted only what she wanted—a chance to feel, to live?

Ever since the old Lord Hunter had tried to unwing him as a whelp, he had believed in the Queen's edict against the Undoing. More than believe in it, he had fought and killed to defend it.

What if he had been wrong?

Certainly the three delinquent *phae* he had confronted had been abroad with nefarious purposes. The crazed dwarf had been hacking down a ring of birch trees that marked the Queen's permanent private gate into the sunlit world. When Vaile had tried to talk to him, the dwarf had cackled, "We must close the circles before we all run out."

Then he turned the ax on himself. Not a pleasant end, and frustrating too since it left many questions in Vaile's uneasy mind.

The very next night, he had found two missing undines at a human watering hole where they had been killing men in their cups—literally. They were crouched over an unconscious man, pouring the frothy contents of a beer can right up his nostrils.

"He was already drowning his sorrows," one of the willowy sprites told Vaile.

"We are granting their wishes when we drown them," said the other.

The undines reminded him of Imogene. They were too skinny and sinuous for his taste, lacking the *sylfana*'s sleek flight muscles, but something about their winsome sideways smiles weakened him. So he followed them to their stream to see why they had left. And it was true, the humans had tossed enough empty beer bottles, snack bags and cigarette butts along the reedy banks to make a path that led straight to their guilty lips.

"You know the Queen won't interfere if you kill men," he reminded the undines. The memory of Imogene agonizing over how she had been made to do worse roughened his voice. "But you can't leave your *phae* waters."

"We couldn't before," said one. "Not when horses crossed our bridges on iron-shod hooves, not when the miller's iron-bound wheel circled through our stream…" The other undine finished, "But now we can. And we will. This world will fall to the steel-born *phae*."

Then, without even counting to three, they pushed him into the stream.

What they lacked in muscle they made up for in ferocity, needle teeth and the slime that oozed from their skin when they were roused to a killing frenzy. They fought him past all reason, past the point where any of them could have stopped. As they coiled around him, dragging him down through the water—that was barely deeper than his waist, damn it—he had a moment where he thought maybe it would be better to let the last of the air bubbles past his gritted teeth. If they were so determined to be free, who was he to stop them? Did he really care that much about living?

Imogene's blue eyes had flashed in his imagination. She hadn't been able to hide that brilliant color—it shone even through her human guise. She had risked everything to live.

As water poured into his mouth, he released the magic in the amber ring. The light—brighter than the sun—exploded through the roiling waves, and the grasping hands fell away from him. He shot to his feet, flailing and choking.

Water streamed from his eyes, and he clenched his wings close to hold them away from the undines, floating belly up beside him. Even as he watched, they started to unravel in strands of algae.

The amber sun was a weapon of last resort. Too many *phae* had been lost during the Iron Wars, and every passing weakened the Queen's power. Although now that she was drawing magics from human collections, perhaps she would kill *him* in a fit of grand annoyance at his failure to bring the undines back alive.

He slogged out of the stream. By all that was dark and shining, why hadn't they yielded? As overwhelmed as the

Hunters were, the undines could have pretended compliance and returned to their killing as soon as his back was turned.

His boots slipped in the mud as his knees suddenly weakened. Was Imogene planning exactly that? He had turned his back on her as soon as the gate had opened to the *phaedrealii*. But he hadn't been able to stop himself from glancing around. Her *sylfana* sisters had bustled forward to surround her, and he caught only a glimpse of her amber hair when she averted her face without meeting his gaze.

If she did escape again, the Lord of the Hunt might send another Hunter—one who would not hesitate to use the amber sun's fatal power against her.

He didn't understand what was happening in the Queen's court, but he knew a certain *sylfana* who hadn't been afraid to step into the unknown.

In a small oxbow of the stream lay the broken circle of toadstools that had been the undines' gate to the *phaedrealii*. He completed the circle with his vial of spores and stepped through.

There was only one more *phae* he needed to catch.

So when guard duty at the Queen's next feast was tossed his way, he just bowed his head in acknowledgment while his brother Hunters jeered, but this time he bit his cheek to hide his smile.

Surely Imogene would be there.

Sometimes the Queen led her courtiers out of the *phaedrealii* to dance in the reflected sunlight of a full moon, but apparently she was loathe to risk any more runners. For this gathering, the shifting walls of the court had drawn back far enough to resemble a poppy field at dusk. As if a summer sun had just set, a warm glow lingered across the illusory sky, but the scarlet blooms were already darkening toward purple.

The Queen held her *phae* in concentric rings. Her attendants lingered nearby with less privileged courtiers farther out. Her inner circle stood close at hand, her goblin chancellor hopping at her elbow while her current favorite—a whispered half-blood with rounded human ears and catlike elvish eyes—solicitously guided her over the rolling grounds. Dozens of other *phae* drifted across the field in small groups, their laughter like distant bells. Someone had even procured a badminton set, and the soft *thwack* of rackets was as indolent as a lazy heartbeat.

Vaile took up a Hunter's stance on the farthest edge of the court. From the small rise beside a spreading tree, he had an uninterrupted view across the crowd.

The vantage point also made him clearly face the fact—despite the idyllic picture—he was not protecting the *phaedrealii* but imprisoning it.

He shifted restlessly, ruffling his wings to create a little breeze in the sultry air. He should curse Imogene for making him realize how unhappy the *phae* were…and how unhappy he had become. But he couldn't close his eyes again; that was not a Hunter's way. He was on the hunt, and his knack would find his answers.

The glow of the sky did not falter, held in stasis by the Queen's magic, but will-o'-the-wisps emerged to dance among the poppies. Their glinting light brightened the crimson petals like the explosions of miniature fireworks, making the shadows beneath his tree seem darker by comparison. Through the heavy drape of leaves, probably no one would even notice him except for the wisps, and they would never tell anyone, except maybe…

The slow wave of his wings halted, but the breeze still swirled around him with a fragrance that haunted his waking dreams.

He turned just in time to catch a flutter of white.

"Imogene." His voice caught raggedly on her name.

She paused, though he had used no force to stop her, and glanced over her winged shoulder. "I didn't know anyone was here."

He wondered if he should believe her. Without his skin against hers, he couldn't be sure. But when he took a step toward her, she sidled back. Her hands fisted in her gold spider silk skirts, whisking the long train away, as if she didn't want any part of her near him.

He stopped. "If you are looking for a place to hide, there's still room under here."

"Is that what you were doing here? Hiding?"

"I was hoping to see you."

She snapped out her wings in a *well, here I am* motion, but she pulled her arms close to tighten the spider silk around her like golden armor. "I have plenty of *phae* watching me. They make sure I don't go anywhere alone, and I don't have access to any gate spores. I suppose you can see me whenever you want since I'm going nowhere."

The glitter in her blue eyes, sharp in the otherwise soft-focus setting, was a clear warning he might see her, but he had better not touch. So he looked his greedy fill.

She was thinner than he remembered, as delicate as the young *sylfana* who had wished his wing whole. His fingers clenched, as if he could gauge the slenderness of her wrists without touching her. Barely any part of her was exposed to touch; her gold gown covered her almost entirely, from the long sleeves ending in deep scallops over the backs of her hands, to the high collar that flared out at the points of her jaw. The red-gold amber of her hair gleamed against the dress, which made her face more wan by comparison. But he supposed she hadn't been out running lately. Even the intermittent Oregon sun would have given her some color.

When she had said she would never feel alive again, he hadn't believed her. Now he did. He had brought her back, but he had left something precious behind.

Remorse nipped him, a sharpness like accidentally sitting on an annoyed wisp. "Hunters are being sent out to retrieve more and more fugitive *phae*. You started something when you bolted."

"There were always *phae* runaways. The only difference is no one noticed before." She glanced down, and the aggressive spread of her wings wilted. "It is only because of me that anyone notices now."

With her attention diverted, he took the opportunity to close the distance between them. When he caught her arm, his fingertips met. She *was* thinner, fading before his eyes.

As he tugged her into the shadow of the tree, the backs of his knuckles brushed the side of her breast through the silky weave of her gown, but he ignored the awareness that sizzled through his body. "If anybody is guilty of turning attention to the runaways, it is me. So go ahead and blame me." He would rather face the bold, angry Imogene than this pensive *sylfana* he barely recognized.

She finally raised her eyes. In place of the cold glitter, her gaze clouded, like the smoky occlusions in his blue amber. "I can't blame you, not when I know why you are so afraid."

"I am not—"

Avoiding his studded Hunter collar, she lifted her hand toward his shoulder, where the knot of scar still twisted over the wing joint. "The Lord Hunter almost undid you, as he came Undone himself."

Vaile stiffened at the almost imperceptible brush of her fingers. "It's nothing. You wished me back together again."

"What did you wish for? To fly? Yet here you are." She shook her head. "I guess I was never strong enough to be a fairy princess."

"Imogene—"

She jerked her hand away. "Don't say my name. It reminds me of…things."

"I want to remind you." He tightened his grip on her arm to draw her up against his bare chest. Sometimes he resented the Hunters' archaic garb—or lack thereof—but now he appreciated the absence of at least that barrier between them. "We don't have to lose what we found out there. We can still have that, here, without the risk of the Undoing."

In the imaginary heat and faked shadows of the *phaedrealii*, only the feel of her was real. When he pressed her close, her breasts were a softer warmth through the gold gown, and the silky folds of the skirt fanned around his leather-clad legs. He slid one hand behind her neck, though the spider silk came between them.

"Hunter..." she murmured.

Her breathy sigh tightened the already-snug fit of his jeans. "Vaile," he reminded her. "Whatever you might think, I am not still that nameless whelp."

"If only you were, then I would still be the thoughtless *sylfana*, and I could forget."

"Forget what?"

"Everything."

He leaned down, angling his mouth above hers. "Even me?"

"Especially you." She stared up at him without blinking. "If you kiss me, I will bite like one of your hounds."

"I almost believe you." He shifted his grip to cup her jaw, just at the edge of her high gold collar. "But not quite."

The soft, shining silk was nothing like the studded Hunter leash around his own neck, yet he thought perhaps they were both bound, in their own ways. He took a breath and ran his thumb over the hollow of her cheek to her lower lip.

"Skin to skin, we cannot lie," he told her, as if she might have forgotten that.

And he covered her mouth with his own.

She did not bite, but her sharp inhalation seemed to yank the air from his body. For a dizzy heartbeat, he felt as if they had gone aloft; every muscle was tight with yearning, his breath and heart suspended. His wings spread in impulsive reaction, rattling the leaves above their heads.

Though he had meant to tease her with the touch, the sensation of her lips softening and opening under his caught him like a gale force wind and ripped away any intention and all thought.

With a groan, he buried his hands in her hair, tangling his fingers in the red-gold locks to tilt her head to his onslaught. He swept his tongue across the inner rim of her lip and sealed their breath between them as he locked his mouth over hers. The taste of her reminded him of their one night in her island cabin, how she had come apart so sweetly in his arms, how she had whispered his name without hesitation, how she had told him she was happy.... His wings arched forward, like a raptor mantling its prey. He wanted that from her again, wanted everything, from her violent release to her sleepy smile.

The bone-deep force of the primal response stunned him into gentling the kiss. He lightened the pressure of his mouth and smoothed his hands down her arms—as much to soothe himself as to apologize for his ferocity. Not that she had ever been afraid of him, or of anything else for that matter.

Maybe she was right, and he was the one who had always been afraid....

Slowly, letting the slick moisture bind their lips until the last possible second, he lifted his head to look down into her dazed eyes.

He skimmed his hands up her gold sleeves to the too-sharp point of her shoulders. "You need chocolate."

She took a shuddering breath—whether at his touch or the thought of chocolate, he wasn't sure—and swayed toward him. "I need only one thing..."

His body yearned toward hers in answer. "Yeah?"

She leaned fractionally closer to him, so her nipples—peaked through the silky gold—grazed his bare chest. "I want you..."

He swallowed hard.

"To let. Me. Go."

She put no magic in the words, but his hands sprang open as if gremlins had wrenched back his fingers.

She stood there a moment without fleeing, poised with her wings half spread. Her unflinching gaze pierced him like the devastating light of the blue-amber sun, shredding him inside. It was he who stepped back.

A faint, mocking breeze swirled between them, bearing a drift of poppy petals. In the shadow under the tree, the blossoms were dark as old blood. He had told her once that his only fear had been not catching her. He had found her—it was his knack, after all—and yet somehow he had lost her too.

She finally averted her gaze, but her words seemed to pin him still. "If my wishes had any power, Hunter, I would wish that I would never see you again."

As she turned on her heel, the obliging breezes billowed the train of her long skirt out behind her as she walked away, leaving him with the withering petals and the wild-sweet taste of her on his tongue.

Chapter Seven

Out in the sunlit world, the moon was waning, thinning the barriers between the realms until the gate magic was accessible even to the weakest *phae*—not that Imogene had seen sun or moon lately, since she lacked the spores to create even the smallest, shortest passage.

But the Queen had summoned all her courtiers to her, which meant some agitation in the *phaedrealii*. Perhaps the restlessness preceded a jaunt across some starlit moor or maybe a wild tear down some unsuspecting Main Street; the Queen's stables provided horsepower in many forms.

Whichever way the *phaedrealii* went, Imogene knew she would not be attending, not since she had declined the Queen's command to procure another victim for her magical dissections.

Imogene hadn't denied the Queen to her face, but the goblin chancellor—who had relayed the command—looked as aghast as if she had.

"You must go." The overbearing goblin slicked back his long, pointy ears in dismay. His sallow skin was more ghoulish yet in the pale blue-green light of the stolen smart phones strung on a cord around his neck. The phones blinked on and off with the images of ghostly faces. The glass and precious metals could be spelled to hold various magics, but Imogene didn't want to know if the faces were leftover avatars of the former owners...or perhaps the former owners themselves. "The Queen says you seem to have a knack for bringing back the most expressively emotive subjects." The goblin peered at her through his tiny white eyes.

No *phae* could force out the true nature of another *phae*'s knack—not even the Queen—though tricking, wheedling and guessing were considered acceptable tactics. But taboo or no, even the most obsequious courtier in the *phaedrealii* would be reluctant to find his knack the sole focus of the Queen's formidable attention.

Imogene forced herself to remain impassive, her wings slack from her shoulders, while her mind whirled at the chancellor's evident interest on the Queen's behalf.

Why had the Queen noticed her? Were the impulsive little breezes a manifestation of a stronger knack? Imogene let out a slow breath to calm her racing pulse. She had always thought merely being *sylfana* had attracted the poor humans who had followed her to their doom. Yet now she wondered... Once, before her wings had unfurled and before the *sylfana* allure and aphrodisiac had fully manifested, she had freed a nameless wounded whelp to fly.

The memory of the full-fledged Hunter under her hands in the ruined cabin—his pulse and his cock rising to her touch—threatened her illusion of detachment. What else could she set free? For a moment, the possibilities diverted her. What if she was not as weak as she had always thought?

Just as quickly though, the truth broadsided her, knocking the breath from her lungs as easily as a tornado shred frail *sylfana* wings.

What she had most yearned for—*to feel, to live, to be free*—had run riot over the humans' caution, loosed their inhibitions, unfettered their emotions…and ultimately meant their magical dismemberment to feed the Queen's pitiless curiosity and need for power. And Vaile had taken a bigger risk than he knew, using her knack against her to ensnare her senses and ultimately her body. If she had Undone his *phae* prohibition against true emotion, he might have become like the old, mad Lord Hunter himself—or another victim of the Queen's gruesome thievery.

Discovering her own power to set spirits free, now, when she was most thoroughly imprisoned, made her laugh until her throat burned as if she had swallowed pure iron.

The chancellor perked his ears and gave her a peg-toothed smile. "So you will go?"

She leaned down to return the smile. "Never, ever again."

To her surprise, he had let her walk away, and the Queen had not pursued the matter. No one was pursuing her anymore. Maybe she had finally become the nothing she had feared, less meaningful even than her errant breezes.

So while the rest of the courtiers made their way to the throne room, she went the opposite direction, down into corridors of the *phaedrealii* she had never roamed. A few wisps accompanied her, and their tiny lights reflected off the old white tiles that lined the walls. When she trailed her fingers over the tiles, pieces flaked away to reveal packed earth. A red worm curved out of the dirt below her hand and plunged right back in, scattering dark crumbs on the cracked stone floor below.

The Queen's illusions had not graced these halls for a very long time, perhaps not since iron ruled the sunlit world. For a moment, Imogene almost understood the need to fill the halls again with *phae* power...until the old tiles gave way to iron doors, staggered at intervals down the corridor into the shadows.

The metal filled the hall with cold power, older than the *phae*, and the wisps whirled in agitation. But Imogene crept to the first door.

It stood ajar, and the cell beyond was empty. She crossed the hall to the next door, two solid blocks of embossed iron. She reached for the small wooden latch in the center of the door and then hesitated.

Even through the iron, she sensed silence waiting on the other side—a silence so vast, the mischievous wisps hung motionless.

Ice rimed the doorway a hands-breadth thick, and as she

watched, words appeared, melting into the white frost to reveal the black iron underneath: *Touch. And die.*

She hurried on.

The next cell was closed with nothing more than a churchyard gate. The whitewash had chipped off the iron bars, and the decorative spear points did not even reach the top of the door frame.

Not that this particular prisoner could escape...

In a rush of sick shock, Imogene wondered why they had bothered to lock the man up when they had taken his second leg.

She must have gasped because he pushed himself up onto his hips to stare at her with his one remaining eye. His collared shirt hung open, framing the ruin of his chest where the Queen had taken her prizes. "You."

Hazel. His eye was hazel, and his hair was sandy; she hadn't remembered those details about him. Now she would never forget, although there was nothing of blame in his eye or the hatred she expected. He was empty—that hatred having been taken by the Queen for her magics.

Imogene sank to her knees beside the gate. The nearness of the iron made her skin prickle like the first sunburn she had gotten on the Oregon coast, but the stone floor sucked the warmth from her palms. "I am so sorry. I didn't know..." She swallowed back the pointless excuses.

"I did." He pulled himself toward her and wrapped his fingers around the bars, immune as any human to the touch of iron. When he tipped his forehead into the gate, the metal rang with a hollow gong. "I knew better than to follow a pretty young girl into the alley, but we'd danced together all night and I wanted to think I'd be getting something more." When he laughed, there was no humor in it, and the sound grated like the broken edges of tile. "I would never have believed this."

She hunched her shoulders to avert her gaze from his mangled remains. "I almost don't believe it myself."

For a minute, they sat in silence. The wisps floated between the iron bars without touching.

Then the man reached out to grab her hand. "Can you make this all a bad dream?"

At the clammy chill of his skin, she felt as if a dozen red worms had squirmed down her spine. "This time, it isn't an illusion."

"I want to go."

"I might be able to get you out of the cell, but you can't leave." She eased out of his grip. "The Queen's magic is the only thing..."

"The only thing holding me together?" He snatched at her wingtip instead, holding on with more force than she thought could still remain in him. "I wish what is left of me would just fall apart, and then I'd be gone."

The crumpled edge of her wing ached, but she was frozen by the tear that welled up in the man's hazel eye. Apparently the Queen hadn't taken everything from him.

The wounds... The tear... The wistful words... Though the white stone hallway was nothing like the blood-soaked Hunter den where the old Lord had come Undone, Imogene stiffened against the intrusive memory.

Except… The broken whelp who became her Hunter had wanted to fly again, and her knack—not just a wayward breeze, but a powerful yearning—had knit *phae* magic and *sylfana* wishes into his wing, just as it had loosed him from his chain.

Could she do it again?

Hesitantly, she closed her eyes. From nowhere, a faint draft ruffled her lashes, and her eyelids fluttered with the effort to restrain herself from the urge to rise and run from this man whom she had once led astray. At least this time he could not follow her. She tightened her hands into fists, as if she could hold herself in place.

"I just wanted…" he murmured.

Of course the poor man had wanted; as a *sylfana*, she had made him want. Now she had to deliver something real, not illusion. And if he wanted to leave the *phaedrealii*, well, she could certainly understand that.

She summoned up the sensations she had pursued in the sunlit world, how she had felt when she was free, the wind under her wings…

The gust that whirled down the hall whipped her face with dust and the stinging ends of her hair. Her clenched fists—and her eyes—sprang open in surprise, and she braced herself against the man.

The dead man.

She sat back hard against the wall, and her knuckles glanced off the iron. She bit back a scream, but the smell of seared skin made her eyes water and she clutched her hand to her chest.

The man had been dead enough before, considering all the Queen had stolen, but something had remained as a spark in his hazel eye. Now that too was gone, leaving him just another pile of dust and dirt in the abandoned cell block. And she had forgotten to ask his name.

"Is this how you wished to be gone?" The whisper of her breath set the wisps dancing. "Because this is not how I meant to free you."

Was she the first *sylfana* ever to kill a man? The court had its share of murderous *phae*, but its fairy princesses would never dream of such mayhem. Though Vaile had told her she had launched an exodus with her escape, she had never wanted to change so much that she became a killer herself.

Her eyes burned with the wind-flung dust and tears she would not allow to fall. No one would share her horror and guilt—except maybe a Hunter who had killed his own Lord.

Of course, Vaile had conjured other feelings in her she wasn't sure the *phae* even had words for...

Thinking of him triggered a hot rush of longing, and she clamped her arms and wings tight as a cocoon around her, as if she could ward off her own wishes.

She didn't want to want—not anymore.

Though everything in her wanted to flinch away, she looked at the husk of the man slumped against the iron bars. The Queen's magic, which had animated him, was gone, and already his remains were crumbling into the exposed dirt between the tiles and broken stone.

This was her other choice. The poor man had his emotions stripped from him by force, but if she backed down, she would be giving hers away for free.

No, she didn't want the burning in her throat, the sick churning in her stomach as she reached down to stroke her fingers over the dead man's lashes to close his eye before the worms claimed him. To avoid such ugliness, the *phae* had relinquished their true feelings to the Queen in return for sheltering under the power of her illusions. But their sanctuary had become a prison.

The man's emotions had been stolen. The *phae* had deliberately forgotten theirs. Was she deluding herself to believe she had any other choice besides these two?

She could sit here beside her last victim until she too moldered, or...

Imogene snapped her wings wide, which yanked her to her feet.

She had run away once. Maybe the time for running had passed.

Chapter Eight

The court was restless. It breathed out of time, and the languid glory that was its specialty seemed to have morphed into a blend of crouched to pounce and poised to flee. The vaulted crystalline walls—the illusion du jour in the *phaedrealii*—resonated with the edgy mood, like a thinly blown glass goblet about to shatter.

Even the will-o'-the-wisps were jittery, their normally drifting flight patterns spiking like a seismograph predicting the end of the world.

Vaile stalked the outer edges of the throne room, equidistant from his brethren patrolling nearby. The nearness of the Queen's magic stripped them of their camouflaging Hunter mist, so he kept his wings folded in a high, tight arc behind his head. The intimidation factor added by the talon-tipped vanes was worth the tension in his shoulders from holding his wings in suspension.

Whispers spooled out around him as he walked toward the throne room doors.

"Hunters…" he heard. "Dirty, dangerous… Shouldn't be in here…"

"…after the *sylfana*…"

He refused to listen to more.

Dirty was justification enough to bar Hunters from the potent beauty of court. As for dangerous, well, some were just better at hiding it.

But they were right; he was dirty. Before he had been abruptly recalled to service the Queen's gathering, he had been tracking a manticore. The half lion, half scorpion had slipped out through an unwatched gate. Although the man-headed creature was clever enough to sneak away unnoticed, that particular gate was unwatched because it opened to an ice field in Greenland. Vaile had found the desert-born manticore half frozen, and only the scorching fire of the blue-amber sun had melted the wretched beast out of the tundra. But he had refused to consider euthanizing the creature, not when it begged for a second chance. Instead, he used almost all his gate spores to sprout a circle of lichens large enough to drag the manticore back to the *phaedrealii*. Who was he to condemn the creature's hopeless but heartfelt desire to run under the desert sun?

The reminder of his own failings stabbed him like the manticore's scorpion tail. With his leathers still dripping from the ice and tracking muddy boot prints behind him, his mood was every bit as foul.

So dirty, yes, and dangerous too… The *phae* were

wise to avert their gazes and step back from his impatient circuit.

From his position a quarter way around the hall from the Steel Throne, he had only a sharply angled view of the enormous double doors. At the moment, the doors were fashioned into two half circles of shining wood etched with steel filigree, closed tight together like an inescapable spiderweb. Within the throne room, the glimmering veins of steel grew ever thinner until they converged on the throne itself. Some other time, the Queen might conjure another look, but this one was a classic. Maybe she, too, felt the restlessness and hoped to keep the rabble in line with a reminder of her abiding power.

Vaile ran one finger under the edge of his studded Hunter collar and flicked out a chunk of ice that had been melting down his chest, unnoticed. When had he gotten so cold?

He cut a glance toward the throne where the Queen sat at the center of all those steel threads, appearing to beam with silvery light. She posed with her head tilted to one side, listening to her favorite courtier, the elf who seemed to be trying to compensate for his rounded human-looking ears with the pompously high points of his collar. Streaks of silver decorated the Queen's black hair, but that too was illusion; her beauty was ageless and infinitely sharper than the elf's collar, a match to the net of honed diamonds that ringed her bared neck.

As a powerfully attractive *phae* and as his liege, she should have won all his attention. Still, his gaze skipped past to the grouping of her attendants. Undines, dryads, nymphs and the squat goblin who served as her chancellor stood arrayed on the tiers of risers that spread out around the throne.

But no Imogene.

As if the ache in his shoulders wasn't bad enough, his chest tightened with misgivings. He hadn't seen her since the poppy field when she had turned her white-winged back on him and walked away, with crimson petals drifting behind her. The memory still burned in his mind.

He touched the blue amber pendant through the front pocket of his leather jeans. Giving her the necklace had been madness when she could have turned its power upon him. He hadn't needed the touchstone on her person to track her; his knack didn't require help. But at least the amber warned other Hunters to stay away, that she had been claimed by one of their own. When she had thrown the necklace back at him, she had lost that protection.

The weight of the steel in his pocket seemed heavier than it should, and he half turned to adjust the coil of links.

He faced the throne room doors just as they blew open.

Heavy as they were, their wood warped with the force of the blow. The steel filigree screamed in the sudden distortion. The Hunter guarding the entry was thrown aside, while the nearest dozen *phae* stumbled backward, hair and wings and tails streaming in a tempestuous wind. Vaile inhaled the scent of ocean touched with a wild sweetness, like some exotic bloom cresting a tsunami.

Imogene. He did not speak her name aloud, not in the

midst of the treacherous crowd, but his heart lingered on every syllable.

Slowed by the tangle of gawkers, he pushed between the *phae* who had recoiled from the newcomer with panicked cries.

Imogene. He might not have recognized her if he hadn't spent one night memorizing her every detail. What had happened to his flighty *sylfana*? The butterfly-winged spirit had left him and returned as something...else.

The wind prowled like an unseen beast to lift the red-gold curls of her hair in a blazing halo and plaster the wintry-blue shift around her curves. The princess in pink had remade herself in fire and ice. The will-o'-the-wisps knew her though and whirled around her in a joyful spiral.

She stared toward the Steel Throne, her eyes bluer than any sky Vaile had ever flown, and his wings flared, instinctively—ecstatically—seeking the storm she had brought. The nearest *phae* scattered from the Hunter mist that spun from his dark vanes.

He cleared only a few steps before the Queen's voice rang out from behind him. "Hunters, stop her! She is Undone!"

The Queen had risen from her throne to point across the room, sending the elf-man reeling back.

The accusation halted Vaile in his tracks, all the momentum leaving his muscles as if the destructive power of an amber sun had gone off within his bones.

Undone? Like the old mad Lord of the Wild Hunt? The

knotted scar behind his shoulder cramped, half folding his vanes.

At the same time, Imogene spread her wings. Against the wide-flung doors with their steel spiderweb filigree, the butterfly scales looked soft and fragile—not dangerous, as the Undoing implied, but endangered.

At the Queen's command, a half-dozen Hunters converged from the far points of the throne room on the lone *sylfana*. Several of them were too young to have witnessed the old Lord's Undoing, and the new Lord Hunter had been away at the time, but he led the phalanx of killers with a brittle smile.

The gathered *phae* scrambled to clear the way, getting more *in* the way. In their haste, slip-sliding on jeweled heels or cloven feet, a few stumbled into Vaile. He pushed them aside roughly to keep his gaze pinned on Imogene.

The chaos churned in waves around her silent form— as if she were oblivious to the Queen's charge of coming Undone, not to mention the charging Hunters.

Vaile's chest burned with the compulsion to cry out her name. He had found her, and he had lost her.

But here she was. Was his knack giving him one last chance to find his way to her?

He had learned to fear the Undoing even before he had lost the whelp's chain. He had taken up other chains since—the Hunter's collar, the hounds' leashes, the steel links of the amber sun—but it was that first chain that bound him still, in knots thicker than the scar that would have kept him from flying if not for a *sylfana*'s fearless touch.

He could not let her get away again.

With a hard snap, he straightened the remembered twist to his wing and launched himself over the heads of the fleeing *phae*.

The throne room, large thought it was, offered little room for maneuvering. His trailing boots made the *phae* below duck and squeal. But the awkward hop put him between the other Hunters and Imogene. He landed with a solid thud and angled himself toward the throne, arms and wings outstretched to ward them away from each other. The Hunters slowed their rush, and their Lord stared at him expectantly, waiting no doubt for the violent undoing of the Undone.

Vaile could not force himself to look at Imogene, though his body yearned toward hers. "Wait." His voice cracked.

"Hail, Hunter." Across the empty crystalline hall, the Queen raised her hand in an elegant gesture. A few dozen of her courtiers lingered near the throne, their personal illusions flickering with their unease. "Once again, you bring us the troublesome *sylfana*."

He inclined his head. "My Queen, I bring you nothing this time. My hunt is over." He took a deep breath. "I have found what I was looking for."

Slowly, he pivoted to face Imogene. The distance in her eyes almost felled him.

When he had flown the Oregon coast, seeking her, he had one night lost track of where midnight-dark sky and boundless ocean touched. He had spiraled for a few frantic heartbeats, out of control, before he found his bearings and righted himself.

He did not think he would be so lucky this time.

He lowered his wings, leaving only one hand outstretched toward her. "You," he said quietly. "I found you."

Her voice was even quieter when she answered, "It would be best for you to pretend you never had."

From her shadowed gaze, he knew she meant not just as a Hunter finds a runaway *phae* but the way, together, they'd found sweet release.

"I can't forget," he told her. "Do you remember you told me once, long ago, that I wouldn't always feel your touch as I did then? You were right. I feel more."

So softly they spoke, and still the word *feel* echoed around them as if it had stolen magic from the very air. Across the room, the Queen descended from the Steel Throne.

Imogene lifted her chin, and her smile at Vaile was cold, colder than an undine's grave water, colder than Greenland ice under a manticore's poisonous quills. "How could you feel anything? I couldn't even see through your glamour, much less touch you."

"Maybe you didn't see that I am a Hunter, but you saw something more. Something I've never shown anyone." The furious pressure of the approaching Queen almost knotted his tongue. "You saw a way to my heart, which had never been touched. Until you."

"A heart can't be touched." At the icy cruelty of Imogene's smile, the nearest Hunter sidled back. "Not unless it is removed from the chest first." The faintest crack appeared in her cold look when she gazed at Vaile. "As for your so-called heart? It was a lie."

"No. You didn't see what I was. But you saw *who* I am. And who I could be."

"And who is that, Hunter?"

"Yours. I would be yours."

The remaining courtiers—who had drifted closer, drawn by the sentiments they had shunned—loosed a whisper of sound, a sigh that vibrated the silver threads of the walls into a single music tone.

"You did touch my heart," he promised her. "You made me love you."

The doubt that turned down the corners of her mouth nearly shattered him. If she escaped him again, this time he would die; like a Hunter who lost his prey would be torn apart by his own hounds, so his heart would be shredded. She wavered, as if buffeted by winds that touched only her. But he felt them too, tearing through his veins. His arm—though honed as the rest of him from centuries of flying and fighting—burned with the effort of reaching out. Maybe it would be easier to tuck close and dive until every sensation was stripped away.

But then he wouldn't have Imogene. He would give her what she wanted—these corrupting, dangerous feelings— even if he had to spin them out of the nothingness of his heart into something real.

Slowly, with her gaze locked on his, Imogene raised her hand.

"No!" Behind him, the Queen's growl was more sinister than any Hunter's hound.

But it was the sound of glass whistling through the air that made him whirl.

The Lord Hunter stumbled into his Hunters' arms as the Queen had shoved him away. The three-sided glass sword of the Wild Hunt beamed in her hand.

She angled the sword toward Vaile and Imogene. "This farce ceases to amuse me."

"Not a farce, my Queen." Vaile took a sidelong step to cover Imogene with his body, but he kept his voice steady. "This is true."

"True love?" The virulence of the Queen's sneer melted the diamonds around her neck. The droplets fell like tears only to congeal again as the temperature in the throne room plummeted. "A figment of your imagination. We sacrificed that to be what we are—powerful, glorious, forever. *Phae.*"

Vaile shook his head. "If we lost it, then I have found it again. Here."

The Queen raised the sword. Its prismatic edges captured light just as it captured magic, and sliced rainbows all around them. A low, ominous drone pulsed from the glass. "That is nothing. Nothing!"

Her hiss curled up in an icy plume, and the prism went dark. The rainbows winked out, sucked into the glass.

Surrounded by suddenly hungry shadows, Vaile reached

for the blue amber necklace. Its power had turned a nameless whelp into a Hunter. Without it, he would be...

Well, if he did this right, he and Imogene would be alive.

The sword flared with stolen light just as he whipped the chain from his pocket. The pendant arced upward like a blue shooting star.

And the pyramid point of the sword—hungrily drawn to magics—tracked its flight.

The Queen cursed. The Lord Hunter launched himself to her side, reaching for her hands to correct the sword's attack.

But the sword had already chosen its prey, and the fire that licked from its tip was brighter than a thousand amber suns.

The pendant disintegrated in a blue mist, surrendering its magic to the entrapping prism, but Vaile was already whirling away, reaching for Imogene. In the stark light, his shadow was blacker than his spread vanes. Her white wings flared as she slapped her palm into his.

A hard wind lifted both of them and spun them between the twisted wreckage of the double doors. He stumbled into her with a distinct lack of *phae* grace, feeling like an awkward whelp again, still seeking his wings.

Until she pulled him into her arms and her lips found his...

This, this *was* everything, everything he wanted, everything he had dreamed.

And it would be the last thing he knew before the Queen's magic blasted them into oblivion.

He deepened the kiss, a wild dance of tongues since he would never have the chance to dance with her to the pipes and bells of the *phae*. Instead, the wind sang around them, whistling through the broken filigree of the doors. The wind lifted their wings, his heart, the edge of her skirt up to her thigh.... He clamped his hand on her bare skin and pulled her hard into his body.

His pulse sang louder than the wind, and his blood burned hotter than any amber sun. Imogene's wisps joined the dance, whirled by her knack. Their little white lights glimmered in the soft facets of the melted diamonds that were caught in the helix winding around them. Between the ruin of the flung doors, Vaile and Imogene were caged in a shine of wisps and diamond and twisted steel.

The Queen's fury lashed out again, sharpened by the glass sword, but the delicate web—hardly more than nothingness—that had sprung up at their kiss caught and scattered the blast of magic in all directions.

And shattered the sword.

The courtiers screamed and fled from the deadly shrapnel. The Queen's shriek was louder yet as the shards of the prism remaining in her hand burned with black flames.

The wisps danced on, free as always.

Imogene raised her hand to Vaile's cheek. "Want to run?"

"Only with you." He yanked the vial of gate spores from his pocket and scattered a hasty circle.

For a desperate heartbeat, he feared he had used too many on returning the manticore, that the crystal floor was too slick, too desolate, for the gate to bloom, but before his eyes sprang up a circle of ivy. The leafy tendrils wove into the steel lattice. Through the barrier, the Queen's cries sounded far away.

Imogene touched the heart-shaped leaves. "Where does the gate open?"

"Someplace we can make our own magic."

Imogene slipped her hand into his. "Take me there, Vaile, my love."

He kissed her, hard and quick. "I've been dreaming of taking you again, ever since that night. But I have loved you far longer than that."

She touched the curve of his lower lip, and her blue eyes glinted with promises of passion. "As I am yours." But she looked back over her shoulder between the wrecked doors. "We *phae* have given up our dreams for illusion. Are they all as lost as I was?"

"You might have been lost, but you found me. You would make an excellent Hunter. Or maybe savior."

"I doubt the Queen will see it that way."

"Her lies and stolen power can't last. I fear it is the court of the steel-born *phae* that will come undone in the end."

He took Imogene's hand and slipped his last piece of blue amber—the ring—over her finger. He raised her hand to his lips, soothing the iron burn across her knuckles; that story would have to wait until they found their new sanctuary.

When the gate magic flared, she raised herself up to kiss him. Her fingers brushed along his jaw and dropped to his neck. The studded collar, long welded in place, sprang open, and he caught his breath.

She half closed her eyes, and the wind of her knack spread his wings with a caress from shoulders to talons. A few wayward wisps tickled under the vanes like bubbles. He had to smile. "I felt that."

Her answering smile lifted his heart as she stepped into his arms and crossed with him into the gate. "You caught me, Hunter. Just as I wished."

* * * * *

HEART OF THE HUNTER
Vivi Anna

A bad girl at heart, **Vivi Anna** likes to burn up the pages with her original unique brand of fantasy fiction. Whether it's in ancient Egypt or in an apocalyptic future, Vivi always writes fast-paced action-adventure with strong independent women that can kick some butt, and dark delicious heroes to kill for.

Once shot at while repossessing a car, Vivi decided that maybe her life needed a change. The first time she picked up a pen and put words to paper, she knew she had found her heart. Within two paragraphs, she realized she could write about getting into all sorts of trouble without suffering the consequences.

When Vivi isn't writing, you can find her causing a ruckus at downtown bistros, flea markets or playgrounds.

Chapter One

The biting wind blew across Jake Conroy's back as he sat waiting on the wooden bench. He pulled up the collar on his leather jacket but it wasn't doing much good. It was damn cold in Calgary in November. He should've been more prepared for the hunt than wearing only his thin leather jacket, leather gloves and boots. Thankfully he was wearing wool socks, so at least his feet weren't freezing.

He turned as his Canadian contact, Ryan, sat down beside him, handing him a tall, steaming cup. "Here. Timmies. It'll warm you up."

Jake took the offered drink. "What's Timmies?"

"Best coffee ever."

Jake took a grateful sip and sighed. It was good. He didn't know if it was the best coffee he'd ever tasted, but on this chilly night, it very well might've been. At least it was piping hot. It burned his tongue, but he didn't care as long as it warmed up his insides.

"Any movement?" Ryan asked.

Jake shook his head, not taking his eyes off the third-floor window of the building across the street. The light was still on and there hadn't been any change. As far as he could tell the demon son-of-a-bitch was still inside the building.

He'd been sitting on the bench on Stephen Avenue for three hours now, waiting for the demon to make a move. According to his contact, the demon had morphed into the body of one Brian Rose, an accountant, who worked until six, then walked down the block to the pub to have a few drinks and scout out his next victim. Jake had been in the pub and checked it out for exits just in case.

Jake glanced at his watch. It was now six-thirty. "You said this guy leaves at six."

Ryan shrugged. "Maybe he's working late."

"Trust me, the demon is not working in there. Do you really think he's going to assimilate this accountant's life so he can do taxes all freaking day?"

"What's he doing then?"

"Planning his next move."

Jake had made the long trip from San Francisco up to Calgary to hunt this demon. He wanted to say he was doing it for the morality of it, but the fact was he was being paid. Demon hunting wasn't a lucrative vocation, so once in a while he had to take paying jobs. Sometimes he did bodyguard work, other times he located missing people, but this time he'd been hired by a wealthy family member of one of the demon's last victims to track it down and kill it. The assignment was right up his alley.

"Do you think he made us?" Ryan asked.

Jake stood and adjusted the harness around his shoulder. He had a 9 mm Beretta holstered there, as well as two silver daggers blessed by a priest with holy water and salt. "Is there a back entrance to the building?"

Ryan shrugged. "There's an alley."

"Damn it." Not waiting for Ryan, Jack jogged down the avenue to the corner, turned it and followed the street until he hit the mouth of the alley.

He peered down the dark lane and saw a shadowy shape walking swiftly away from him. Ryan came up behind Jake. "Is that him?"

"Don't know, but I'm going to find out."

Jake started at a slow jog, but as soon as he was halfway down the alleyway, the shadowed shape began to run. He guessed he had his answer.

He chased the spectre down the lane. The demon was fast, faster than a normal human. But Jake was in great shape and had trained for years for this type of activity. He was able to stay up to speed. He'd never outrun the demon, but he could at least see where it was running to.

The demon in the accountant suit, rounded the corner to the left and dashed down the sidewalk. As Jake came around, he nearly ran into an old woman with a walker. She yelled at him but he didn't have time to stop and make sure she was okay. By the ire in her cracked voice, he didn't think she was in any immediate danger or pain.

He watched as the demon dashed across the street, jumping over the cars and on top of them. There were honks and tires screeching, but no accidents. Jake had to wait a bit before he could follow. After the last car raced away, he ran across the road and picked up the demon's trail.

It wasn't hard to find, since the demon was swinging from the white metal decorative structures that lined either side of the trendy shopping district. Like Spiderman, the demon swung from one to the next, but there was no webbing holding him up, just sheer supernatural strength.

Incredulously, Jake ran after him, careful of running into anyone. A bum sitting on one of the benches watched as the demon swung over top of him.

As Jake sprinted by, he yelled, "Are you guys making a movie?"

"We sure are," Jake responded, hoping to keep this strangeness out of morning papers. He also didn't need the police around either. They'd just want to arrest the man, when Jake needed to kill him. They'd probably arrest Jake as well. There were laws against carrying concealed weapons in Canada.

The demon was nearing a glassed-in walkway that spanned the shopping lane. Instead of dropping to the ground and going under, it jumped onto it, breaking glass panes as he went, and landed on the other side at full throttle.

Jake's boot crunched the glass fragments as he ran under the pedestrian bridge. The police would definitely be alerted now. The damage wasn't immense but it was enough to draw attention. He had to end this quickly.

He had to get the demon off the streets.

Reaching under his jacket, he withdrew a weapon. It was a small crossbow he had modified especially for this type of work. It was already cocked and loaded with a silver-tipped arrow blessed with holy water. It might not kill the demon, but it would slow him down enough that Jake could drag him off the public street and deal with him in private.

The demon rounded the corner before Jake could get an arrow off. Running with his weapon at his side, Jake sprinted after it. It ducked down another alley. This was perfect for Jake, except now it was dark and he couldn't see much. He only had four arrows with him, so making a bad shot and losing an arrow wasn't really an option at this point. He needed all the weapons he had to complete his job.

As he ran, he kept an eye on the shadow bouncing around in front of him. Then the shadow bounced up and kept going skyward. Was it flying? He'd never heard of a demon with flight ability. But as he got closer, he could see a set of fire escapes leading to the roof. Damn it. He really didn't want to go up there. He hated heights. It wasn't that he was afraid; it was the chance of falling he didn't relish.

Jake reached the bottom rung of the metal ladder and pulled it down. He mounted the steps and climbed as fast as he could. In a matter of minutes he was at the top and clambering onto the seventh-story rooftop.

It was lighter up top so he could see fairly well. The

demon was nowhere in sight. He didn't hear it jump off so it had to be up here somewhere, hiding, waiting to spring out at Jake and rip out his throat.

Cautiously, Jake moved across the gravelled roof, careful not to make too much noise. But it proved difficult especially with the crunching of stones underfoot. Pointing the crossbow forward, he did a sweep of the area, tensing at every shadow.

He neared a large metal box on the roof. It probably contained electrical equipment for the building, or was an air filtration system. Either way it was a perfect structure to hide behind.

Sweat soaked the back of his shirt under his jacket and it beaded on his top lip. Adrenaline pumped through his body, making him keenly aware of every movement, every sound around him.

That was why the slight swish of fabric on fabric made him stop and spin around.

Its face twisted in rage, the demon levelled its razor-sharp claws at Jake's throat. As if in slow motion, Jake could see the arc of its hand. He hoped he could pull the trigger on his bow before it reached him.

The arrow zinged by the demon, narrowly missing its shoulder. An error that would likely cost Jake his life.

"Conroy! Drop!"

Instinctively, Jake dropped to the ground.

He heard the knife *swoosh* through the air, but he didn't see it. But he did hear the telltale thunk of the blade hitting its mark. Turning his head to the side, he saw the demon stumble backwards, and its shriek of fury and pain echoed over the rooftop.

Its claw wrapped around the hilt of the knife and it pulled the blade out of its chest, dropped it to the ground and turned and ran the other way. It dashed to the edge of the roof and jumped.

A pair of black boots came into Jake's view, and he rolled over onto his back and looked up at his savior.

A woman with fire-red hair and golden eyes looked down at him, a bemused expression on her face. She offered her gloved hand to him.

"Need some help getting up, Conroy?"

Jake sighed. Just what he needed. His ex-girlfriend, Gianna Morgan, saving his life.

Chapter Two

Gianna pulled Jake to his feet. What he secretly wanted to do was to pull her down with him, just to be childish and spiteful—two things she accused him of being years ago when they broke up.

He wiped at his jeans, trying to be cool. "What are you doing here?"

"What, no thank-you for saving your ass?"

He stared at her, not wanting to give her any satisfaction. "What are you doing here?"

"Same as you. I'm hunting."

"This is my demon."

She shrugged. The movement gaped open her jacket, revealing her ample cleavage. Despite his dislike of her, his gaze dropped to her breasts. That was one thing he'd always admired about her. Her bustline.

Gianna caught him looking, and then zipped up her

jacket. She shook her head. "Why does that look not surprise me?"

"Because I'm a guy."

"That's always your excuse." She sniffed, and then bent down to retrieve her blade. She wiped the blood off on her pants then sheathed it back into her ankle holster.

"Yeah, well I can't help it if it's true."

She glanced at him with one eyebrow quirked up as if thinking, "You are such an idiot."

"Like I said, this is my demon. I'm being paid to hunt him down and kill him."

"So am I."

He gaped at her. "What? By who?"

"I'm not at liberty to say. You know clients are confidential."

"Don't give me that shit, Gi, just tell me." He flinched inwardly at using his nickname for her. If it bothered her, she didn't show it.

She gnawed on her bottom lip, which was a sign she was seriously thinking. She'd done that right before she tossed him out of her apartment along with all his clothes and his toothbrush.

"Daniel Frost."

Jake sighed, then clenched a fist and banged it on his leg. "Damn it."

"I take it he hired you as well."

He nodded.

"Well, I guess I can't blame the guy. He wants to find whoever killed his daughter. I can get behind that."

Jake wanted to bitch and complain about the situation, but the fact of the matter was he didn't blame the guy, either. His daughter had been tortured and raped and killed, left in a dumpster like day-old trash. Jake would've done everything in his power to find her killer, too.

"What now?" he asked.

She shrugged. "Don't know about you, Sport, but I'm going down and tracking this bastard again." She turned on her boot heel and headed toward the fire escape.

"Wait. We should work together. It'll be easier and we can pool our resources."

She stopped midstride and turned to glare at him. "No way. I remember the last time we worked together."

"That was different. We were sleeping together then. Mixing business and pleasure never works out well."

She eyed him as if she were dissecting him. He used to love that look from her. Her gold eyes were so bright and intense that they usually gave him chills. Before it was a look of desire, hard lust, saying she wanted to rip his clothes off and have him right there and then. Now, the look just said: I don't trust you anymore.

Some two years later, it still hurt.

"All right. But we are in this fifty-fifty. You don't tell me what to do."

"Okay. That goes the same for you."

"Fine."

He smirked. "Do you want to shake on it? Or we could hug and kiss, if that's what you want."

She shook her head. "Not likely." She turned back to

the fire escape, but not before Jake saw a slight lift of her luscious full mouth.

He knew she was fighting a smile. He could always make her laugh. And that was probably the problem. He always looked for the humor in the situation to diffuse the tension. Even when he knew deep down that humor was the last thing Gianna was looking for.

He followed her down to the alleyway. Ryan was waiting for them at the bottom. Jake jumped from the last rung. "I hope you saw where it went."

Ryan shook his head. "Was I supposed to?"

Gianna smirked. "Who is this, your minion?"

"My contact."

Ryan followed close at Jake's heels as they all went out onto the street. "Hey, I didn't know I was supposed to track this dude. I thought I was just the scout. I find the location, you do the chasing and catching and killing."

"So find us another location."

"I need a place to plug in." He lifted the bag hanging around his shoulder. "And a warm place so my fingers don't freeze off." Jake knew Ryan always carried his laptop. It was like an extension of him. Jake supposed it was like his 9 mm to him.

Fifteen minutes later, they were seated in a local fast-food joint, drinking bad coffee and eating bad hamburgers. Ryan was doing his thing on his laptop at a separate table. He was searching for all known places of business and home addresses related to the accountant who was housing the demon. Jake hoped they could track it down before it went underground. If it did that, the chances of it resurfacing any time soon would be slim to none. They'd have to wait weeks, possibly even months, before they got another shot at taking it out.

Jake dunked a couple of fries into the ketchup blob on his hamburger wrapper. He noticed Gianna watching him. He popped the fries into his mouth and grinned at her. "Do I have something on my face?"

She smiled. "Just wondering if you're going to eat all of those." She gestured to his pile of fries.

He shook his head, and pushed them toward her. She grabbed three at once and dunked them in his ketchup. She folded them into her mouth. A spot of ketchup was left on the side of her mouth.

He grinned again. He'd always loved that about her: the fact that she ate like a guy. She didn't fuss and obsess over the calories she was putting in her body. She liked to eat and cook. When they'd been together, she'd cook him huge meals with several courses. Sometimes he'd help her in the kitchen, and usually it would end up with them making love on the counters, or table, or he'd pick her up and carry her to the bed. And afterward, they would return to the kitchen and continue on making the meal, feeling more joy than they had to begin with.

His smile faded. Jake missed those times more than he cared to admit.

Gianna noticed. "What's wrong?"

He shook his head, and wiped his greasy fingers on a

napkin. "Nothing. Just hoping we can track this bastard down again."

"We will. Despite everything, we're both really good at our jobs."

He nodded, realizing she knew what he'd been thinking about. Them. Their failed relationship. "Well, I can think of something else we were both really good at."

She smiled around more fries. "Sex was definitely not our problem." Was that a mischievous gleam in her eyes?

"Nope, it certainly wasn't." Jake became uncomfortable in his seat just thinking about the two of them together. The fun they had; the passion that had always swelled between them. "You know, my hotel room has a king-sized bed."

There was that gleam again. She licked her lips and tilted her head to look at him. She opened her mouth to answer, when Ryan stood up and declared, "I know where the demon's going."

Chapter Three

Gianna walked beside Jake as they followed Ryan to his car, parked three blocks away on a dark side street. They left her rental where it was. They didn't need to take two vehicles.

She tried to keep from glancing at his profile. He was a good looking man, Jake. Built like a linebacker but not busted up like one. His nose was still perfectly straight, and he had an amazing smile. It lit up any room he was in. It also made her stomach flip to see it. Even after all this time apart, she found her belly clenching when he smiled at her. It was a dangerous feeling.

It was how they'd got involved in the first place. A smile across a dark and dirty bar, as both of them had been scouting out their next hunt.

She wouldn't let it go down that road again. She couldn't do it and not get hurt. There were still pieces of her heart missing. Pieces she knew she'd never fill again. And spackling them over with some amazing sex wasn't a healthy choice.

It might make her feel extremely good and satisfied. And would definitely work off some of the tension and stress she'd been feeling lately. And frankly it had been quite a while since she had sex....

Gianna shook her head. She had to stop thinking about Jake. It was a bad idea. She needed to concentrate on the job at hand; taking down this demon was all that mattered. Everything else could wait until she had a clear head to figure out what she wanted to do with their relationship.

They piled into Ryan's Toyota Camry and drove for maybe ten minutes, Ryan chatting the whole time.

"I realized that the demon would need a good quiet place to torture and kill his victims, and I figured his nice suburban condo probably wouldn't work. So I cross referenced any holdings with the accountant's name and any relatives." He raced around the corner, tires screeching. "I came up with an address in Ogden. It's an older area of town, which has had problems in the past with drug dealers and prostitutes. It's being gentrified now, but there are still some houses that are nearing condemned status. One such address belonged to the accountant's mother, who conveniently passed away last month."

Convenient, my ass. Gianna bristled at that. The demon was systematically disassembling this guy's life. Killing his relatives, and basically making him one of Canada's most wanted. Even though the demon had only been possessing the host body, Brian Rose could never go back to his life. If he didn't get arrested, the trauma of it all would definitely send him to the nearest nut house.

Ryan pulled into an older neighborhood, with huge trees lining the cracked road. In the dark, Gianna thought it looked peaceful and even idyllic. But she imagined in the daylight, a person could see all the potholes in the road, the craters in the sidewalks and the disarray of all the houses. Paint peeling, lawns unmowed, abandoned cars up on cement blocks. She'd seen countless neighborhoods just like this one all over North America. It was a prime spot for demons and other undesirables.

Ryan rolled to a stop along one street and parked on the curb. He pointed to a house about four houses down.

"That's it right there."

Both Gianna and Jake got out of the car and came around to sit on the hood, as if they were doing nothing but minding their own business. Gianna eyed the small blue-and-white bungalow. It had two garage doors instead of one large one, which was common in the seventies when the house was built. The lawn was weed infested, and the walkway was cracked, a couple of the stones were even missing. It didn't look like anyone had lived in it for years. But of course that wasn't the case. If Ryan was correct, the demon inhabiting Brian Rose's body was inside licking its wounds and planning its next move.

The demon was vulnerable right now. They needed a good plan of attack so they could take it out. This might be their last chance.

"So what do you think?" Jake asked.

She eyed the house and the surroundings. "We're on his turf. There could be traps all over the place. He might have a bolt hole in the basement. It's going to be dangerous."

"It's always dangerous, Gi." He nudged her in the side with his elbow. "That's why we love it so much."

"True."

"We can't let this hellspawn escape again. We have to take it out here and now."

She nodded. "How about we salt the front and back doors and the doors to the garage? We step over the lines, but essentially it can't cross to get out. It would be trapped inside."

"With us trapped in with it."

She smirked. "Yup, just the way we like it." She pushed off the car hood. "Let's load up."

They walked around to the trunk of the car. Ryan popped it open for them. Jake unzipped his bag and started pulling out all his tools of the trade. She did as well. By the time they were done, it looked like they were big-game hunters, with all their weapons and harnesses and bags strung over their shoulders.

Jake closed the trunk quietly, then went to the open driver's side window to talk to Ryan. "Stick around as long as you can. Keep the motor running in case we've got to get out of here fast."

"What if it comes out?"

"If it gets out of that house, then that means we're likely dead and you should get the hell out of Dodge."

Ryan nodded, then rolled up his window. Gianna could

see him shivering although she knew the car heater was going full blast. She wondered if it was the kid's first hunt.

Together, she and Jake crossed the street. As they approached the house, they stopped near the big oak tree on the east corner. It provided good cover for the moment.

"I'll take the back," she announced.

Jake frowned. "Like hell you will. I'll take the back, Gianna. We don't know what's there. There could be a hellhound running around for all we know."

"I told you I'd only share this job if you didn't tell me what to do."

"It's not like that, and you know it. It's the best way to go. I'm bigger and make more noise. In the back I'll be away from prying eyes. We don't need the cops all over this until we finish it."

She sighed. He was right. She just hated having to admit it. He usually gloated about it afterward. "Fine. Let's do it." But before she could step away from the tree, Jake grabbed her arm and pulled her toward him. She looked up into his face. "What?"

"I just want you to know that I've thought about you every day for the past two years. For me, you and I will never be over."

"Jake. Do you really think this is the best time to talk about us?"

"It may be our only time, and you know it."

Gianna didn't know what to say to him. What would be the point in admitting that she thought about him as well? That she'd kept pictures of them together, and to this day looked at them when she was alone. Telling him wouldn't change anything. They couldn't be together. It was too hard. Too much work.

She was about to open her mouth to say something, anything, but Jake pulled her closer. He wrapped a big hand behind her neck, his thumb nuzzling against her jaw, and tilted her head up to his. Leaning down, he claimed her mouth.

He kissed her hard. She wanted to push him away, knowing it would be the right thing to do, but she couldn't. His lips felt too good on hers, his breath hot and steamy, and the taste of him was like ambrosia.

She lifted her hands and buried them in his hair and kissed him back. It was a long, wet, hot kiss that she wished would last for hours. But it soon ended and, out of breath, she ran a hand down his chest and tried to smile.

"I missed you, too," she said. And then, dropping her hand, she turned and headed for the house.

Chapter Four

They moved toward the bungalow, staying in the shadows. Gianna kept an eye on the house next door, where lights still burned bright in the windows. The last thing they needed was for the cops to show up and arrest them for trespassing or worse, breaking and entering, which is what they were planning to do.

Gianna took up a position in the front as Jake rounded the corner to head to the back. She told him she would wait five minutes for him to get prepared before she drew the last line and picked the lock on the front door.

But she was never one for waiting.

She took out her lock-picking tools and got to work on the lock. In one minute flat, she had the lock disengaged. She took out her salt bag and poured a thick line along the bottom of the door frame. There was no way the demon was getting out the front door.

Carefully she turned the knob and slowly pushed the

door open, praying it didn't squeak. She hoped that Jake was also gaining entrance to the back of the house. If he wasn't, she might very well be in some deep trouble. Although she'd been in that kind of situation countless times before.

Once in, Gianna paused in the front foyer to get her bearings and adjust her eyesight to the dark inside. She also paused to attune her hearing. The house wasn't completely silent. Nothing ever was. There were some noises she could discern. The hum of the furnace kicking in, the tick of a clock probably hanging on one of the walls, and the tell-tale creak of a door opening. Jake was inside.

Quietly, she crept across the living room and met up with Jake in the kitchen. He had his crossbow loaded with a silver-tipped arrow. It was ready to fire. He pointed to the closed door in the kitchen. It likely led down to a basement.

She nodded, and then put her hand on the knob. "On three," she whispered.

He nodded.

"One, two…"

The door slammed open and the Brian Rose doppelganger came rushing out, pushing Gianna with the force of the door. She stumbled back hitting the far wall.

Before she could recover and come at him, the demon had already cut Jake. Thankfully it was across his forearm and not anywhere vital. Still it bled like a crimson river. And it was enough for him to drop the crossbow. It skittered across the kitchen floor.

"Gi, get the crossbow!" Jake yelled as he fought off the demon who was trying desperately to give him a matching gash on his face.

Gianna skirted round the demon and scrambled for the crossbow. She managed to scoop it up and turn in one swoop. Except Jake was in the way. She couldn't get a clear shot.

"Shoot it!"

Grinning like a maniac, the demon had Jake up against the kitchen counter, its claws pressed to his throat. Even in the dark she could see the blood beading on Jake's skin.

"I'll hit you," she said, her hands starting to shake.

"Do it! It's our only chance."

Gianna raised the bow and aimed for the demon's back, just below his right shoulder blade. The arrow would pierce its heart, killing it, but the tip would go straight through and likely pierce Jake's chest as well.

"Now, Gi!"

Holding her breath, she pulled the trigger.

The arrow sang, straight and true, through the air. A nanosecond before it hit its mark, Jake shoved the demon backward. The arrow shot into its back and the tip shot out its chest. The silver tip just touching Jake in the sternum.

Gianna let the breath she was holding out in a quaking rush as the demon collapsed to the kitchen floor, its eyes still open and staring lifelessly out through Brian Rose's dead body, or what looked like him. She had to remember that it wasn't really him. That she hadn't killed an innocent. It was still sad to see.

Jake pushed away from the counter, letting out the breath he was holding as well. He looked down at the body. "That was damn close."

She inspected his arm, which was coated in blood. "This looks bad. You're going to need stitches."

"We need to salt and burn the body first. My arm can wait."

As she grabbed her bag from where she'd it dropped earlier and took out the bag of salt, Jake kicked the body over onto its back. Before she salted it, he took out his cell phone and snapped several pictures of the body. It was evidence that they had done the job for the client.

Starting at the head, she liberally sprinkled the salt until she reached the feet. She shoved the remaining salt back into her bag. Jake squirted lighter fluid all over, then lit a wooden match and dropped it. The flames were instant.

In silence, they watched the demon burn until there was nothing left but ashes. It didn't take long as the salt and the demon's own physiology increased the burn rate. Jake bent down and brushed the remains into a small wooden box.

When it was done, they collected their equipment and Gianna wiped up the blood Jake had dripped on the counter and floor. After everything was clean, she shoved the dirty cloths into her bag and followed Jake out of the house and down to the car. Jake got in the back while she slid into the passenger's side.

Ryan glanced at her, then at Jake. "So? Did you get him?"

"It's done," Jake said. "You can drop us at the hotel."

"Okay." Ryan put the car in gear and pulled away from the curb.

Gianna turned in her seat to tell him where he could drop her off but she caught Jake's gaze. All thoughts of going somewhere else, away from him, dissipated like fog in the morning sunshine. She had other things she needed to do, but this was where she wanted to be.

Chapter Five

Jake and Gianna didn't talk as they took the elevator up to the Jake's hotel room on the fourth floor. Ryan had dropped them off with a promise he'd return in the morning to tie up any loose ends for the job.

The elevator dinged, the door slid open and they shuffled out and down the hall to his room. He slid the key card in, waited for green, and then opened the door. Gianni walked in, dragging her bag. He followed, making sure to lock and bolt the door behind him.

After dumping her bag on the floor, she turned to him. "Take off your jacket and your shirt."

"Whoa, baby. Let's have a drink first and get to know each other."

She gave him that look, the one that said she was going to knock him in the nose if he didn't do as she asked. He had to admit he loved that look. Her gilded eyes flashed in annoyance.

He chuckled. "Can't a guy joke around?"

"You can joke all you want after I stitch you up."

"Okay, okay, but your idea of foreplay is not what I remember." He slipped his leather jacket off, dropping it to the floor, then as carefully as he could he stripped off his shirt. "The Gigi I used to know was all kinds of fun."

He sat on the edge of the bed as she gathered the first-aid kit. She unzipped it and took out the alcohol swab.

"You ripped all the fun out of me, Jake."

She wiped his arm with the wet medicated cloth. The sting was instant but he sucked it up. As she worked the pain abated a little. He watched her, searching her face, mentally tracing the lines at her eyes and the determined tilt of her mouth.

"I'm sorry I did that to you."

She looked at him, surprised. "Doesn't matter. It's in the past. Anyway it wasn't as horrid as I made it sound."

"It was horrid enough for you to stop loving me though."

Looking away, she didn't comment and continued to clean his arm. Was that a tick of her eye?

"You did stop loving me, right?"

Gianna tossed the swab in the trash can and reached into the kit for the needle and thread.

He touched her hand. "Gi? You don't love me, right?"

"Can we just get your arm fixed, please? I'll feel better when you're not bleeding all over the place. Because I ain't cleaning it up."

He dropped his hand and nodded, letting her do her thing. Although he hated any type of needle, he watched her poke the steel tip through his skin and stitch it. She was good with the needle. Always had been. Every scar he had was from a wound Gianna had sewn up. When he looked at them, he remembered her fixing him up, putting him back together again.

"Hey, remember that time in Boston when you had to stitch me up on the subway?"

She smiled. "Yeah, gave those other passengers quite a show."

"Hey, I couldn't help it if I got clawed across the derriere."

"That was definitely my best work.'"

They laughed together at that.

He watched her nimble fingers complete the last few stitches and wished she would touch him in other places. He didn't realize how much he'd missed her touch, her smell, her voice, everything about her, until now. He had been walking around broken since they'd been apart.

"You know after that last time on the subway, I haven't gotten wounded. Not like that. Not like this. Just small cuts and bumps and bruises."

She tied off the thread and cut it. He flexed his arm. It was good, tight work as usual.

"I guess I knew I didn't have you to piece me back together anymore. So I better not get hurt."

She set the needle back in the bag. "I'm not sure what to do with that, Jake."

He shrugged. "Me either."

Gianna zipped up the kit, picked it up, and went to set

it back into her gear. "I guess we should contact the client and tell him we've completed the job."

Jake stared at her, willing her to stop moving about. He didn't want the job to end. Because then they'd be done. Again. He didn't want to leave Canada without her.

Her back was to him when he spoke. "My old man never laughed. He was a really serious man."

She slowly turned and looked at him.

"I'd never seen him smile or laugh. Not once. And I vowed as I grew up I'd never be like that. I told myself that I would always laugh. Always find the fun in life. Especially when everything else seems so dire. I supposed I take it too far sometimes."

Gianna settled down on the bed beside him. "I never knew that. You never talked about your father."

"I know. I never opened up to you and I'm sorry for that. Maybe if I had…"

"It's okay." She patted his hand then stood.

Jake grasped her arm before she could put distance between them again. "I'm still in love with you, Gi."

She met his gaze. He searched her face, looking for the same emotion in her eyes. Something was there, he was sure of it. But he wasn't certain it was love. He hoped it was.

"Tell me you don't love me, and I'll let you walk out of my life again. Tell me that, and I'll accept it and move on."

There was a long silence before she spoke. "I can't."

His heart thundering, he pulled her to him and wrapped his arms around her waist. He buried his face into her chest and inhaled her scent. He wanted to sink into her, to submerse himself completely. It was here, with her, in her, that he could find peace and salvation. She did and always had possessed his heart.

Sighing, Gianna buried her hands in his hair. "Jake, I don't know if this changes anything."

"I don't know, either. But I want a chance to try again."

She pulled his head back and gazed into his face. She shook her head, her lips twitching into a reluctant smile. "You are hard to resist."

"Then don't."

She licked her lips, then leaned down and covered his mouth with hers. It was the only answer he needed.

The smoldering kiss ignited every nerve ending in her body from the top of her head to the tips of her toes, and all the parts in between. Fiery tingles radiated over her thighs, surging dangerously toward her center.

Gasping for breath, Gianna broke from the kiss. Her hands raced over his back, feeling the soft skin and hard muscles beneath. Jake was indeed a beautiful man.

He pulled her down. "Kiss me again."

He moaned as she traced the tip of her tongue around his mouth then finally stopped to nibble on his full bottom lip. After playing, she dived into the kiss, pulling, and teasing, and taking what she could from him.

The man could kiss. The hard press of his lips and the provocative way he moved his tongue over hers in a slow torturous dance sent bolts of red-hot pleasure surging over her body. He had one hand wrapped in her hair and the other at her hip. He feasted on her mouth, ripping gasps of pleasure from her with every nip and nibble. She dug her short nails in while he moved over to nibble on her chin, then down to her neck.

Finally he stood and, wrapping his arms around her, tossed her backward onto the bed. She landed in the middle, willing and ready, just as hungry as he was.

He unbuttoned his jeans and pulled them off. His erection made a tent out of his boxer shorts. Hooking thumbs in the band he quickly removed those as well. Some men would be quick to lie on the bed, cover themselves almost, but not Jake. No, he was damn proud of his form and he wasn't afraid to let her devour him with her eyes. Which Gianna did, readily.

"Take off your clothes," he growled at her.

She loved it when he took charge in bed, when he demanded things from her. That was one of the reasons the sex was so good between them. She trusted him completely to please her however he could. In different ways he knew she liked.

Sitting up, Gianna stripped off her T-shirt and tossed it to the floor. She then unhooked her bra and took it off, feeling the full weight of her breasts. Jake's eyes dilated and she knew he was drinking her in.

She unzipped her jeans, then arched a brow at him. "Little help?"

He gripped her pants and in one yank he had them off her and on the floor. That just left her panties. Kneeling on the mattress, Jake hooked his fingers in them and tore them away, leaving her gloriously naked and hot for him. The ache between her thighs was so intense it nearly made her moan in anticipation.

He raked her body with his ravenous gaze. He looked like a starving man in front of a buffet for the first time in his life. He looked like he didn't know where to start. Gianna lifted her arms and hooked them over his shoulders. She longed to feel his heavy weight on top of her.

Instead he leaned down toward her breasts and took one rigid peak into his mouth. Bowing her back, Gianni gloried in the pleasure surging through her as he sucked on one nipple and rubbed the other with his fingers. After lavishing avid attention with his tongue and teeth to one aching peak he moved onto the other, giving it equal consideration. When he was done and shifted his notice to her navel, she was throbbing inside every crevice.

Leaning down, Jake pressed open mouth kisses to her belly, his tongue dabbing at her every now and then. It tickled but she tried not to move. She liked what he was doing and hoped he'd venture lower.

"Are you hot for me, baby?" He nipped at her navel.

"Why don't you find out for yourself?" She grinned.

He returned her daring smile, and then shifted himself. He nudged her legs apart and positioned himself between. He placed a hand on each of her thighs, pressing his fingers into her flesh.

She found it hard to breathe as he leaned down toward her aching sex. Lust pooled at her center. By the time he lowered himself to her, Gianna was nearly mad with desire. She bit down on her lip to stop from begging him.

Her breath hitched in her throat as his fingers brushed over her mound. He was careful not to touch too much too soon. He was teasing her, and it was driving her insane. She was at his mercy, but she liked that. Relenting power to him was something she could only do in bed. But it was because she trusted him so much. And she had to admit, she was able to trust him outside of the bedroom, too.

Jake continued to tease her with light brushings of his fingertips. She rose up to meet him, hoping he would end her suffering. That he would lick and suckle her, and fill her with his fingers, his tongue, anything to urge her over the edge to a mind-blowing orgasm.

She didn't have to wait long. Lying down on his stomach between her spread legs, Jake parted her with his thumbs. He nuzzled his face into her. Lightly at first, he trailed his tongue up and down her slick channel, swirling the tip as he reached her opening. But then he picked up the pace and she nearly lost her mind.

Heaving, she thrashed about on the mattress as he nudged her clit with the tip of his tongue. He pressed her down to the bed with one hand on her stomach. He tried to keep her still as he feasted on her.

With ease, he slid two fingers into her, manipulating her with quick hard thrusts. The scorching heat between her legs was quickly nearing unbearable. Gianna was close to climaxing. The muscles in her belly and thighs tightened, preparing her for the overwhelming rush that would eventually come.

As he continued to thrust his fingers in and out, pushing as deep as he could go, Jake sucked on her. With one final stroke of his tongue, he pushed his fingers deeper. Clamping her eyes shut against the sudden rush of ecstasy, she cried out as he found her most sensitive spot. He pressed hard just as he clamped down on her clit with his lips.

She came in a hot liquid rush and she couldn't catch her breath. Thrashing about, she grabbed onto Jake's head, grasping for something...*anything*...to release her from the hold he had on her. Relentlessly he continued to manipulate her, stroking his tongue over her and moving his fingers inside, prolonging her orgasm.

She tried to fight it but it was pointless. So she dropped her hands, closed her eyes and rode the soaring waves of pleasure until she was spent.

Chapter Six

Jake loved to watch Gianna as she orgasmed. It was when she was the most unguarded. It gave him an ego boost to know that he was able to give her that much pleasure.

She opened her eyes and gave him one of her saucy grins. "Play time's over. It's time to get serious."

He crawled up her body and hovered over her, his arms braced on either side of her body. Leaning down, he kissed her. Soft at first, then hard and fierce and hot.

She gave just as good as he did, darting her tongue in and out of his mouth. He nibbled on her lips as she dug her fingers into his back and pulled his body down. He couldn't resist the enticement any longer. He ached to lay with her, to be inside her—deep.

The moment he covered her with his body, her hands ran over his back, urgent and eager to possess. Cupping the back of his neck, she deepened the kiss, moaning into his mouth. He swallowed down each gasp, each heave of breath, willing and wanting to hear more of her groans. It was a powerful thing to pleasure a woman. Especially one as strong and formidable as Gianna.

Unable to hold himself back any longer, Jake nestled between her thighs, kneeing them apart, and, gripping his cock in one hand, guided himself into her. She opened for him easily and he slid all the way in.

He closed his eyes against the initial fierce assault on his body as he began to move inside her, finding a rhythm. She was so hot, so wet; it nearly did him in right there and then. Soon he was grinding on her, against her, in her. It felt so good that he moaned her name.

She wrapped her legs around him as he picked up the pace. With every thrust she dug her nails into him harder. It wouldn't surprise him if she drew blood. He didn't mind. They'd always been this fierce when they made love…

And it was love, not just sex between them. No matter how much she denied it, he knew the truth.

Kissing her mouth, her neck, her shoulders, Jake thrust harder, faster, burying deep inside. She gasped as he rammed into her again and again, lifting her pelvis up to meet him each time.

Muscles clenched with strain, his legs started to twitch. He was close, so close. Clamping his eyes shut, he drove into her as hard and as deep as he could, pulling her to him as he did. She raked her nails across his back and he knew there'd be divots in his flesh.

Then he heard the words that he'd been waiting to hear, that he hoped to hear.

"Oh God, Jake," she whimpered. "I love you so much."

In that moment, he climaxed in a violent surge, emptying himself completely. Even his mind failed to function as his body convulsed in long, hard tremors.

For several minutes, Jake lost himself. But then blinking back the oblivion, his gaze focused on Gianna and he knew he'd found the only place he ever wanted to be. With her. Beside her. Inside her.

If she allowed it, he'd never leave her side.

He drew a finger across her forehead, pushing aside the sweat soaked hair. She blinked up at him, a dreamy satisfied look on her face.

"Why did we ever break up?" he asked as he traced the usual hard lines of her jaw.

"You know why."

"What if I promise to change, that I'll be whoever you need me to be?"

He could see the glow starting to dampen as he spoke. But he couldn't keep silent any longer.

"Jake, that's the great sex talking." She pushed him over and rolled out from under him. She sat up on the bed and started to reach for her clothes.

He rolled with her and grabbed her arm to stop her. "It's my heart talking, Gianna. I love you. I don't want to go another moment without you."

She dropped her arm, and sighed. She glanced at him over her shoulder. "I don't know. How do I know it will be different? I don't want to risk my heart again, Jake. It hurt too damn bad last time."

From behind, he wrapped his arms around her and kissed her shoulder. "I promise you it will be different. I will do anything to not lose you again. Anything, Gi. You just have to tell me."

She covered his hands with hers and relaxed into his arms. He kissed her shoulder again, then her neck. Then he heard her sigh again…which wasn't a good sign. He knew her sighs well.

Dropping her hands from his, she stood and moved away from the bed, gathering pieces of her clothing along the way. "You've caught me off guard, Jake. I don't know what to say."

"Say you love me."

She stopped in the middle of dressing and turned around to look at him. "I do love you. But I don't know if it's enough."

She finished pulling her clothes on, grabbed her bag, then looked at him again. "I need to get back to my hotel and gather my stuff and check out. I'll call the client and make sure we each get our payment." She moved toward the door but stopped with her hand on the handle. "Look, we can talk about this again back in San Francisco. I fly out tomorrow."

"I'm not going back right away."

That shook her a little. "Oh, okay. When will you be back?"

Jake scooted to the edge of the bed. "I don't know. I'm taking a little holiday. Going out to the mountains."

"Oh. Well, then, I guess you can call me when you return." She turned the handle.

"Come with me, Gi. We've never taken a holiday together before. No work, no demons. Just you and me, hanging out."

She frowned. "I don't know, Jake…"

He put his hand up to stop her protestations. "Tell you what, I'm leaving tonight around seven. Be here, if you want. If not, then cool, I'll see when you I get back to town. No pressure, okay?"

"Okay." She opened the door and left, shutting it firmly behind her.

Jake didn't know how long he sat on the edge of the bed and watched the door, waiting for her to return. All he knew was that he was damn cold when he finally stood and got dressed.

Chapter Seven

In her hotel room, Gianna shoved clothes into her bag. Anger fuelled every push and shove on her stuff to make it fit into the leather case. After everything was crammed inside, she zipped it up and collapsed beside it on the bed, her fists still curled tight.

She was so mad at Jake she could spit. How dare he show up and make her love him all over again? It wasn't fair. She'd worked hard to exorcise him from her mind and from her heart. So what if it didn't take too well? At least she'd tried. At least she was resigned enough to know that he might never be completely gone from her psyche, but it had been enough where she could've moved on.

Jerk. How could she move on now?

The sex had been spectacular. That hadn't really been a surprise. They had always had good sex. But it was the force of his passion that had surprised her. She'd always known in her mind that Jake had loved her, loved her still obviously, but this was the first time she really *felt* it. It had skimmed along her skin, moulded every curve and filled every part of her body. She had felt it deep within her belly and deep within her soul. And she couldn't shake the sensation.

It was as if his hands and lips were on her still, caressing her, loving her....

She stood, trying to shake it off. She didn't need this. Not now. She had a lot of money sitting in her account, thanks to the fast transfer of funds by the client, and was planning a vacation of her own. Somewhere warm, with long white-sanded beaches, and cabana boys in small shorts happily serving drinks with little umbrellas in them. The Caribbean would be perfect this time of year.

A trip to the snowy mountains of Alberta didn't sound like the perfect getaway to her. What the hell would she and Jake do out there in the cold? She didn't ski, neither did Jake. What was there to do then, in the cold, when a person didn't want to go outside and freeze?

Images of sizzling fires and hot tubs came to mind. As did images of Jake naked in that tub with his sexy grin on his remarkable face.

A shiver vibrated up her body. She tried to tamp it down, but it was useless. It was just the afterglow of amazing sex; it was not future thoughts of amazing sex with Jake that made her quiver. Her thighs clenched, calling her a liar.

"Damn it." She picked up her bags and left the room.

She had to get out of there. Sitting around thinking about Jake wasn't doing her any good. She had to do something to get him out of her mind. Anything would be better than pining away for him like a lovesick teenager.

Jake sat in his rental vehicle, an SUV made for Alberta winter driving, and played with the heater controls. Full blast. Off. Full blast. Off. He couldn't decide if he was freezing or not. He was definitely cold but he wasn't sure it had anything to do with the weather outside the vehicle.

He glanced at his watch again. It was one minute to seven.

She wasn't coming.

He leaned his head back against the seat and closed his eyes. He had been certain she would change her mind. She'd said she loved him.

So why wasn't she here?

To him it was easy. He loved her, therefore he wanted to be with her. He didn't understand why she continued to push him away. He knew he'd done some stupid, senseless stuff before. But he promised he'd change. And he always kept his promises. Gianna knew that. Didn't she?

He wasn't so sure now.

He opened his eyes and glanced at his watch again. It was seven-o-one. Squinting, he peered out the front window and the sides, then out the back. She wasn't coming. She obviously didn't love him enough to want to work out their problems. He'd overestimated what he'd sensed from her earlier.

He pushed on the radio, setting it to something hard and fast, and tried to push down the hurt rising inside him. He'd never gotten over Gianna, and he knew he'd never be able to fully move on. He'd found his one true soul partner and he wasn't allowed to be with her. He'd heard of heartache but never knew that one's heart could actually shatter. It felt like a thousand bloody shards were piercing him from the inside out.

Jake put the SUV in gear and let his foot off the brake. He coasted out of the parking stall but stopped when the light from his headlamps illuminated Gianna standing in front of the vehicle, her bags in her hands.

He braked and put it in Park and just stared through the windshield at her. Gianna smiled, and magically his heart pieced back together.

She walked around to the passenger side door, opened it, tossed her bags in the back, and then slid into the seat. She shut the door and turned toward him.

"Am I too late?"

Without a word, Jake reached for her, cupping her neck and pulling her to him. He covered her mouth with his and kissed her so damn hard he hoped she'd feel it for her entire lifetime.

Because God knew, he definitely did.

* * * * *

THE DEMON'S
FORBIDDEN PASSION

ZOEY WILLIAMS

Prologue

Gripping the steering wheel so tight his tendons bulged, Ethan Phillips winced at the sight of every car quickly dodging out of his way, their tires screeching. The siren wailed louder and louder overhead as Ethan eyed the speedometer, its pin inching closer and closer to ninety miles per hour. He had *definitely* never driven the truck that fast before. But he had never responded to a call at 52 Crawford Place before either, an address within a gated community that he had been trying to forget for a decade.

As he hit the brake to turn the corner, he wished he could press the pedal just a bit farther, delay the inevitable, make time morph into slow motion. His stomach clenched, dread settling into his body. He pulled up to the scene, where five other fire trucks were already parked, their crews surrounding the house and attempting to fight the monstrous flames. He sat motionless, his seat belt still buckled. Adrenaline pumped through his veins and he could feel it begin: his body temperature rising above the flames in front of him, the crystal blue of his eyes transforming into yellow slits. His forehead ached, his horns desperately wanting to break through his skin—the skin that, although his uniform obscured it, he knew was turning from a deep tan to a blistering red. His teeth sharpened into points and he ran his tongue over them in a desperate attempt to suppress the transformation.

Regain your control, he reminded himself. *Don't get angry.*

Another wicked clap of thunder vibrated through the sky, just as he had been hearing all night, and still no rain had come. It was a tease—one of those hot, stuffy summer evening thunderstorms that didn't hold the promise of rain. And what Ethan would do right now for rain. The house, a gigantic three-story mansion, was fully engulfed in flames so tall he couldn't tell where the angry bursts of fire ended and the deep vermilion sunset began.

Ethan exited the truck and bolted toward the house with incredible swiftness despite his heavy uniform and equipment. As he clomped toward the front steps, the gravel driveway crunching beneath him, he could feel the air vibrating with the spray of the immense hoses that were on full blast all around him, a slight coolness emanating from them, before he surged into the blazing heat ahead.

"Hey!" one of the men called out to him. "We haven't secured an entrance yet—" But Ethan had already slipped into the residence, his pace never slowing. It was as if his body simply turned to smoke and the house had breathed him in.

Once inside, Ethan maneuvered around the smoldering surroundings, trying to ignore the wave of crackling and popping that flooded his ears. He needed to focus, to find whoever lived here before it was too late. He did a sweep through the first floor, but found no one. Through the thick, dark smoke, his heightened vision helped him find his way to the staircase.

At the top, a beam—white-hot with flames—crashed down from the ceiling, hitting Ethan's right shoulder with a powerful smack. He grunted, but pressed on.

The first door he approached was off one of its hinges, and leaned precariously in the door frame. The door easily gave way when Ethan knocked it down with a powerful kick from his heavy boots. It revealed a massive library—shelves stretching from floor to ceiling, the pages of its thousands of books flapping in the blaze like frantic birds.

"Saunville Fire Department. Anyone in here?" he called out. The room seemed to crackle louder in response. "Speak to me if you can!" he shouted, his eyes desperately searching for any sign of movement, any sign of life.

He wasn't sure if he was imagining things, but after hearing no response for a few seconds, an unmistakable sound finally reached his ears: a cough. It was coming from under a mahogany desk, flames licking one of its panels.

In one fluid motion, he lifted the massive desk and tossed it aside, feeding it to the inferno around him. It revealed a young boy, lying in the fetal position, one tiny hand pressed hard into the crook of his opposite forearm. Ignoring the sharp pain in his shoulder, Ethan picked the boy up and hugged him close. The boy cowered.

"I'm going to get you out of here, buddy," Ethan said. "There's nothing to be afraid of."

"M-my eyes," the boy stuttered, his voice thick with trepidation.

"I know they sting from the smoke, keep 'em closed for me, okay?" They needed to get out of there now. Valuable time was ticking.

"No, it's not that," the boy replied. "My eyes…they just…my eyes do the same thing. And I can't control when they do it, either."

The words sliced through Ethan like a knife, stopping him dead in his tracks. Ethan forced himself to look down at the boy cradled in his arms. The same golden color of his eyes reflected back at him. Just for a flash, and then they went back to the same crystal blue as Ethan's.

The boy wasn't a regular demon. He was a Half Blood, just like him. An anomaly. Ethan had thought he was the only one sentenced to such a fate.

The last fire to happen on demon territory was in this very estate, to the only mixed couple—and their Half Blood son—on the block. A sense of horror still seized Ethan's body. Because now he knew the scene was an *exact* replica of a terrible event that drove him away ten years ago. And he had joined the fire department *specifically* for this night, if it would ever come. And now, it *had*.

Chapter One

Tina Driscoll could barely keep her eyes open as she shuffled to lot *D*, the parking lot on the farthest end of the hospital where she worked. Her legs were stiff from standing on them for twelve hours straight and felt heavy, like they had lead weights tied to both feet. When she finally found her car, she leaned on the side of it, digging into the pocket of her sweat-stained scrubs for her keys. But a different sensation met her palm. A buzzing. It was her phone vibrating…and the last name she wanted to see at this very moment was flashing on its screen.

"*Nooooooooo*," she groaned, drawing out the word until it turned into a whine. "Not tonight," she said, her eyes cast heavenward. As much as she wanted to shirk her responsibility, pretend she never felt her phone in her pocket and head straight home, she knew she couldn't ignore the call. It was the kind of thing that was simply part of the job.

"Gus, you've got to be kidding me."

"Ah, you're still here! Fantastic," Gus exclaimed on the other end. The voice was hoarse and gravelly. Despite being Tina's boss and head nurse, Gus still hadn't given up smoking. Or baking decadent desserts for the entire staff. A smoking nurse with an atrocious sugar and fat-laden diet: the ultimate irony. He continued on before she had the chance to protest. "I know, I know, *I know*. Let me explain."

"Now you told me I was absolutely, one-hundred-percent *off* the schedule tonight. You promised me that Kendra had it *covered*." Tina tried her best to sound annoyed, but it was hard to be annoyed at goofy, lovable Gus. The one guy who took a chance on a wrong-side-of-the-tracks kid with no family and a degree from a less than reputable community college. But it was because she was good. And he noticed her potential right away.

Gus coughed throatily into the receiver. "I'm so sorry, hon. Kendra called in sick not even a minute ago and something big just came up. Real big. I promise that you will be absolutely, one-hundred-percent off the schedule *next* Saturday night."

Tina tried her best tough-guy voice. "She better be *really* sick, Gus."

"Incredibly sick," Gus confirmed.

"Like projectile-vomiting-pea-soup-while-pus-drips-out-of-her-eyes kind of sick?"

"Yes, I swear. Now you know I'd never bother you unless it was an absolute emergency and I need your expertise tonight. You're the—"

Tina smirked. "I know, Gus. *You're the bee's knees, the cream-of-the-crop, the best nurse on my staff,*" she said, repeating all of Gus's usual lines. This wasn't the first time he'd called her back in after giving her the night off. But his words did have some merit to them. Tina had never lost a single patient—even the ones with the grisliest injuries. She had managed to help heal them all—everything from stage-three pancreatic cancer to a drowning victim who'd been pronounced dead for seven full minutes. And Gus knew this.

He barked a short laugh. "Damn right you are. Now get your butt over to 52 Crawford Place in Saunville," he instructed. "The Mezza Estates."

Demon territory, Tina realized. She bit her lip. "A residence?" she asked, her voice quavering slightly. "But Gus, you never have me go directly to the scene."

"I know, but tonight we can't waste any time. This one's bad, honey. Real bad. I need you to get there as soon as you can."

"What happened?"

"Another fire," Gus replied. Tina heard a flick and the crackling incineration of the end of a fresh cigarette.

"But that's the like—what? Sixth one this week?" Tina asked incredulously.

"It's summertime in Los Angeles, doll. The trees and grass are dry and all it takes is one little incident—a flash of lightning, even—and *poof.* And these estates also happen to border on a national park that caught fire ten times within the last year alone."

Tina considered for a moment. "Throw in a box of your famous éclairs and you don't have to start a chain of un-welcomed phone calls tonight."

"Done," Gus laughed throatily. "I'll even raise you a butter tart for your trouble."

Tina removed her opposite hand from her pocket and opened her fist. She looked at the car keys she had been gripping so tightly that they had left little indentations in her palm—she had been *so close* to having the night off. She placed the keys on the roof of her car and sighed. Pinching the bridge of her nose with her thumb and fore-finger, she said, "I'm heading over there now."

Chapter Two

When Tina eyed her dashboard and saw the green line on the screen of her GPS get shorter and shorter as the blue dot of her car approached her destination, a tightness started to grow in her chest. She stopped at a red light and glanced at her hands, which were now trembling fiercely as they rested on the steering wheel. *What is going on with me*, she thought. Nothing about tonight was out of the ordinary, aside from Gus requesting that she go directly to the scene. She'd seen fires—and their resulting burn victims—dozens of times and never lost her cool, calm demeanor. Sure, there were always the nerves that riddled her before pulling back the curtain of an exam room, the buzz of anticipation of what she'd have to do for her next patient. But this time it was as if her body was trying to tell her something. To warn her.

Though she was still a few miles away, Tina could see the black mass come into view through a thick patch of evergreen trees, the smoke pluming upward and outward across the now darkened sky. "Wow" was all she could manage to say. It had to be one hell of a fire to create such an incredible amount of swirling smoke, the black clouds so large they looked like an entity. A living, breathing monster. Unsurprisingly, when she finally arrived on the scene, there were dozens of firefighters. They were still armed with hoses, eliminating what were presumably the remaining hot spots in the ash, while three ambulances sat parked across the street, out of harm's way. There must have been only a few residents in the house, Tina thought with a sigh of relief. She searched the ambulances for any kind of flurry of activity, but the first two appeared to be empty. The third held a small, vague outline of a patient sitting on its gurney. Tina threw her car into Park and jogged over to it.

The child inside the only occupied ambulance looked to be about five, Tina guessed. The shirt of his cowboy pajamas, its edges charred and sooty, was unbuttoned to accommodate the panels of a heart rate monitor that beeped like a metronome in the corner of the ambulance. His short black hair was mussed and his crystal blue eyes—which peered from above an oxygen mask that slightly concealed the rest of his face—looked bright with wonder. Tina thought of the resilience of kids until she saw that his left hand was pressing down into his right forearm; the gauze under his fingertips was stained deep red with blood.

Tina stole a glance over her shoulder at what was once

this boy's home and shook her head, astonished that he made it out alive, that only his arm was injured.

She recognized the EMT taking the boy's vitals. "Hey, Nikki."

Nikki's short gray curls bounced when she glanced up from the stethoscope pressed to the patient's back once she had finished listening to his breathing. Her silver-framed glasses sat low on her nose, making her look like Mrs. Claus, which was quite fitting, Tina thought, as Nikki was just as cheerful. "Hey, Tina! Surprised to see you here, girl. But happy none the less." She smiled.

"Gus said you'd be needing back up," Tina explained.

"And Gus would've been right." Nikki nodded to the crumbling house. "With these giant mansions, you can never tell if there's one person inside or fifty. But luckily there were only three people, including my friend here."

Tina turned to the boy. "And who's this fine, young patient?"

He smiled up at her, beaming at the compliment.

"Name's Danny," Nikki answered. "Vitals are stable. Third-degree burn on his arm. Pretty bad—the bleeding hasn't stopped yet. I don't hear signs of any serious smoke inhalation, but I'm giving him a little oxygen to be on the safe side. We're definitely going to keep him overnight for observation."

"Gotcha. It's nice to meet you, Danny. I'm Tina. I'm going to be your nurse when we get back to the hospital."

"My cowboy PJs are ruined," Danny said mournfully, sticking out his bottom lip.

Tina gestured to her frizzed hair and the grungy pair of sneakers she now noticed had a spot of baby spit-up on the toe. "Well, I'm not looking so fancy tonight myself."

The boy laughed softly.

"I'm looking a little ugly tonight, huh, Danny?" Tina teased.

"No," Danny giggled as his face blushed, cheeks burning. "You're not ugly." He looked down.

"Thanks, bud. Do you mind if I take a look at your arm?" Tina asked.

Danny, still bashful and smiling at the ground, stuck out his arm.

Tina carefully removed the gauze, revealing a patch of bubbling skin slick with blood. She could see Danny's eyes well up when he turned to look at his injury; she knew it must hurt so badly. After slipping on a pair of gloves, she removed the bloodied gauze from his arm and replaced it with a fresh piece.

"You're being such a brave boy. Now are you sure you're not feeling any pain besides your arm?"

He shook his head. "Nope."

"So the only casualty is the cowboy pajamas. We can work with that. I'll see if your parents can get you another…." Tina bit her lip, stopping herself.

"It's okay," Nikki said. "His parents were taken to the hospital about an hour ago. Critical but stable condition. They're going to be okay."

"The fireman saved them!" Danny interjected, his eyes lighting up. "He saved them right after he saved me."

"He must be a really awesome fireman then," said Tina.

"He is!" Danny agreed. "And Nikki said he's a hunk!"

"Nikki!" Tina laughed in surprise. "What about Bill? You know, your husband of thirty years? Does the name ring any bells?"

She put her hands out in front of her in mock surrender. "Hey, I can look!"

"But not touch," Tina playfully admonished.

Nikki waved a hand. "Yeah, yeah, yeah."

She tugged on Tina's sleeve and leaned in. "But seriously though, I've seen him at the scene of a couple of other accidents and *girl*, he is fine," she stage whispered.

Tina rolled her eyes and put a hand on Danny's shoulder. "Which one is he, sweetie?"

"He's over there!" Danny pointed emphatically to a group of fifteen firemen.

"The tall one with the black hair," Nikki added. "I think his name is Ethan."

Tina followed Nikki and Danny's gazes and gaped despite her best efforts. Like Nikki said, the man was *fine*. Strike that, Tina thought, the man was *gorgeous*. Though he was standing far away, Tina could tell he had the same striking blue eyes as Danny, which was curious. Ethan stood with arms crossed, his eyes pinned on the ambulance he knew held the boy he rescued. His face had sharp features; his nose was straight and narrow, his cheekbones were high and strong, and his jaw line could cut glass. With his olive complexion and raven hair, he was the definition of tall, dark and handsome.

He had the impressive muscular build that most fire-fighters had. Although his uniform obscured most of it, Tina could tell that underneath, Ethan's body must've been nothing more than one hundred and seventy-five pounds of pure muscle. And, oh, that uniform, she thought. Though she adored a man in uniform, she found herself wondering how much fun it would be to remove all doubt of what lay underneath the thick, yellow-brown garb. To feel the strength of all the perfect body parts that allowed him to save the world night after night. A tight, rippled abdomen, biceps so beefy she wouldn't be able to wrap both her hands completely around them, two sharp hipbones, that thin trail of hair between them—her favorite part of a man—that would direct her gaze downward, teasing at what it led to... Tina shuddered with naughty thoughts.

But she was jolted from her fantasy when she realized that Ethan's eyes were now fixed upon hers. She quickly averted her gaze, her cheeks flushing with embarrassment. Just before turning her back to him and burying her chin to her chest, she noticed a smirk lingering on Ethan's face.

"What did I tell you?" Nikki laughed. "Rumor has it he's a real ladies' man, too." She leaned in closer to get out of Danny's earshot. "Word at the station is even though he's a demon, he doesn't act like one. Takes a different woman home every night."

Tina didn't know how to feel about that. Demons were renowned for their monogamy and their tendency to want to date within their own race. That's why they tended to live in gated communities. But regardless of his heritage, a different woman every night? Half of her felt like rolling her eyes…but, judging by his looks, the other half of her felt like she wouldn't mind becoming another notch in his bedpost.

"Know anything else about him?" Tina asked quietly.

"Not really. Only interacted with the guy once. I remember trying to convince him to go to the hospital last year when he got caught in a collapsed porch. Twisted his ankle pretty bad, but said he was fine. Wasn't sure if it was just him being macho, but it didn't feel like it. It seemed like he had something against hospitals. No matter what I said, I just couldn't convince him."

Tina shrugged. Everyone had their phobias, and she knew full well that plenty of people were scared of hospitals, but she couldn't help wondering why such a strong, powerful man—especially a firefighter who stared down death every day—would be so averse as well. Her mind started to fill with all the ways that she could comfort him. Coax him the next time he needed to go. Maybe she'd volunteer to go to the scenes of fires more often.…

"Hey!" Nikki exclaimed, interrupting her thoughts. For a split second, Tina worried that she had voiced her fantasies aloud. But instead she pointed to Danny's gauze, which was as white as a piece of paper. "Would you look at that. Your bleeding completely stopped, kiddo. Nice job, Tina."

"Ready to go?" she asked, turning to Danny.

But the boy didn't hear her. His gaze was fixated on Tina as he regarded her with a mixture of awe and wonderment. "You fixed my boo-boo like my mommy does."

"She sure did, honey," Nikki said. "Now say good-night to Miss Tina while I go tell the ambulance driver it's okay to take us to the hospital now."

Danny's gaze refused to leave Tina. "Okay..." he said softly. "You're a lot like my mommy, Miss Tina. Except for your hair," he blurted pointedly, as only a five-year-old could.

Nikki chuckled, shaking her head as she walked to the front of the vehicle.

Tina laughed. "Is mine messier than hers? I'm sure it is."

"No, it's the color," he said solemnly. "Just the color."

Tina twirled a chestnut strand in her fingers as Nikki returned to the back of the ambulance. She switched places with her as Tina stepped off onto the grass, which was now wet with dew.

"You're not coming with us?" Danny demanded.

"No, sweetie. It's time for me to go to bed. But I'll be there first thing tomorrow morning. Bright and early."

"Can you bring the fireman with you?" he asked hopefully.

Tina turned back to where Ethan was standing, but he was gone.

"I don't think so, kiddo, but if I see him, I promise I'll ask."

"I just never got to say thank you for saving me and my parents, that's all," he said softly.

His kindness, after all of the events of the evening, touched her deeply. Whatever his parents were doing, they were doing it right. "Oh, honey," Tina said. "It's his job to save people. Even if you don't get to say it to him, I'm sure he knows you're grateful."

"I know. But still ask him if you see him, okay?"

"Okay," Tina answered.

"Promise?"

"Promise." Tina reached out and lightly ruffled Danny's hair before saying good-night. Nikki gave a small wave before closing the doors toward her with a metal *click*.

Tina stood with her hands on her hips as she watched the ambulance pull away from the scene, lights flashing, but lacking the deep whine of the siren. She gave a quick phone call to Gus, letting him know that the last victim of the fire was on his way and that she'd see him in the morning for the early shift. After hanging up, Tina took a deep breath, the charred air tickling the back of her throat. When she turned around, she was nose to chest with Ethan.

Chapter Three

For the first time in his life, a fire had shaken him. But *she* had shaken him more. Lucky for her, Ethan thought, he always hungered after a fire.

It plagued him after every rescue, the demon part of him begging him to satisfy the demands of his birthright, balance all the good he had just done. And so every night he yielded to the plea from deep within him by finding a woman to satisfy and carefully leaving as soon as the deed was done. Tonight wouldn't be any different. And this one? Her allure was too powerful to deny—he had to have her.

While almost three hours had passed since he'd rescued Danny and his parents from the house and delivered them to the ambulances, he was still trying to shake the feelings and memories that sprang to the forefront of his mind when he first saw the community after all this time. Unbeknownst to the boy, he was a painful reminder of what Ethan was, of the terrible events that had taken away both of his parents, and the fate their attacker reserved exclusively for him. The curse still pulsed through Ethan's veins—and though no one could tell of his fate by just looking at him, his skin began to feel itchy, as if the curse was apparent on his face, just as noticeable as a birthmark.

And what a distraction she would be. He could tell immediately that this woman wasn't like any of the others he pursued. She was more than just a pretty face. He had overheard the entire exchange between her and Danny and the kindness she showed toward one of his kind. She was sweet, she was calm and she was *lovely*. It was the only word he could think of to describe her. Standing there in her wrinkled scrubs and messy hair, she was ten times more attractive than any woman in a low-cut dress and stilettos. Something about her exuded power and competency. She was serious about her job and cared about others. It pulled the heartstrings of his lighter side. He watched her from afar until he couldn't stand being away from her any longer, the force between them when they exchanged glances too magnetic.

But that was dangerous territory he was creeping into. *That's not why you want her*, he reminded himself. *Personality doesn't matter. Just seduce her and be done with it.* And now that he was up close to her, he could tell that wouldn't be difficult. Her emerald-green eyes were as large and innocent as a doe's, and the full, cherry-red pout of her lips just begged to be kissed. And not to mention the dangerous curves that he only got a hint of at the seams of her scrubs. He knew exactly what he was capable of doing with them... after all, practice did make perfect.

Tonight she would be his.

"Oh! Sorry!" Tina laughed nervously, breaking him from his trance. "You startled me."

He put his hand on her forearm to steady her, then slid his hand down her arm and into a firm handshake. Smiling a gleaming white smile, one he knew could make any woman weak in the knees, he felt the muscles in her hand tense. He could tell she was holding in her breath.

"I don't remember seeing you before. Are you a new EMT?" Ethan asked. "I'm sure I would have remembered you." He let his tongue moisten his lower lip flirtatiously. "I'm Ethan Phillips."

"Oh, I'm Tina Driscoll. I'm a nurse, actually. It's very nice to meet you, Ethan," she said, her gaze dropping to his mouth.

The sound of her saying his name sent a ripple right through him. The sweet melody of her voice, the way she said it so breathlessly, was incredibly charming. While he usually felt bored at the lack of challenge, there was something about her nervousness that excited him.

"The pleasure's all mine."

Tina's cheeks flushed slightly. "You did an amazing job tonight. I've heard a lot of nice things about you."

"Like your coworker thinking I was a hunk?"

Tina's eyes widened. "How did you—"

"Ears like an eagle, the guys on the force always say."

He smiled bigger, showing off the dimples. They always loved those.

Tina opened her mouth to say something, possibly to try to backpedal her way out of it, but thought better of it, her cheeks burning brighter. She laughed, and the sound of it was like music.

"But what I was unable to decipher, unfortunately for me, was if you agreed with her."

Tina clamped her lips, but was still smiling. "Hmm," she responded.

That's it, Tina. You're better at flirting than you think.

"So I'll never know?" he asked, feigning a frown.

"I guess not," she said, smirking.

"Wow, that really hurts, Tina," he teased. "My self-esteem is hemorrhaging points as we speak."

"You measure your self-esteem in points?" She raised an eyebrow, amused.

"Yes…yes, I do."

"How many was it at before this conversation?" she asked.

"Seven hundred and forty-two," he responded, not missing a beat.

"And now?"

"Twelve."

She laughed again, obviously entertained by his answer. "Ah, don't be so hard on yourself," she said, giving him a playful pat on his shoulder.

He winced without meaning to, a small grunt sounding in his throat.

Tina's eyes widened. "Oh my god, I didn't mean to… Are you okay? Did something happen during the rescue tonight?" she asked.

He hated feeling weak in front of her, but, on second thought, realized playing the sympathy card would probably work to his advantage. "Oh, yeah, I'm fine," he replied. "A beam fell on my shoulder when I made it to the top of the stairs."

She had touched him, which was an encouraging sign, but now he had to go in for the kill. "You can examine it if you like."

Before she had a chance to answer, he took off his shirt and heard a sharp intake of breath escape Tina's lips. His abdomen, glistening slightly with sweat, was rock hard. Flashing the abs *always* worked. He let her take a good look at him before turning so that she had a better view of the back of his shoulder. "It's somewhere around…there."

He glanced behind him. Tina stood there, dazed. It took a few moments before she slowly lifted her arm and finally spoke.

"Oh, um…" She shook her head as if to clear her thoughts. "You have a, uh…a welt. A particularly nasty one, too." She lightly placed her fingertips on the back of his shoulder and Ethan felt fire. Not pain radiating from his injury, but a fire that raged deep within his brain. Her touch. It felt amazing, it felt like heaven. He turned his head forward and closed his eyes, grateful he had his back to her as he silently willed her not to stop.

She continued. "The skin is terribly bruised and I have

no doubt that the muscle underneath is a little bruised as well. But it should heal in about three weeks or so, I'd say…." Every word she uttered lessened in volume until she finally trailed off altogether. "I, ummm…wait, what was I saying?"

She was so cute when she got flustered. "You were talking about the healing time," he said innocently.

"What? Oh right, I'd, um, avoid putting any pressure on it in the meantime, so it doesn't get any worse." She removed her hand from his bare flesh and he felt a flicker of disappointment at the lack of contact.

Ethan turned to face her, giving her one last look before he put his shirt back on. "Are you sure your cure doesn't involve a one-on-one care type situation?" Ethan asked.

She laughed. "I can't say it does." Right then, Tina's stomach growled loudly. She clutched her midsection, as if that would lessen the rumbling. She laughed nervously. "I came here straight from my last shift and didn't have any time to eat dinner," she explained. Her stomach groaned again, even louder. "Ugh, that is so gross," she said, still laughing.

Ethan smiled internally. He finally found an in. "Well, it may be—and I'm using your word here—*gross*, but you're in luck," he said impishly. "Because I happen to know the cure for that unfortunate condition."

"Oh, you do?" Good humor sparkled in her eyes, washing away her embarrassment. "What do you prescribe, doctor?"

"Plenty of food. Stat," Ethan answered solemnly.

"And do you have any? At your place?"

"Unfortunately, no," he lied. "It's been such a busy week I haven't had time to stock up."

Her face dropped. He'd told millions of lies to millions of women, but for the first time his conscience felt the tiniest twinge of guilt. Though his house, with a fully stocked refrigerator, was not but ten minutes away, he had to follow the first rule: always take her back to *her* home, not yours. You can't ditch someone the next morning when it's your own place. He couldn't make any exceptions, even for Tina.

"But I'd be happy to cook anything you have at your place," he offered.

She took one agonizing moment to consider, but then her face lightened again. "I have to be back at work in a few hours, but I guess I can stay up. I'm probably too wired to sleep anyway."

Yes, Ethan thought. *Feeding time.*

"Perfect. Let's go," he told her, before she had a single second to change her mind. "I'm always up for pulling an all-nighter."

Chapter Four

The twenty-minute car trip passed in a blur, as she tried to focus on the road ahead of her instead of the gorgeous man who sat a mere two feet away in the passenger seat. *My patient's sinfully hot firefighter rescuer is sitting just beyond that armrest*, she thought in amazement. She couldn't believe her luck. Despite the radio being turned up and the rush of air resulting from all the rolled down windows, she could feel a palpable energy coming from Ethan, and suspected that the wheels in his head were turning just as fast as hers. So many thoughts were rushing through her mind: that uniform, that smile, that *touch*. First he had put his hand just below her shoulder, a genuinely sweet gesture she knew was meant to calm her down, but all it did was put her nerves on full blast. And when he thought better of it and ran his hand down her arm, his fingertips, which she expected to be rough and calloused, were deliciously smooth. His soft touch sent a shiver up her spine and, even now, she could still feel goose pimples where his hand had lingered ever so slightly before turning his gesture into a strong—goodness, how strong—handshake.

And when he'd decided to take off his shirt then and there...well, she nearly fell over when he did that. She knew he was in shape, but she couldn't have anticipated just how perfect the muscular physique was that lay hidden under his uniform. Just the sight of his naked torso created an ache between her legs. An ache she hadn't felt in a very long time. An ache she wasn't sure she was still capable of feeling, it had been so long.

She had been so confident just moments before, but now her nerves were kicking in. Her eyes focused on the road, she didn't dare to look over at him. What was he thinking about right now? Was he just being friendly when he asked to eat with her? It was completely innocent, right? But something in the way he looked at her made her think that he was hungry for more than just the pathetic leftovers that sat plastic-wrapped in her fridge.

She was so distracted she nearly drove right by her place, but jammed on the brake just in time. Her apartment was actually the lower level of a small house. She felt slightly embarrassed taking him to the fairly rundown Colonial. She undoubtedly could've afforded something much better on her current salary, but old habits died hard. Never having money growing up, she wasn't willing to fork over more for higher rent. She threw the car into Park and led Ethan up the front steps to the porch. Expecting to find a quizzical or disgusted look on his face, she turned around to steal a glance at him. But he wasn't looking at the house—he was only looking at her.

His focus on her made her stomach give an excited flip. After nervously fumbling with her keys, she finally opened her apartment door and kicked off her sneakers, instantly regretting her second nature action as soon as she heard Ethan give a small chuckle behind her. She turned around and smiled sheepishly. Her body was bone-tired from her jam-packed week and the events of the evening, but she now had a buzz circulating through her body that made her feel as if she had just sipped ten shots of black espresso.

She looked at Ethan, and it suddenly hit her that he was there. Alone. In her apartment. His gaze, which was warm, was also filled with something else—anticipation? she wondered—and Tina got the distinct feeling that Ethan wanted her to kick off more than just her shoes. She couldn't say she didn't want the same thing, but now she could only stand there frozen, lost in the beautiful amber eyes of the man standing in her living room. Amber? *I thought his eyes were blue.*

"Sit down, make yourself at home," she offered and Ethan walked in a slow circle, getting the full scope of the place, before taking a seat next to her. The heat from his thigh touching hers radiated up the length of Tina's body. Her scalp tingled and she began to talk faster.

"Well, this is my place," she said. "It's not much, but—"

But she could not get out the rest of the sentence. Because when she stretched out her forearm to gesture to the room like she was presenting it as a prize on a game show,

Ethan had taken her hand and planted the most feather-light kiss in the middle of her palm.

Tina's mind reeled.

It had been a *long* time since she had been with a man, and here was Ethan, sitting in her living room, making her legs turn to jelly as he kissed her hand. It wasn't exactly sexy—it was beyond that: tender, sensual, tantric almost. In that one gesture, he affirmed that he wanted exactly what she did, even though she wasn't brazen enough to admit it.

But Ethan had picked up on her slight hesitation. "You're a very beautiful woman and I want you very much, but I'll stop if you ask me to."

She didn't know what to say. No one had ever been that direct with her before. She tried to find the words. "Trust me, it's not that I don't... It's just that I've never...uh..." She tried to phrase it in the gentlest way possible.

"You're a virgin?" he asked.

I might as well be, Tina thought as she tried to calculate how many months it had been since she'd last had sex. She couldn't.

Tina shook her head. "It's just that...Nikki told me that there's a rumor that you're a..."

"Demon," Ethan answered flatly.

"Yes." She cringed, not wanting to hurt his feelings.

"And I bet the other part of that rumor is that I'm quite the Casanova?" His tone was light.

"Well, I don't know about that—"

"Both accounts are true," he answered.

Tina was a little shocked at his openness, but would be fooling herself if she didn't find it to be incredibly sexy. If he was as experienced as Nikki said, that would surely make him *very* good at… But Tina stopped herself. Because even though there were demons out there that were nice enough—she had treated enough of them, like Danny, to know—they were still *demons*. And since they tended to never sleep with humans like her, she had no idea if she was making a giant mistake.

"So you're—you're a demon?"

"Does it scare you?" he asked.

"No, I've just heard a rumor that some demons are more…uh…aggressive than others."

"That's true. But it depends on what kind. We have clans for each deadly sin," he explained.

So the folklore was true, Tina thought. But now she had to know which kind of demon she was about to invite into her bed. She almost didn't want to ask the words, but she had to. "Which one are you?" she asked, her chest tight.

Ethan leaned in and whispered his answer against her lips. "I'm a Lust."

She leaned her neck forward and kissed him, hard. His lips were soft, but the force behind them matched hers. He kissed her back expertly, nibbling and sucking on her lower lip, letting his tongue dart into her mouth, deepening the kiss so much that Tina felt dizzy with excitement. Suddenly his hands slid down the length of her body to cup her ass and he drew her over to straddle him right there on the couch. He massaged the back of her thighs, squeezing her, stroking her over the fabric while never breaking the kiss. His fingers explored every inch of her thighs and, before she knew it, he was moving his hands up to the bottom of her snap-front scrubs. He tore open her shirt with one forceful tug and tossed it aside. A surprised laugh escaped Tina's throat and she could feel his lips smiling against hers in response. Her bra exposed, she felt the slight chill in the air around her, but not for long.

Ethan slipped a thumb under each bra strap and slid them slowly off her shoulders until they hung loosely on the sides of her arms. His kisses traveled down her jaw line to the smooth of her neck. She could smell the spicy, cinnamon scent of his skin, feel his warm breath caressing the crook of her neck. Tina closed her eyes and sighed. Goose pimples began to prickle all over as she reveled at the pleasure of being kissed in her favorite spot. She lightly closed her eyes, a soft groan echoing in her throat.

"Mmmmm," she cooed.

"You like that?" Ethan whispered against her skin. His deep voice vibrated against her skin and she could feel herself getting wet.

One of his hands slithered underneath the cotton drawstring of her pants and he pressed his palm over her mound, over her panties. He cupped her, no doubt feeling the soaked lace. He continued to kiss her while his other hand pulled down one of the cups of her bra, exposing the creamy-white skin of her breast, its pale pink bud already pebbled and aching. He lowered his head and sucked on it, teasing it to a harder peak. When he bit down on it gently,

Tina let out a gasp and tilted her hips into his hand, urging him to touch her inside her most intimate place.

He pushed her bra down farther, and moved to the other breast, kissing it slowly before letting his tongue run all the way down its sloping curve. Ever so lightly, he kissed the underside. Tina nearly jumped, shocked at the amount of pleasure it gave her. As he continued to kiss her there, Tina felt his other hand push aside the lacy material of her underwear and stroke the smooth lips between her thighs. He traced a circle around her entire mound, building her up until he finally touched her between her lips, running his finger up and down her cleft before settling on her clit. He rubbed it with small, fast circular motions, making it swell and pulse with intense pleasure. Tina thrust her hips faster over him, tilting her head back. Ethan lifted his head to kiss her neck before he slipped his middle finger inside her, his thumb, slick with wetness, still rubbing her clit.

She clenched her muscles around his finger. He curved it into a "come hither" gesture, hitting her g-spot with every stroke. She could hardly breathe, the double stimulation almost too much for her. Her climax built up so quickly, so intensely, that when she peaked, she screamed, digging her nails into Ethan's chest. After she came, she bent her head down into the crook of his shoulder, trying to catch her breath. No one had ever made her come that quickly before. If his foreplay was an indication, the rest of her night with Ethan would be incredible.

She leaned back, her legs still spread on either side of his lap. When she looked up at him, he brought the hand that was inside of her to his lips and, without breaking eye contact, licked his middle finger. "You taste so good."

Tina felt light-headed. Was this real or was this a dream? The man was a stone cold hottie *and* knew how to push all the right buttons. All while, she noticed right then, fully clothed. They hadn't even gotten to the good part yet. She kissed him, tasting herself on his tongue before rising off of him and silently leading him to her bedroom.

Tina lay down on her bed, arching her back slightly as she reached behind her to unfasten her bra. She threw it at him playfully before shimmying out of her pants, pulling her underwear down with them. Ethan still stood at the foot of the bed, his chest rising and falling faster as he drank in the sight of her.

"Come here," she purred.

He climbed onto the bed on all fours, crawling exaggeratingly slow, smirking, until Tina grabbed him and pulled him on top of her. He kissed her, sucking gently on her tongue when it swirled into his mouth. He dragged his mouth down her neck, licking straight down from the hollow of her throat to her stomach before he settled in between her legs. She parted her knees wider, splaying herself open for him.

The instant she felt his tongue on her, she had to stop herself from crying out. He licked the length of her slowly, in long strokes. The muscles on the inside of her legs were shaking, and when his lips pursed around the sensitive nub of flesh at the top, she almost jumped off the bed. His tongue swirled around and around her core, now glistening even more from her wetness and his mouth, before he brought his lips to her clit again and continued sucking, harder this time. Her pussy was now even wetter, aching with an incredible need. His tongue felt amazing, but it was only a taste of what she wanted most.

"I need you inside me," she said, barely able to find her voice.

Ethan lifted his head from between her legs and looked up at her. He kissed her there one last time then slid down to the end of the bed and stood up. He licked the corner of his mouth before he began to strip. He slid the thick black suspenders of his uniform off his shoulders until they hung limply on either side of his hips before removing his shirt. For a flicker of a second, a grimace flashed across his face as he pulled the white T-shirt up and over his head. Tina knew a zing of pain must have radiated in his shoulder, but it didn't stop him. He slowly lowered the thick yellow pants of his uniform to the floor and stepped out of them. Though she could barely think straight, she took a minute to admire him. She had to admit he was breathtaking. His body, obviously chiseled from every physical encounter he faced in his daily job, was pure muscle: from his solid, powerfully built legs to washboard abs to his perfectly defined chest. Every inch of his body was rock solid…and, to Tina's delight, the pronounced outline in his boxer-briefs indicated that also included the one *particular* part of his anatomy that mattered the most.

"Are you ready for me?" he asked softly.

Tina sat up and touched the lines of Ethan's obliques,

letting her finger run down each of them before slipping her index finger into his waistband and pulling his boxers down. She gasped. He was big.

Strike that, Tina thought. He is *enormous*.

"Yes," she gasped.

Ethan took both of Tina's hands in his and leaned into her until she was laying flat on the bed, pinning both of her wrists on either side of her head. She loved the feeling of him on top of her, the heaviness of his muscular physique against her delicate frame. He was assertive, but gentle at the same time. Using his knee, he gently pushed her legs farther apart to accommodate his massive body settling between them. She felt the amazing pressure of his erection on her thigh.

"You have to say 'pretty please,'" he teased, a wicked glint in his eye.

She lifted her shoulders off the bed just enough so that she could kiss him. "Please," she murmured against his lips.

At first, he merely let the tip of his cock brush up and down the length of her, rubbing it a few times over her clit. The feel of him against her was exquisite. But when he shifted his weight forward and entered her, it was another feeling altogether—one that stole her breath away. His thickness filled her so completely she wasn't sure her body would be able to accommodate the breadth of him. Ethan must've sensed this in her. He released her wrists. "You okay?"

Tina could barely speak, only nodding in response. She

wrapped her arms around him, her fingertips trailing down the length of his back before settling on his ass. She pulled him closer, pushing him deeper inside of her. Ethan's hips moved against her grasp as he pulled himself almost all the way out of her before surging in again. The feeling was so intense Tina had to shut her eyes with every pump. It seemed like every time he surged into her, she climaxed with every stroke. It was beyond belief, almost mystical.

"Is it all right if I go a little faster?" he asked.

"Oh, please, yes," she begged.

Gradually, Ethan upped his speed, exploring her deeper and deeper. She screamed his name with every plunge, their bodies writhing in unison. Soon he was bucking into her with wild abandon, but her hips moved in rhythm with his, urging him on until they came together, a climax so powerful it seemed to rattle the walls.

Chapter Five

Tina was in a daze. More than that, she was stunned. It was the same reaction every woman he'd slept with before had, but he usually never felt any connection to it. But this time a swell of pride rose within him for pleasuring her so thoroughly. It felt good to see her happy.

Ethan fell back on a pillow, his arm folded behind his head. The deed was done, the demon part of him completely satiated. The next night he'd do the same, and the night after that, and the night after that. But as he looked over at Tina, her skin absolutely glowing, contentment practically shining through every cell of her, he found himself silently hoping that that wasn't the case.

"That," she said with a breath, "was unreal. You are—" She wheezed, taking another gulp of air. "Wow." She curled up into the crook of his arm and sighed. One of her hands rested lightly on his torso, her long fingers lazily twirling the dusting of dark hair just above his belly button. He found himself absentmindedly rubbing the small of her back.

Ethan had never cuddled before, and the feel of a woman's naked body against him in repose was a new sensation. It wasn't turning him on—not to say that *she* wasn't—it was just...different. It was surprisingly comfortable. And he was finding that he kind of liked it.

"You're not winded," Tina noticed.

"One of the perks of being a Lust," he shrugged. But it didn't outweigh the downfalls, he thought bitterly to himself.

"Does that mean we can go again?" she asked, her eyes filling with desire. When she looked at him like that, he wished they could just stay like that forever. But after ten years of this lifestyle, he knew what would come next. Having been forced to live like this for so long, he had been finding it was becoming easier and easier. Yet, as her green eyes bore into his, the part that was usually the easiest had suddenly become hard: leaving.

"I wish we could but, babe, you're exhausted," Ethan observed.

"No, I'm not! I'm just—" She stifled a yawn. "Okay, I'm a *little* exhausted. But I've had a long week. Trust me, if I could go again, I would." She gave him a small smile that hit him to the core. "You're incredible."

And so are you, he thought to himself. *But I have to get out of here.*

"You're allowed to be sleepy." He looked over at the bedside clock. "It's almost three."

"Oh god, I have to be at work in two hours," she groaned, covering her eyes with her hand.

"All the more reason for me to just let you sleep then," Ethan said as he tried to smoothly shift his weight from under her. "I don't want to bother you."

Tina's hand gently squeezed his shoulder. "You don't have to leave. We can get some rest together."

"I snore like a banshee," he lied.

Tina laughed. "Then we don't have to sleep. We can just relax right here." The look she gave him stirred a wild desire within him. "I quite like having your arms around me."

With that, he couldn't say no to her. While it was against all of his better judgment, if she wanted him to stay, he was going to stay. *Just this once*, he told himself. He let arms drape over her once again.

"I like it, too," he murmured, his lips grazing the top of her head.

She sighed against him and he shivered slightly as her exhalation tickled his bare chest. He looked down at the rumpled, pale blue bedspread, then lifted his head to survey the room around him. A small wooden nightstand on his left, one bookshelf with three toppled books, her modest collection of clothes peaking out from the large closet's slightly ajar door. He realized that he had never taken the time to notice his surroundings during his past conquests. Tina's bedroom, while fairly barren, was cozy.

"It's a nice place you've got here," he commented kindly.

"You don't have to be polite," she yawned against him. "I know it's a little sparse."

"But it *is* nice. A lot of room. I like it," Ethan said earnestly. "I just noticed you don't have a lot of decorations...." His gaze wandered to an empty row of picture frames sitting on the sill of her window.

"You mean I don't own a lot of stuff," Tina corrected.

That was exactly what he'd meant, but he didn't want to hurt her feelings.

"Well, growing up, I bounced around a bunch of...*modest*...homes. I learned to never carry a lot of things with me because I was so used to constantly packing up, never sure where I was going next. I've never lived in a place this big in my entire life," she explained.

"Army brat?" Ethan guessed.

Tina yawned again and it her next words breathy and an octave higher. "Foster care. My mom died when I was born. Never knew my dad."

A pang of sympathy made Ethan's gut clench. He couldn't imagine what that must've been like, but he knew exactly what it was like to be without parents. But he had at least known his for a little while before they were...gone.

"How long have you been on your own?" he asked quietly.

"You get kicked out of the program when you're eighteen. Went to Kent Community while working a couple of jobs. Graduated last year and moved here."

Ethan cleared his throat. "I've been on my own for a while, too."

Tina tilted her head up to look at him. "Yeah?" There was a sense of tenderness in her gaze.

This whole talking afterwards thing felt weird to Ethan. But something told him he could confide in her. "You know that development we went to last night? I used to live there with my parents. Before the accident."

Tina paused and Ethan knew she was wondering how to phrase the inevitable next question. "What, if you don't mind me asking..."

"They were murdered. Someone set fire to our house." Even after all this time, saying the words still triggered a dull ache in his chest. His parents, the two most wonderful people in the world, disappeared forever when he was just a teenager.

He felt her shudder against him. "I'm so sorry."

Ethan remembered the house in all its glory: the exquisite stained glass windows on the second floor, the white wicker swinging chair on the porch, the brass knocker on the front door that resembled a stoic lion. Before tonight, it was the only house in Mezza Estates to ever burn down. He frowned.

"Did they ever catch who did it?" Tina asked.

"It was my father's best friend, a Gluttony. After it happened, he was run out of town and no one saw him ever again. His actions shocked the demon community—they never thought he would go to that extreme."

Tina looked at him with disbelief. "That's terrible. Why would his friend do that?"

"Because my father was a demon and my mother was an angel." Bile rose in his throat at the reminder of how close-minded demons used to be.

"An angel?" Tina wondered aloud. "They really exist? I thought they were just a myth."

"Oh, they exist. But they are very rare. Most of them are healers. At birth, they are marked with a strip of platinum blonde hair near their temple so that people know they could go to them whenever they are in danger."

Tina shook her head. "Why would his friend do that to him?"

Ethan sighed. "It seems ridiculous now, with demons, angels and humans living peacefully yet fairly separately among each other, but in my parents' generation there was a hatred toward mixed marriages in the demon community. My father's best friend spearheaded this movement, this discrimination. What would happen to the demon community if there were people with mixed blood out there? His platform was that we had to preserve the traditions and values we uphold."

"And what are they?" Tina asked, genuinely interested. "The traditions."

"Demons were stigmatized for so long, that the darkness we bring to the world is bad, is wrong. But we were created to balance the dark and light in the world, to provide a yin to the yang in life. Angel blood would lighten our darkness. Many demons take this role very seriously, but some took it too far, becoming corrupt, taking pleasure in the pain they bring humans. They ruined it for others, like me, who just try fulfill their duty, never taking advantage."

"So your father's best friend was one of the bad ones?"

"Yes. And at first my father agreed with his friend. But

then he met my mother and fell hard for her, and his mind changed about mixed relationships. He knew he'd be ostracized by his clan, so he fled with her."

"But he found them."

"It took him eighteen years to track them down. When he found out I was their child, that a half demon, half angel existed, he was enraged."

"You...were there when it happened?"

Ethan nodded.

"And you somehow escaped?"

No, he had a different punishment in mind for me. "Yes," Ethan lied. "The last time I saw them was in the basement of the hospital, the police forcing me to identify them, they were almost burned beyond recognition." Ethan swallowed as the image of his parents' charred bodies occupied his mind, their melted skin sticking to the white sheet laid over them.

"The morgue," Tina said. Then she looked up at him, her eyes widened in understanding. "And that's why you don't like hospitals. That's why you became a firefighter—to protect that development so no one would have to go through what you went through."

Ethan didn't say anything. Though Tina remained silent, he noticed a flurry of thoughts behind her eyes, that she was trying to work something out in her head. She bit her lip.

"You want to say something," Ethan prompted.

"No, I—"

"You can say it, it's okay."

"I just remembered that I kind of promised my new favorite patient that I'd get you to come to the hospital with me if I could, but I don't want to pressure you," she confessed.

"Your new favorite patient?" he asked, confused.

"That little boy you saved tonight. Danny. He really looks up to you." She averted his gaze. "But like I said, if you don't want to go…"

Danny. The mention of his name gave him chills. But as he looked at her, he knew in that moment she could ask him to do anything and he'd say yes. He was powerless against it.

"I'll go," he said. "If you promised him, I'll go."

She smiled. "Thank you. I know it'll mean a lot to him." Her body relaxed against him once again, her eyelids drooping. Before she drifted off into sleep, she said, "I'll be there for moral support if that makes you feel any better."

He smoothed her hair as he whispered, "It does."

Ethan found himself so enraptured by watching Tina as she dreamed. She was more beautiful than ever, if that was even possible. She was still in his arms, her legs intertwined with his as her head lay across his chest. He smiled to himself when he felt her take a deep breath in and sigh contentedly in her sleep. He pointed and flexed his toes, happy to feel the sluggish ache that racked all the muscles in his abdomen, the back of his thighs, his buttocks—all from their passionate lovemaking. His brain felt foggy and sluggish, too, like he'd taken a drug that calmed all the senses.

He continued to watch the rise and fall of her chest as she slept. He tilted his head down slightly and breathed in the scent of her silky chestnut hair. It smelled fruity and tropical, like sand, coconuts, pineapple. It immediately made him think of a sun-drenched island. And that's exactly how he felt when he was around her, like he was on vacation, like he didn't have a care in the world.

But that was just it—he did have cares, big ones. The curse that raged within him never took a holiday. It forced him to lead the life of the perpetual bachelor—rescuing Danny reminded him of that. There was no way he'd be able to commit to a woman—any woman, including one as perfect as this one—without the curse making sure that she suffered. He knew the rules and had learned to live with them. But that was before he met Tina, the self-reliant, incredibly sexy, sweet, wonderful Tina.

She has to mean nothing to you, he chastised himself. *Get out of here before it's too late.*

Careful not to wake her, he slowly bent his knees and twisted his torso until he could plant his feet on the hardwood floor of her bedroom. Then he wiggled his shoulder out from under her, carefully moving her head from his chest to the nearest pillow before he fully sat up. Sitting there on the edge of the bed, he stretched his arms above his head.

And then it hit him.

The welt on his shoulder. He couldn't feel it. A pang of

terror stabbed his stomach as frantically padded over to the full-length mirror that hung on the back of her closet door.

He stood with his back to the mirror and looked over his shoulder, frantically searching for the angry purple welt that had blossomed on his back the night before. When he saw it, he noticed it had faded considerably. And within the light yellow-green pigment of the now rapidly healing bruise were flesh-colored fingerprints. Her fingerprints.

His worst fear was becoming a reality. The faces of his mother and father—contorted in pain, their eyes widened in desperation as they clung to life—flashed through his head and he heard the laugh, the deep belly laughs of the man who had cursed him, the man who had murdered his parents out of ignorance and fear. Ethan doubled over, gnashing his teeth as waves of nausea washed over his body again and again. *Run, run, run*, his brain chanted. When he was finally able to stand, he gathered all his clothes and bolted out the door.

Chapter Six

When Tina woke up to her alarm an hour later, her head was pounding and her bed was cold...and empty. She tapped the clock off and bolted upright, searching the room around her. But the moment she sat up the ache in her head intensified into a sharp pain, as if a butcher knife cleaved the front of her skull in two. She blinked a few times, trying to shake the heaviness of sleep from her eyes, but her vision was blurred.

"Ethan?" she asked groggily. There was no response, no sounds of the shower running or breakfast cooking to greet her, only her headache pulsing harder in her ears.

She called his name again. Even the sound of her own speech aggravated her headache further. But her physical pain was quickly replaced with devastation when she realized that Ethan was nowhere to be found. He had slipped out sometime while she was sleeping.

Tears of embarrassment and mortification stung her

eyes. *The first time I open myself up to someone, the first time I let my guard down, and this is what it gets me?* He said he'd go to the hospital with her in the morning. He'd *promised.*

You can mess with me all you like, but don't jerk around the emotions of a five-year-old kid, she thought resentfully.

She threw on some clothes, popped double the recommended dose of aspirin and headed to the hospital. She'd gone into work under worse circumstances before; a migraine wasn't going to make her call in sick. If he wasn't going to go and see that sweet Danny, she was. Her promise to get Ethan to come with her was out of her hands. She hoped Danny would forgive her; she knew the look of disappointment on his face would be enough to send her over the edge.

She drove there in silence, replaying the night before in her mind. *Did I do something...say something...? But all she could think of was her and Ethan's naked bodies tangling in the sheets, the way he looked at her with something in his eyes that was more than desire, something deeper. The way he rubbed the small of her back as she fell asleep. What had gone wrong?*

She was still agonizing over the question when she looked at the master chart and saw that Danny wasn't in a normal room, but the ICU. Confused, she jogged to the east wing of the hospital. When she found his bed, she gasped. Gus was standing over the boy, who was out cold, as he attached an IV into the back of his tiny hand. A bag of what looked like morphine dripped silently nearby.

Tina's mind began to spin. Besides the burn, Danny had been fine when he left in the ambulance. All of his vitals were textbook, he was sitting up and talking without any problems. And now he was laid up in bed, the starchy white sheet pulled up to his chin, on pain meds. The boy, who was already small, now looked frighteningly gaunt, like he'd lost ten pounds overnight.

Gus turned around and frowned.

"What the hell happened?" Tina demanded. "Why is he like this?" She was practically hysterical, having never seen such a deep decline in a patient before.

"I'm at a loss for words myself, kiddo. He fell asleep last night and never woke up." He sighed heavily.

"But he was fine, Gus. He was alert and speaking—" Tina was interrupted by an electric tone from the intercom above the doorway.

"Nurse Diaz, please come to the nurses' station. Nurse Diaz, please report to the nurses' station," buzzed a voice thick with static.

Gus sighed impatiently. "Karen, what could be so urgent?"

"We've found another discrepancy in the schedule that you need to take a look at immediately."

"You've gotta be kidding me," Gus muttered under his breath. He turned to Tina. "Do you mind staying here for a second while I take care of this?" He gestured at the speaker.

"Of course," Tina answered.

"That's my girl," Gus replied, patting her on the shoulder once before leaving her and Danny alone. "I'll be back in a jiffy."

She was still frozen in her place. She willed her now stiffened legs to walk over to the bed. Pulling a chair up to the bed's rail, knowing that he couldn't hear her, she whispered more to herself, "What happened to you, Danny?"

The hum of machines was all that answered her. Tears welled in her eyes.

"Wake up," she pleaded into his ear. "Wake up for me. Please."

Nothing. He continued to lie there like a body in a casket.

She reached out to him, hoping her touch would will him back to life. But the moment she smoothed his hair away from his face, his eyelids fluttered. Hope surged within her chest until she saw his face twist in pain. His eyes closed tightly and he bared his teeth, grunting wildly.

The heart monitor in the corner started beeping like mad; his pulse was skyrocketing. Tina stared back in horror. "What's going—"

Tina removed her hand and, in the blink of an eye, the sense of stillness took over the room again. The beeping stopped and Danny fell gently back to sleep.

Tina looked down at her hands; they were pale and clammy. She spread her fingers wide and studied them, as if something on her skin could explain what had just happened.

When Gus entered the room again, the look of pure terror on her face stopped him dead in his tracks, causing him to block the doorway.

"What's going on?" he asked.

"I gotta go, Gus," Tina said, panicked. She made a move to walk past him. "I can't explain it, but something is just not right with me today."

He planted his feet firmly, still standing in the doorway. "Listen, Tina, I know you haven't lost a patient yet and that this may be the first time you've ever seen someone suffer. This must be hard for you, but it's—"

"I know, part of the job." Her voice was cracking. "But I—"

"That's right," Gus said, stopping her. He took one of her hands in his. "And Lord knows I've been through this plenty of times. The first time is always the hardest, I know."

"I feel like it's all my fault. That I've done something wrong."

He looked her dead in the eye. "Now you listen to me, Miss Driscoll. You're the most talented nurse on my staff, but everyone hits a wall sometimes. Sometimes it's just out of your hands, do you understand me?"

Tina sniffled. "Yes."

"Why don't you go to the waiting room, grab a cup of coffee and calm yourself down before going home? Take a rest, work this out."

Tina took a breath. "You're right, Gus." She smiled faintly. "As always."

"That's right," Gus laughed softly. "I'll see you later, okay?"

"Okay."

Tina walked down the corridor toward the waiting room, trying to steady her breath. She thought about how lucky she was to have such a supportive boss like Gus. She knew he gave her preferential treatment and she was appreciative. It came in handy on tough days like today.

But the moment she dug into the pocket of her scrubs for a rumpled dollar bill, her fleeting sense of relief crumbled. The waiting room was empty except for one person sitting in the far corner. He was there. Ethan was sitting in the waiting room, his gaze on the shiny, polished floor.

He looked agitated, his left knee bouncing up and down with nerves. She knew it must've taken a lot for him to come here. *At least he made good on his promise*, a small voice told her. The waiting room was probably the farthest he could make himself go, she thought sadly. But her pity for him didn't damper the intense blaze of anger that flickered within her. The moment she walked into the shadow he cast on the floor in front of him, he looked up.

"How nice of you to show up," Tina said.

"You're angry. You have every right to be angry—" Ethan began.

"Why did you run out on me this morning?" she asked him point-blank.

"Listen, I should've explained—"

"You're damn right you should've explained," Tina countered, raising her voice slightly. "First we share one—"

she paused, looking Ethan up and down before continuing "—*memorable* night together, we stay up half the night talking, and then the next thing I know you're making your perfect getaway as I sleep?"

"That's not what it was—I swear, I didn't mean for it to be a getaway. I just saw the welt on my shoulder and knew you were in grave danger—"

Tina shook her head. "What? What are you even talking about?"

"I need to talk to you," Ethan said, taking her hands in his and gently pulling her down to sit next to him. "You know that bruise you saw on my shoulder last night?" he asked evenly.

"Yeah…" Tina drawled, her patience wearing thin. "What about it?"

"It looks different today."

"What does that have to do with anything?" Tina asked with a helpless laugh. "That's usually how bruises work. They fade from black to purple to—"

Ethan squeezed her hands, massaging her palms with his thumbs. "No, no, it's more than that. There are fingerprints visible in the bruise. Wherever you touched me healed and the skin around stayed as it should." He pulled down the collar of his shirt, revealing his shoulder. He was right—there were her small ovals within the bruise, and they were just as smooth and pink as the rest of his back. The same size and shape of her fingerprints. "I don't feel *any* pain there anymore. None. Your touch healed me, Tina."

When she didn't answer, he asked gently, "You've never lost a patient, have you?"

"No, but I—"

"You're an exceptional nurse. You're smart, you're nurturing, you care about your job. But even the best nurse can't help everyone."

Tina didn't move a muscle. He continued.

"But there's a reason for all of that. A gift. You're an angel, Tina. You're one of the most powerful healers on the planet."

"I don't—" But Tina stopped herself. She thought to all the patients she'd ever saved, an internal Rolodex flipping in her brain. All the times her coworkers stared at her in amazement after helping a stroke victim walk again, a case of pneumonia clear up overnight, even the most destitute of drug addicts' withdrawal symptoms vanishing minutes after she soothingly rubbed their backs while they retched over the toilet. How even Gus, a man with so much more experience on the job than she had, seemed to lose more patients than he saved. Losing a patient had happened to everyone, except her. That is until, it seemed, with Danny, today.

"Listen, even I didn't think so at first. But the healing you did to my shoulder is undeniable."

"But didn't you say last night that angels have a marking?" She pinched a strand of her hair between her fingers. "I don't have anything, Ethan."

"I did. Full blood angels have a streak of white-blond hair near their temple. But then I realized something this morning. That there's a possible explanation as to why you don't…"

Tina opened her eyes wider, urging him to go on, but he was hesitating, perhaps to spare her feelings. "What is it?"

"It's because the marking is given to angels after their mother's first embrace."

"*Mother's first embrace?*" Tina asked uneasily. "Do you mean the first time a mother holds her child?"

"And when you told me you were a foster child, that your mother died in childbirth, I realized…"

"That my mother never got to hold me."

Tina's mouth went dry. Danny's words echoed in her head. *You look like my mother except for her hair. Danny!* she suddenly thought again. She couldn't be a healer.

"You're wrong," Tina said, raising her voice. "I wasn't able to heal Danny today. So you're wrong."

"What do you mean you weren't able to heal him?"

"I touched him and it seemed to make him worse." His pained face flashed in her mind and her headache came back stronger than ever.

"Oh god, it's already starting," Ethan moaned. His hands balled into fists. "You're an angel and that's why we can't be together. I'm not supposed to be with anyone, but the consequences for angels are especially more perilous. Just as you've found out today."

"What do you mean perilous? What are you talking about?" She was starting to panic.

"There's something I didn't tell you last night." He looked up at the ceiling as if debating to continue. "Something I usually don't have to tell anyone because I never stick around long enough," he added softly.

"Ethan, you're scaring me. What on earth is going on?"

The hurt on his face was undeniable, but he continued. "When my parents died, the attacker didn't spare me. He didn't kill me because he had a more torturous, more sadistic punishment in mind. He wanted to make an example out of me, he was so incensed that his best friend would have a Half Blood child. And so he cursed me, Tina. He put a curse upon me that dictates that I never fall in love with anyone."

Tina's brows knit in confusion. It seemed Ethan could barely look at her when he uttered the next sentence.

"Because if I do, it will end up killing them."

Tina felt like she was going to faint. "Killing them?"

"That's why I have such a reputation, that's why I sleep with a different girl every night. Not because I want to, but because I figured out a long time ago that it was the only loophole in the curse. It was the only way I could control my needs as a Lust and prevent me from getting attached."

Tina couldn't believe it, refused to believe it. "Ethan, this is all crazy talk. If you want to break promises, that's fine. If you don't want me around, that's fine. But please don't make up some fantasy. First you're a demon, then you tell me I'm an angel—I can't wrap my mind around any of this."

Ethan looked at her with a distinct sadness.

"You're not feeling well, are you?" he asked quietly. "You felt different this morning, right? Sick? In pain?"

Terror seized in her chest. "How do you—"

"I've feared all my life that this day would come. I'm telling you the truth."

Tina wanted to fight back, but she couldn't argue with anything Ethan was saying. It was all true, every word of it. She felt her heart sink as she considered the striking contrast of the two incredible sensations she felt in the last day—the unbelievable pleasure of being with Ethan and now the agonizing pain as her headache pounded in time with her quickening pulse. And he was telling her that these two sensations were connected, irrevocably linked. Forever.

"You're telling me your love for me will take away my powers...and ultimately kill me." Tina's voice shook. "But how is that possible? I'm already feeling pain."

Ethan looked down. "That's because I've already started falling for you."

She shut her eyes, unable to look at him another second. When she opened them, she rose from the chair, trying hard to keep her composure. She had been crushed before—it was a running theme in her life. She had learned, time again and time again, to pick herself up by her bootstraps and move on. But this was different. This was the last straw. She had been disappointed one too many times and her heart couldn't handle one more devastating blow.

As she walked away from him, she heard his voice echoing down the hall behind her.

"Tina, wait!" Ethan called out, but she couldn't bear to look back at him.

Chapter Seven

The skies had opened and it was pouring outside. Tina could barely see—her tears blurred her vision and the pounding of raindrops on her windshield didn't make it any better. *How could this have happened? I finally meet someone and it could kill me.* Her heart ached. It ached for Ethan, for Danny, for herself, for never having anyone to call her own.

By the time she got home, she was sobbing, gulping for air. She had let her guard down, opened herself up to someone and experienced the most intense pleasure of her life, and her heart was stomped to pieces. She should have known it had been too good to be true.

After entering her apartment, she immediately sunk into her couch, not bothering to close the door behind her. She laid down face-up, wrapping her arms around her face, letting her tears gather into the crook of her elbow. She forced herself to take a few deep inhalations and felt her breathing hitch, hiccupping as she tried to calm herself down. "You're n-not going to do th-this," Tina admonished herself between breaths. There was no way she could ever be with Ethan again and crying was not going to change that. She took a few more deep inhalations until her breathing finally evened.

While other people may say it was unlucky, she considered herself fortunate that she had been disappointed by people countless times over the course of her life. It taught her how to bounce back and bounce back quickly. It was the only way she got through her ever-changing childhood homes, how she got through being the new kid at schools, how she got through life. She did it all on her own and she didn't need *anybody*. Her mini pep talk, one she had told herself time and time again, suddenly strengthened her, but even as she thought it, a flicker of doubt took root in her mind.

She unwrapped her arm from around her forehead and noticed the slight slick of oil left glistening on her arm. Surveying her body—greasy hair, dirty fingernails—she realized she hadn't showered in almost forty-eight hours. The grimy feeling was definitely worsening her already soured mood. Sighing, she rose off the couch and walked to the bathroom to turn the bathtub faucet on full blast while she walked around her apartment, first plucking a celebrity gossip magazine off her coffee table, then a jar of mud mask off her bedside table, and, lastly, one—very large—bottle of red wine.

When the tub filled, Tina undressed and daintily dipped

her toes into the steaming bath, barely submerging them, and issued a small sigh. With both feet submerged, she gripped both sides of the tub as she slowly eased herself into the water, savoring the warmth as it crept up the length of her body. Every tiny hair stood up on end as her skin adjusted to the temperature. She looked down, surveying the slim body that lay under the steaming surface of the water: long and lithe as a ballerina.

Tina reached her hand up to the back of her head and undid the purple hair clip that was now uncomfortably digging into her scalp. Once released, her dark brown hair tumbled into the water beneath her, where it swirled like a mermaid's. She let her head dip below the surface for just a second, savoring the feel of the water caressing her face…the tip of her nose, her full lips, the delicate skin of her eyelids.

The moment she had seen the luxurious tub when touring the apartment—her *first* apartment, she thought with a little surge of pride—she knew it had to be hers. Growing up, she never was able to take baths. Usually the homes had multiple foster kids and time only allowed for a five-minute shower each. Even when she finally got out of the system and miraculously made it to college, her dorm room never had a bathtub. It had been a year and she could still not get over how different it was having her own place—no foster kids or coeds constantly milling around. On one hand, it was peaceful. But on the other, it was quiet, maybe too quiet—a total and utter soundlessness she had never experienced in her entire life. And now, after the apartment had been filled with the screams of ecstasy, the scent and sexual energy of Ethan less than twenty-four hours ago, she noticed the silence more than ever. She was alone. Again.

She grimaced. Not bothering to dry her hands on the towel nearby, she reached for the wine, her wet fingers causing rivulets of water to slide lazily down the glass bottle. She brought it to her lips and took a swig. If anything could erase the memories of Ethan in this apartment, alcohol had the most potential.

After returning the bottle to its place on the closed toilet lid, she picked up the magazine, her fingertips leaving dampened indentations on each page as she flipped through the latest gossip. After a flurry of bored page turning, she settled on a three-page spread of the "Sexiest Man in Hollywood" featured on the cover. The movie star was most known for playing the bad cop in a series of crooked FBI flicks and his pictures featured the shirt of his faux police uniform unbuttoned dangerously low. It was so positively cheesy, but Tina felt her breath grow shallow. Because at the sight of this bad boy in uniform, she couldn't help but be reminded of Ethan. Though she didn't want to, she immediately pictured Ethan in his fireman's garb, slowly stripping each piece off one by one.

Before she knew it, Tina's hand had dipped beneath the water while the other gently massaged her breasts, teasing each nipple to a peak. For a few moments she rubbed her clit into a tight, pulsing bud, picturing Ethan's head nestled between her thighs, his tongue lapping at her core. She continued to stroke, but knew she could not bring herself to full satisfaction this way. She needed warmth, pressure; she needed more.

Sliding her body down to the end of the tub, she bent one leg at the knee, planting her foot firmly on the porcelain beneath her. She draped the other leg over the wall of the tub, her soapy foot dripping noiselessly on the tiled bathroom floor. The maneuver was a little tricky, but she steadied herself by placing one hand behind her for support. She turned the faucet back on. After adjusting the temperature, she turned the faucet on full blast before letting her hand join the other one that was braced behind her. She was able to push her bottom a little off closer to the drain and use her upper-body strength to lift herself up so that she half balanced, half floated in the water while she lay back, spread-eagled, her knees resting on each side of the tub. A dull throb pulsed down below, anticipating what would come next.

She thought of Ethan plunging into her as she let the rushing water settle on the juncture between her legs. The sensation was intense and she tilted her hips, rocking them back and forth so that the water pressure ran up and down the length of her pussy. Slowly she rocked, letting the powerful stream of the warm water touch every inch of her sensitive flesh with incredible pressure. She tilted her behind down slightly, letting the warm stream of water settle on her clit. A few seconds was all she could take, as the pleasure built so quickly. Teasing herself, she slowly circled her hips in a clockwise motion, letting the water pulse on the inside of her right thigh, down to the bottom of her splayed legs, and straight back up to her clit. The varied sensations were almost too much to handle, and when she just couldn't take it anymore, she let the water again settle on that sensitive nub of flesh, feeling the orgasm build higher and higher, until she came with a soft moan.

It was satisfying, she had done it many times before, but after knowing the pleasure that Ethan had given her, it just couldn't compare. It merely felt like foreplay.

Trying to savor the release, she submerged the back of her head, closing her eyes. A lump rose in her throat and she furrowed her brow, trying to shake off the emotion. It was going to be a long night if she kept on thinking of what she had just lost. Huffing out a frustrated breath, she sat up in the tub and opened her eyes. Immediately she screamed.

There was Ethan, his good shoulder leaning against the door frame of her bathroom. As if he had simply materialized from her thoughts into the physical realm.

She gasped. "What're you—How did you—" She stopped herself, trying to gather her thoughts. "How long have you been standing there?"

He looked away. "You look beautiful." She detected hurt in his voice and though *she* was still hurt, his expression tugged at her heart.

"What are you doing here, Ethan?" she asked. "You said we could never work."

"I just couldn't leave you that way. I wanted to let you know that this situation absolutely destroys me."

"Is that all? Tell the truth. Are you still thinking of me like I'm thinking of you?"

"Of course. But I just wanted to say goodbye properly and make sure you understood. I have no part in this, it's just the way it is." His shoulders slumped, the lips she kissed just last night pressing together into a thin line.

Tina felt her voice rise slightly. Not from anger, but from desperation. She couldn't picture herself not kissing that mouth ever again. "So you're saying there's absolutely *no way* to break the curse? There's *no way* we can be together?" Whenever she had been told no she had found a way to overcome it. There had to be something she could do.

"The only way would be to kill the Gluttony who killed my parents. But I told you—he disappeared right after the attack and no one has seen him since. The first few years after the attack I tried, I searched, but it was useless—"

"Well now you'll have another person to help you. We'll search together. We'll hunt him down if it means that—"

"Tina, I'm begging you to understand. It's *impossible*. Please don't think that I don't wish—don't pray—that that wasn't the case." He rubbed his face with his hand. She noticed he hadn't shaved, his five o'clock shadow making him look even more rugged than when he was in uniform.

A moment of silence hung between them. He was right—there was no way to argue the point. They could not be together. Slowly, she stood up in the tub and climbed out, shivering as the coolness of the tile met the soles of her feet. After wrapping herself in a white towel, she stared him down. "You care about me. The pain I woke up with confirms that you do. And you're going to ignore the most amazing thing that has ever happened to both of us and just walk away?"

"I don't have a choice," he whispered. "I'll hurt you more. I can't bear to hurt you."

"If being able to be with you means these bouts of pain and discomfort, I'll do it. I'll soldier through. I can take care of myself." Tina was choking up again. "I'm strong."

"You *are* strong," he said gently. "But this is out of our hands."

"Everything's been out of my hands, Ethan. My whole life has been constantly filled with other people making decisions for me. And right now I want to make a decision for myself. To hell with the rest."

"Tina—" Ethan began.

"I don't care," she answered. "Right now I just want to be with you. I need to feel you next to me again. Last night just can't be the last time. It just can't."

She walked over to him and draped her arms around his neck. He stiffened. She tried to kiss him, but Ethan stopped her, wiping the tears on her face away with his thumb. Looking into his eyes, she saw the inner battle that must've been waging within him, saw him trying to work it out in his mind. She knew stopping her took a lot of will-power—that he wanted to kiss her, but knew he shouldn't. Before he could make up his mind, she pressed her mouth to his. His hands trembled as he slid them under her towel, his cold fingers jolting the bare skin of her back. She kissed him harder, pressing her hands against his chest, massaging a nipple through the fabric of his shirt.

She dove a hand in the front of his pants and grasped his shaft, which was already hard and ready for her. The delicate skin was smooth, soft like velvet, and she curled her fingers around it, pumping her hand slowly. She heard a groan of pleasure in the back of his throat and she broke the kiss. She put a finger to his lips, then lowered herself until she was kneeling in front of him.

"Don't think. Just let me do this."

She unbuttoned his fly and pulled his boxers down, revealing his massive shaft. She kissed up the length of his cock before taking all of him in her mouth. He was so big, so thick, her eyes watered when his tip touched the back of her throat. Then she pulled away painstakingly slow, her lips curled tightly around him, before sucking up his length again while her hand cupped and squeezed his sack, the inside of his leg, his lower abs, stroking, fondling. Pulling back her head, she circled her tongue around the tip a few times before sucking his foreskin in and out of her mouth. Ethan bit his lip with a moan and that turned her on more.

Suddenly, Ethan took a step back. "You're very good at that, but I want more. I want you right now."

When Tina stood up, Ethan pulled her close to him. He kissed her all over, devouring her with the fervor of a dying man with his last meal.

"After we do this, we can't ever do it again. Please tell me you understand," he asked.

She'd tell him anything if it meant one more time with him. "I understand."

With that he gently turned her around and bent her

over the back of the sink. She couldn't drop her towel fast enough.

Feeling him from behind was amazing. His hands massaged her ass, gently pulling her cheeks apart as he thrust into her again and again. He reached one hand around her waist, finding her clit. With every stroke, he pounded her harder from behind, his thighs slapping into hers with incredible force. Her ecstasy soared to new levels, her heightening orgasm peaking with an intense climax.

"Yes, yes, yes," she called each time he thrust into her.

But in the middle of her chant, her knees buckled. She felt the contents of her stomach slosh.

Ethan stopped, pulling himself out of her. "Tina?" he asked anxiously.

"I'm fine, I'm fine. Keep going. " She tried to sound convincing, but her voice was barely above a whisper as her body lowered farther to the ground, causing her to sit with her feet tucked under her.

Ethan kneeled in front of her and placed the back of his hand against her forehead. "No, you're not," he insisted. "See what's going on? It's getting worse. We can't—"

Ethan was interrupted by a loud rattling sound against the tile. It was coming from the pile of Tina's clothes on the floor. Tina shifted her weight, reached for her scrubs, pulling them over to her, and fished around the heap of fabric. Her mind running a mile a minute, she found her phone and automatically answered it. She heard a hoarse voice on the other line.

"Gus, I'm sorry but I'm—"

"Tina, you have to come to hospital right away. There's no time to explain."

"Gus, I can't do—"

"Meet me in Danny's room," he said urgently before hanging up.

Oh god, what's happening now? She turned to Ethan, bringing her hands to his face.

"We have to go. It's Danny," Tina breathed. She grabbed onto the sink and rose to standing, her legs wobbling under her.

Ethan still sat there on the floor. "Tina, you are in no condition to drive. And you won't be able to heal him." He looked away.

"Ethan, I have to make sure he's okay after what happened this morning," she pleaded. "Please help me get dressed and take me there."

Chapter Eight

The ride over to the hospital was tense. Ethan had no idea what they were going to do, the obstacles in front of them insurmountable. But for now, he would support Tina as she went over to find what was wrong with Danny. Danny, the Half Blood just like him. He had to look out for his own.

But when they entered the designated room in the ICU, the boy was nowhere to be found. The only person standing there was an incredibly tall, fat man in a pair of blood-stained scrubs, his lips pulled into a sneer as he bared his yellow teeth. His gravelly voice seemed to echo in the room. "Well, hello there, lovebirds," he greeted them cheerily.

Ethan recognized that voice. It intermingled with the screams of his parents on the night of their death as the house popped and crackled around them with flames. A wave of nausea suddenly washed over him and he knew. Though he may have changed his earthly form, there was no denying that the man standing in front of them was the man he'd thought vanished for the last ten years. The man that had had killed Anne and Matthew Phillips. The man who had cursed his and Tina's love.

It was him. Gustavo Diaz.

"Why, the last time I saw you, Ethan, you weren't but this high." Gustavo raised a hand just above his bloated stomach. "Did you really think that after spending all that time trying to find your despicable parents that I would ever let you out of my sight again?"

Tina turned her head to Gus, then to Ethan. "What's going on?" Her voice was barely a whisper. She swayed beside him and Ethan caught her elbow to keep her on her feet. He was still too stunned to speak.

"Ah, I see the curse is working just fine. I had almost lost hope that I would ever see it in action. I saw her powers backfired this afternoon, but you've weakened her even further. Good man."

Ethan growled. "You son of a bitch."

Tina fell to her knees, it suddenly dawning on her. "Is this? Is that him?"

"Why, yes, Tina," Gus confirmed. "I am certainly the man of the hour."

Fury flared deep within him and it took every modicum of restraint to not go over and attempt to beat him to a pulp. But he needed answers first. "Why are you back, Gustavo?" Ethan demanded. "Why now?"

Gus laughed maniacally. "You really are stupid, aren't you, Ethan? I never left. I've been here all this time, watching you." His eyes narrowed to slits. "Watching you night after night not succumb to my curse. Watching you out-smarting it. But then I grew tired and decided to channel my focus into something else. Torturing patients at the hospital was all great fun until *this* one came along, healing everyone she met." Gus cocked his head. "I was very angry, but then one day I realized *these two should meet.*"

Ethan's throat went dry. "You—"

"Set the fire," Gustavo said simply. "*I've* been responsible for all the sparks that've been flying around. Both literally and figuratively, that is."

"It was all a setup," Ethan whispered to himself, desperately trying to wrap his mind around everything Gus was spewing. "You knew I would respond to the call and come to my community's rescue. And then you called Tina, making her think they needed her for backup."

"Quite an ingenious plan if I do say so myself."

Ethan felt like he was going to be sick. "You knew that by bringing us together, you'd kill two birds with one stone. I'd finally become victim of your curse and ultimately destroy Tina and her powers."

"Oh, no, my boy," Gus said in a singsong voice. "Not destroy, *weaken*. I couldn't defeat her in her current state."

"Because she's too strong," Ethan spat.

Gustavo snarled. "That may be true, but not anymore. And now I'm ready to do the honors…and it's all because of you."

"You're sick," Tina breathed, her arms wrapped around her.

"You know that saying 'glutton for punishment'? Well,

I just so happen to be a glutton for other people's. Including yours."

"I won't let you," Ethan said.

"Oh, yes, you will. Need I remind you that you're nothing more than a weak, disgusting Half Blood? You will never be a match for this."

At that moment, Gus snapped his fingers and his body began to morph. His skin became a sickly green, his tongue turned black and forked, darting in and out of his mouth like a snake. Two enormous horns broke out of his skin. They were thick, the color of charcoal, and deep with ridges as they curled back and grew behind him like a ram's. His horns were like a headpiece, like armor. Then his irises went completely white, and Ethan knew that he was pure evil. The eyes were the window to the soul and Gustavo Diaz did not have one.

"Lucky for me, I don't have to wait to get angry in order to fully transform, you little Half Blood. You little disgrace."

Fuming, the transformation quickly overtook Ethan's body. Canines sharpened, skin brightening, the two points of his horns poked through the top of his head.

Gus laughed loudly until he coughed. He choked, spitting a wad of phlegm at Ethan's feet. "That's it? That's all you got, Half Blood? Absolutely pathetic."

As the two stood there staring each other down, Ethan finally faced what he knew all along: there was no way he could beat Gustavo. He didn't have nearly the powers he had. In fact, he only had half.

But he had to try. If he didn't, Tina wouldn't have a chance.

With his arm outstretched, Gustavo took a step toward Tina. Ethan tried to intervene, to create a physical barrier, but Gus backhanded him so hard he flew into the opposite wall, his body crashing into the concrete. Dust and rock fell around him, making the room fill with a cloud of white. For a moment Ethan saw double, every inch of his body hurting like hell. As he struggled to get back up, he found he barely had the strength to push himself to his knees. He shook his head, trying to focus. When the dust settled, he saw that Tina was no longer lying in the middle of the floor.

Gus had his beefy hand around her throat as he slammed her against the closed door, sliding her up until her toes left the tile. Tina's face grew paler as Gus applied increasing pressure to her throat. Then her frantic, scared expression started to dim. Her eyes drifted to close, her head bobbing limply to her shoulders.

"Say goodbye to your little girlfriend," Gustavo laughed. The same echoing laugh Ethan had heard while the demon lit fire to his parents' home, all of them still inside. The laugh Ethan had heard in his head his entire life—every night, haunting his dreams. Gustavo had stolen away any chance for Ethan to have a normal life. Any chance to not live in fear. Any chance to find a woman to love.

Something bubbled up within him and Ethan somehow found his footing. Gustavo, thinking he was dead, still had his back turned to him.

He bent his head down before running his skull into the demon's back, letting his horns pierce Gustavo anywhere they could. He howled and turned around, breaking his grasp from Tina's neck. Her limp body crumpled to the floor.

Placing both his hands on Gustavo's shoulders, he headbutted him. His horns sliced open his enemy's face and broke his nose. A putrid-smelling, thick black liquid spilled from the places Ethan had gouged him. Gustavo stumbled on his feet, bringing his hands into his face as if he was trying to put it back together. The thick sludge now dripped through his fingers, splattering onto the floor.

Unable to see, Gustavo couldn't defend himself. Ethan punched him with a powerful right hook and heard one of his massive black horns crack upon impact. The liquid gushed thickly from that puncture, too, running down, coating his arm. Gustavo screamed in agony.

"You son of a bitch," he choked out. "You son of a—"

But those were the last words Gustavo would ever say. Because when Ethan kicked him square in the middle, Gustavo fell backward, his wounds weeping heavily onto the tile. The sludge had turned as thick as tar and sizzled, searing all of Gus's skin. After the floor stopped shaking with his massive weight, Gustavo Diaz's body turned into a thick green fog and evaporated.

Epilogue

Though nearly an hour had passed since she and Ethan returned from the hospital, Tina was still thinking about Danny and his parents' faces after she healed them all. There was a look of amazement in Danny's gaze when he saw his parents awaken and scoop him up into a warm embrace, tears misting in all of their eyes. To witness the love the three of them had for each other was beautiful. A warmth filled her chest as she thought how she had helped reunite a family…and how she was currently nestled against the man who helped her do it.

They now sat groggily in the bathtub, the steam and exhaustion of the day forming a powerfully intoxicating lull. Ethan agreed with a sly smile that since he had interrupted her previously, it was only fair that he owed her a bath. Tina leaned her head back against Ethan's shoulder as he wrapped his arms around her. In his arms she felt protected, like nothing could ever hurt her ever again.

Ethan squeezed the soapy loofah over Tina's chest and neck and she groaned with pleasure.

"That feels so nice."

Ethan leaned in close to her ear. "I know something that'll feel even nicer."

Despite the heat of the water, Tina shivered. "Feeling wicked after committing an act of valor? This whole duality thing seems to have its benefits."

Ethan laughed. "Perhaps. Or perhaps I just want to love my woman without any consequences."

My woman. He had called her *my woman.* Her throat became tight with emotion. She turned her head until her lips were on his. Softly, sweetly, she kissed him, relishing the feel of them. She reached her soapy hand up to Ethan's face and rested her palm on his cheek. His two-day stubble tickled her skin and a deep sense of relief flooded over her as she realized that such a showing of love would no longer be able to hurt her. They were free.

In a flash of movement, Ethan slid out from under her and lay between her parted legs. She felt him smile against her lips.

Grasping with both hands, she tugged him gently, pulling him inside of her. She still wasn't used to the fullness, how he filled her up so completely, the wonderful pressure his manhood inside her. He wasn't like any man she'd been with ever been with before. No one could compare.

Chuckling, she threw her head back, breaking the kiss. He was a million times better than any fun she had by herself in the bath.

"What is it?" Ethan asked. She saw a flash of confusion cross his deep amber eyes.

"It's okay, it's okay," Tina assured him. "I'm just amazed at how I had almost given up hope of finding someone until I found you. You're everything I could hope for."

"And so are you," he said firmly, no trace of uncertainty in his voice. He pumped into her slowly, taking his time, savoring the slick tightness of her, no doubt. He closed his eyes dreamily and Tina almost cried out at the tenderness of it all. His hands were exploring every inch of her body, fondling her lathered breasts, massaging the sides of her hips, stroking between her legs where he entered her. Water splashed over the rim of the tub with each powerful stroke, coating the tiled floor with a thin layer of soapy water.

Gradually he increased his speed and pressure until her body sung with satisfaction, every muscle shuddering with the most powerful orgasm she had ever experienced. The orgasm only Ethan could give her. She shut her eyes tightly and screamed, bursts of light appearing on the inside of her eyelids.

Ethan crumpled into her, kissing her neck before raising his head to meet her eye. After removing himself from her, he kissed her lightly on the lips, holding the kiss for a few seconds. She had butterflies in her stomach. Every time he kissed her, it felt like the first time.

But when he turned to her now, his face lacked all humor. He was serious.

"And now for the test." Ethan's hand shook slightly as he brought his hand to his mouth. A fang peeked from behind his lips. Pricking his pointer finger with the tooth, a small droplet of blood formed on his fingertip. Tina knew what he wanted her to do and it scared her. Her gut tightened in response and she heard Ethan's breathing become ragged.

"But Gus is dead—the curse is lifted," Tina said, trying to reason. "You saw me heal Danny and his parents right before we left the hospital."

"Just to be absolutely sure," Ethan said quietly. There was a pleading look in his eye and Tina understood; after almost half a lifetime of being cursed, he needed there to be no shadow of a doubt. She hesitated.

"Do it," he implored.

Tina placed his finger in the palm of her hand and wrapped her fingers around it. She closed her eyes, hoping with everything within her that her powers were still there. That everything was fine. That she could move on with her life and the man lying with her would be able to stay by her side, take care of her, love her without any consequences. Without any reminder of the prejudice that had destroyed a family.

Tina hesitated, but when she finally opened her fist and looked down, she gasped.

In a span of seconds, Tina and Ethan watched in awe as the droplet of blood on Ethan's finger grew smaller and smaller...until it vanished. Completely.

"And how are you feeling? No pain?" Ethan whispered excitedly, hope surging in his voice. He reached to tuck a piece of hair behind her ear and let his thumb linger to caress her cheek.

Tina's eyes sparkled with relief. "Never felt better."

* * * * *

DEMON LOVE

GEORGIA TRIBELL

Georgia Tribell has been an avid reader of fiction since she learned there was more out there than the books that were assigned in school. She loves to be taken away from reality and shuttled into the future or dropped into the middle of a contemporary adventure, murder mystery and of course a romance.

She is a Texan, but you'll seldom see her in a cowboy hat or boots. She lives in the same town she grew up in with her husband, two boys and two dogs. When she's not being housekeeper, chauffeur, chef, plumber or wife, you'll find her with her laptop, typing away and ignoring the mayhem that seems to constantly surround her.

Chapter One

Kendra Morton pulled the trigger twice in quick succession on the demon-blaster she held. The first shot was a direct hit to the beast nearest her, but round number two, unfortunately, only wounded the second hellhound. The angry creature from the parallel world of Torlin was determined to destroy as much of downtown Houston as it could.

It was like this every full moon. The rips in the fabric of space and time would open, allowing access to the living, breathing demons from Torlin. Torlin demon-hunters assigned to this universe, along with those humans willing to risk their own lives, fought off the evil spirits that made their way through. The majority of the demons who crossed over tonight would return to their world before sunrise or die. The few who didn't die or return would be hunted down before the next full moon and terminated. Then the process would start over, a never-ending cycle.

Kendra raised her hand and aimed at the demon charging her. She didn't hesitate to fire. Her heart skipped a beat when the weapon misfired. She pulled the trigger again and still nothing.

Dropping the gun, she pulled the silver dagger she kept in her boot and crouched low. The creature was coming at her fast, running on its hind legs with wings spread wide and eyes of deep crimson. She'd get only one chance to send it straight to hell or she'd be pushing up daisies by sunrise. The monster roared as it spread its forearms and dived for her. For the briefest moment, the demon revealed its vulnerable spot and Kendra took advantage, shoving the dagger deep into its wicked heart.

There was a soft popping sound as the hellhound erupted into a cloud of black ash that rained down on her like dirty snow. Holding her breath, Kendra stood and brushed the powder from her clothing and hair. It was said that inhaling too much of the dust was like taking a wild LSD trip that you never returned from. She retrieved a medical mask from her coat pocket and slipped it on. The cover would stop her from inhaling any more powder while she waited for a cleanup van and crew. From another pocket, she pulled a small GPS transmitter and activated the emergency frequency.

After only a few minutes, she heard the familiar low rumble of a motorcycle and frowned. Being ashed was bad enough, but having to deal with her overbearing, but very sexy, boss was enough to make a girl want a very strong drink or a cold shower.

The bike rounded the corner and came to a stop a

good ten yards away. Enough distance so the motorcycle wouldn't become contaminated. She watched as all six foot three inches of solid maleness swung his leather-clad leg over the bike and stood. She swallowed and tried to slow her runaway heart as he took off his helmet and placed it on the seat before he stalked toward her.

Thor Kensington's black hair and onyx eyes were common to his race from Torlin. He was one of the few from that realm to make an alternate world his home and was a man of overpowering presence. He was a natural born leader, a take-charge man that others didn't dare question. He'd trained her and the other elite humans to fight the monsters that traveled from his world to this one. It was during the training course that she'd learned exactly how cold and unbending he could be. Thor had nearly worked them to death, and he gave new meaning to the term *drill sergeant*. Despite this, her heart still sped up every time he was near.

"Morton, are you okay?" Thor's deep baritone voice echoed across the empty alley.

She watched him approach and steeled her nerves. He only called them by their surnames, but a small, deeply buried part of her longed to hear him use her first name. "I got dusted, but I'm good. You need to stay back."

Thor stopped in front of her, his gaze narrowing as he looked her up and down. "I'm immune to the effects of ash, but you aren't, and it's all over you. Take off your clothes."

She blinked a couple of times, not sure she'd heard correctly. "You want me to do what?"

"Take off your clothes. And quickly." The look in his eyes was hard and unyielding.

"No." She crossed her arms over her chest and met Thor's glare.

Thor leaned down, getting closer to her face. "The cleanup wagon is held up at another site and will be a while. The poison can travel through your clothing, to your skin and straight into your system. So either you take that contaminated clothing off, or I'll strip you myself."

He was correct and she had no doubt he'd do it. "Fine. But I'm not walking around naked."

"You can wear this." He shrugged out of his black trench coat and held it out to her.

"Okay, but turn around. You can hand me the coat over your shoulder when I ask. I don't want you watching."

He studied her for a moment before he turned his back to her. She paused. For a brief moment she thought she had seen a glint of worry in his eyes and that was very un-Thor-like. She shook her head and started undressing, setting her mind on the task at hand.

She removed her long duster, kicked off her shoes and pulled down her jeans before tugging the shirt she wore over her head. She used the shirt to wipe herself down, before dropping it to the ground along with the rest of her clothing. She considered removing her bra and panties, but couldn't bring herself to do it. Looking up to ask for the coat, she found dark eyes staring down at her. Her breath caught in her lungs as her body heated under his intense gaze.

"Turn around. I'll help you slip the coat on." His voice was rougher and deeper than normal.

Her eyes dropped to his lips and not for the first time she wondered what it would be like to kiss Thor Kensington. Would he stay cool and in control? Or would he let go and enjoy the ride?

She turned her back to him and let him slip the coat up her arms. The backs of his fingers skimmed across her skin causing her breath to catch as the coat settled about her shoulders. His scent and residual body heat wrapped about her like a lover's caress.

Kendra mentally shook herself. These feelings were crazy. Thor never ever gave her any reason to believe he thought of her as anything more than a team member, a soldier to rid the world of demons. Maybe she'd inhaled more ash than she thought and it was wreaking havoc on her emotions.

Thor let his fingers brush the soft skin of Kendra's neck as he moved her long blond hair out from under the coat. He needed the physical contact to convince himself she was fine. When her alarm had sounded on his radio, pure fear had raced through him. Only now, after touching her, did his wrecked nerves begin to calm. His job here was to handpick and train those who were going to keep the demons at bay. This wasn't his first off-world assignment and he wasn't a wet-behind-the-ears rookie, but every time he was this close to Kendra, he felt like one.

Dropping his hands, he stepped back and turned the fear he'd felt into anger, something he knew how to deal with. "What the hell happened here?"

Kendra faced him, tilted her chin up and arched an eyebrow at him. It was her way of letting him know she didn't like his tone. "My blaster malfunctioned."

Good. He could handle this angry proud woman much better than the one who looked as if she wanted him to hold her. "This is the third time in two weeks you've had equipment failure."

Kendra rose up on her toes, pulled the mask from her face and waved her arms as she spoke. "No kidding. Now why don't you tell me something useful? Or do you believe the rumors about me sabotaging my own equipment? Well, let me set the record straight, I don't have a death wish."

Thor's temper spiked but he held on to it as he snatched the mask from her hand and snapped it back over her head and face. "I know you don't, because if you did, you wouldn't be on my team. Why didn't you follow procedure and pull one of your other weapons? The silver daggers are our last resort."

She stepped back away from him and wrapped the coat tighter about her body. "I thought about it, but I knew if my secondary weapon failed there wouldn't be time for anything else. I didn't have a choice, Kensington."

"I'm not sure I agree." He turned and retrieved her duster from the ground. The coats were made from a high-tech material from his world that made them lightweight in addition to helping repel demon magic, but they didn't protect from everything and they were useless against demon ash. The inside of each coat was customized to carry the preferred weapons of each hunter. He pulled Kendra's secondary weapon and pointed it at the concrete wall, released the safety and pulled the trigger.

Nothing.

He fired again.

Nothing.

His stomach rolled and he felt ill. He dropped the gun back into its pocket, and then turned to Kendra. Even in the milky moonlight, he could see her pale face. Above the mask her large blue-green eyes filled with terror. He started toward her, but at that moment the decontamination unit rounded the corner. "Don't say a word about this to anyone. Do you understand me?"

"Yes."

Her voice was soft and carried a note of uncertainty. He clenched his fist to keep from going to her and pulling her into his arms. He forced his voice to be hard when he spoke. "After they're finished with you, have Midnight drive you home. You're done for the night."

The converted motor home stopped as close to them as it could. She looked at him with sad eyes before she turned away and started walking to the unit. He watched her disappear into the motor coach and wondered what the hell he was going to do about Kendra Morton.

Kendra ate popcorn and watched as Fred Astaire and Ginger Rogers danced across the TV screen. She loved old sappy movies and their happy-ever-after endings. After all, wasn't that what everyone was looking for in this imperfect world? She sighed as Fred took Ginger into his arms and for a brief moment, the pair on the screen turned into her and Thor. It was a wonderful little fantasy to take her away from the horrifying night she'd just had.

The shrill ringing of the doorbell ended her musings. She glanced over at the clock and wondered who would be visiting at five in the morning. She stopped the movie and then put down the bowl of popcorn on the coffee table. She stood and cautiously walked to the door. With a quick look through the peephole, she spotted Thor on the other side. She ran nervous fingers through her hair and adjusted the pajama bottoms and old college sweatshirt she wore. Wishing there was time to change, but knowing there wasn't, she opened the door.

Thor stood there wearing a black turtleneck, tan trousers and black loafers. She was so used to seeing him in his hunting gear, which consisted of leather pants, T-shirt, boots and duster, all in black, that she felt she was now looking at someone she didn't know. Butterflies started to dance in her belly. "Hello."

"Sorry to bother you, but I figured you would still be up, and I wanted to see how you were doing." His eyes moved over her slowly before returning to her face.

The look he gave her felt more like a sensual caress than a health checkup. He might be here on the pretense of business, but she was sure his eyes had lingered on her unbound breasts. "I'm good. You could have found that out with a phone call."

"True, but I couldn't discuss this with you." He held out his arm.

It wasn't until then that she noticed the coat draped over his arm. Disappointment replaced the butterflies when she realized he was truly there on business. She had to stop filling her mind with pointless dreams. "Come on in. I can put on some coffee if you want."

"I'd rather have a strong drink if you don't mind."

She closed and locked the door behind him. "I've got ten-year-old scotch, some bourbon, or beer."

"Bourbon on the rocks."

"Not a problem. Have a seat, and I'll be right back."

Kendra walked as calmly as she could to the kitchen and, once she was out of sight, turned to stare in the direction of Thor. She'd known the man for over five years and worked directly with him for the past eighteen months. In that time, he'd never come by her house, not even for business. If he needed to talk he'd call. Heavens, they'd never even been to a work-related function together. It was a joke among their coworkers that you got either Kendra or Thor, as they never showed up anywhere together. She had the strangest feeling that tonight would change their lives forever. She quickly fixed his drink and returned to the living room.

He was seated at one end of her sofa with his feet propped on the ottoman in front of him. The drapes were open behind him, allowing her to see the nighttime sky. Soft music and candlelight were the only elements needed to make the scene romantic, she thought as she crossed the room. She quashed that idea as she handed him the drink and reminded herself this was business. "You look worn-out."

"I haven't slept a lot recently." He put the glass to his lips and swallowed.

She seated herself in the oversize chair across from him and tucked her feet beneath her. "So, what prompted this visit? You could have returned the coat to me at our team meeting later tonight."

His eyes were as black as the night sky behind him. "I could have, but I didn't want your guns going through the normal distribution process. The odds don't seem to be in favor of you receiving working equipment. I'm hoping to change that."

She arched an eyebrow. "After tonight, I'm certain the malfunctions aren't an accident."

He reached over and pulled the demon-blaster from her coat. "No, there was no accident. Midnight and I inspected your weapons piece by piece and found where three of them had been sabotaged. Your primary weapon had been set to allow only two shots. Whoever did this was smart. They knew it would give you a sense of security."

She glanced at the weapon then back at Thor's face. His expression sent a shiver down her spine, making her very glad she wasn't the one he was angry with. "That's the exact number of rounds I got off before it misfired. Had my backup weapon been impaired?"

Thor returned the gun to its pocket in her coat. "The firing mechanism on your backup had been disabled. You wouldn't have gotten off a single shot."

Kendra swallowed hard at the thought. "Good thing I pulled my blade."

"It's a damn good thing." Thor's voice was rough.

Dread settled in the pit of her stomach; he wasn't telling her everything. "Was anything else messed with?"

Thor took another drink, draining the glass before he answered. "The timer on all of your Particle Grenades had been reset to zero."

"If I'd used them I'd have been incinerated instantly." She sat perfectly still absorbing this new bit of information. She wrapped her arms about her midsection. Her close call with death had been a lot closer then she'd realized. "Who wants to kill me, Thor?"

"Hell if I know, and it's all I can seem to think about."

Chapter Two

Thor watched as Kendra processed the information he'd given her. She was a warrior at heart with a gift for leading people, but even these traits didn't prepare a person for being targeted by an unknown assassin. With this in mind, he'd mentally prepared himself for the possibility of hysteria, or weeping, or screaming, or any combination of the three. What he wasn't ready for was her total silence. "Morton."

Her eyes were empty when she looked over at him. "You need a refill."

She stood and he followed her with his eyes until she'd walked out of sight. He sat there for a minute and realized there was no sound indicating a drink was being poured. In fact, there was no sound coming from the other room at all. He stood and followed the path Kendra had taken only to find himself in a nice and tidy, but empty, kitchen. Well hell, he thought as he eyed the back door. It stood open and he walked toward it. He heard the slight tick of a gun's safety being released as he reached the door.

He froze and cursed his own foolishness for falling for such a two-bit trick. "I'm not the enemy."

"How can I be sure? Someone has tried to kill me three times now. That same person had access to my equipment."

He looked over his shoulder and noticed the gun she held steady in her hands. She was as cool now as she always was under pressure. "I'm going to turn around, so don't get jumpy."

He didn't speak again until he could clearly see her face and read her expression. "And you think that person is me?"

She narrowed her eyes. "You have access to all equipment. You showed up at the site tonight before anyone else and then you didn't let anyone else touch my coat. That's suspicious enough, but out of the blue you show up on my doorstep. You have never been here, not even for parties. Don't tell me you didn't come here with a purpose."

"You're right, I used bringing the coat to you as an excuse, but I couldn't stay away. I needed to see you and hear your voice, otherwise I'd go crazy tonight with worry." Thor took a deep breath and forced his eyes away from the gun. It was time he said what he should have months ago. "I've wanted you for a long time. Not as a coworker or friend, but as a lover. I know our work condition makes it impossible, but considering how I feel, the very last thing I want is you dead."

He watched as her face flushed bright red but her hand never wavered. "I'd be a fool to fall for talk like that."

Thor sighed. So much for the truth helping. "True, but

think about this. If I came here to kill you, I would have done it first thing. I wouldn't have taken the time to enjoy a drink or show you the weapons. And I sure as hell wouldn't have given you a chance to get the drop on me."

Emotions played across her face as she slowly lowered the gun. "I hope I don't die regretting this decision."

He crossed the distance between them and gently removed the gun from her hand before placing it on the kitchen counter. He brushed a strand of blond hair back from her face and looked into large turquoise eyes. Her lips were parted, making her look so damn sexy he wanted to take her to bed and not leave for days.

Instead, he let the backs of his fingers graze the soft warm skin of her neck before stepping back. "I'm going to leave before I do or say anything more that's unprofessional. See you at the office later. Bring your coat and don't let anyone else touch it."

Thor didn't stop as he made his way to the front door, afraid that if he did, he would give in to the urge clawing at his insides to take her. He'd almost made it safely out of the house when he heard her behind him.

"You do know I wouldn't mind some unprofessional behavior between us."

He closed the front door behind him and walked away. It was the hardest damn thing he'd ever done.

"Are you sure this is what you want?" Midnight asked from the other side of his desk at the United Realm Security building.

No, Kendra thought as she tried not to show her true

feelings. Midnight had the uncanny ability to read a person and to know when they were lying. And she totally sucked at telling lies. "Yes, I've given this a lot of thought and I want a transfer."

Midnight reviewed the paperwork in front of him and then looked back up at her. "I'll see what can be done, but it might take some time."

"I understand." Hearing a noise behind her, Kendra fell silent. Turning, she noticed the hard look in Thor's eyes as he stood in the office doorway. She turned back to Midnight as she stood. "I need to get ready for the briefing. Thanks for your time."

Thor didn't move from where he stood, so Kendra was forced to squeeze by him to get out the door. As she did, their bodies brushed against each other causing heat to pool in her belly.

She made her way past him without saying a word or making eye contact and headed straight to the break room for a quick cup of coffee before the meeting started. There were four team leaders in the Houston area, Midnight, Navida, Erik and, of course, Thor. All were from Torlin and all were master demon-fighters. At the evening briefing, the teams were given their area to patrol and updated reports on what was happening at other invasion sites around the world.

With the cup of steaming coffee in hand, Kendra went to her desk and opened the folder that awaited her. Each team consisted of eight people who worked to cover a ten square block area of downtown Houston. The territory didn't sound large, but when you were chasing, or being chased, by several madder-than-hell demons, it was a lot of ground to cover. As second-in-charge, it was her job to be as prepared as Thor. Which normally wasn't a problem, but tonight her mind wandered to Thor and his visit. After he'd left, she'd been unable to fall asleep until much later. She truly hoped he meant what he said, because that had spurred her into coming in early to speak with Midnight about a transfer. She'd decided to take the first step, because it was painfully obvious he wasn't going to do a darn thing but be professional.

There were other relationships between team members. Some were open about them and others kept them on the down low. The only regulation against such relationships stated that Lead Hunters could not be involved with a direct report. Even if something did happen between Thor and her, she wouldn't be held accountable, but Thor could lose his position and/or be forced to return to Torlin. Not liking either of these options, she'd come in early to request a transfer to another team.

There was a noise at the opening to her cubical, and looking up she smiled. Noah Campton, a teammate and friend was standing there. "Hey, what's up?"

"I was checking to see how you were doing after getting ashed," Campton stated as he leaned one shoulder against the opening.

"I'm good."

"Are you sure?" Campton asked with honest concern in his voice.

She smiled. He reminded her of an overly protective

brother. "Yes, I'm positive. Now, you'd better get a move on or you're going to be late to the briefing."

"Yes ma'am." Campton stood straight and gave her a little salute as he turned and walked away.

With a slight laugh and a smile, she took both the coffee and folder with her as she headed to the briefing room, also. The room was almost full so she took a seat at a table in the second row.

Erik, the fourth Torlin team leader, walked in and went directly to the front, taking charge of the briefing. The chatter in the room immediately silenced when he stepped up to the podium. Kendra did a quick scan of the room and spotted her other team members, but no Thor. She started flipping through the folder as Erik spoke, jotting down notes as he went. She jumped when a warm body slid into the chair next to her. The unmistakable aroma of soap and earthy cinnamon assaulted her senses and she knew without a doubt it was Thor.

He leaned into her as he reached across her and pulled the paperwork closer so he could see it, too. He stayed with their shoulders touching and she felt as if an electric current was flowing through her body. Beneath the table, his warm thigh pressed against hers and her heart rate sped up. She glanced to the right and saw Thor's strong profile and wondered if he felt the heat between them the way she did. From all appearances this was just another meeting to him. Then he turned his head enough that she could see his eyes. Black and silver swirled together filling his eyes with a passion that took her breath away.

The meeting ended and Thor spoke for the first time. "Stay."

She closed her folder and gathered her items as the others cleared the room. There was something in his tone she didn't like. "Is there a problem?"

Thor looked about the room before making eye contact with her. "You're going to ride shotgun with me tonight. It was decided earlier you shouldn't be out there alone."

Kendra felt anger ignite deep inside her. "You've got to be kidding. I haven't ridden shotgun since earning my first badge, and I'll be damned if I'll do it tonight."

She pushed her chair back and went to stand. Thor's hand shot out and wrapped about her arm, keeping her in place. "Let me go."

His face was nothing but hard angles. "Not until you listen to all I have to say. We all ride second seat at different times. This has nothing to do with your ability. It's purely a safety factor."

Kendra pulled her arm away from his grasp. "It's a slap in the face and you know it. It will make everyone think you don't trust me to do my job, no matter the reason. I won't let that happen."

Thor's eyes narrowed. "You ride with me or you go home until we have this situation resolved."

"Home!" She looked around to make sure no one was within listening range. "You never said anything about this when you dropped by my house earlier."

He moved slightly, blocking her view of everything but him. "The decision wasn't final until Navida, Erik, Midnight and I met a couple hours ago."

She was so angry at this turn of events that she didn't know what to think. "You can't take me off the street."

"We aren't doing that." His voice softened ever so slightly.

She stood, unable to stay seated any longer. "You might as well be, and you know it. This one move strips me of all the respect I've earned as a hunter. Especially in the eyes of the Torlin team members."

Thor stood and took a step closer, but she didn't move. There was no way she was going to give an inch. "Believe what you want, but at the team lead meeting this afternoon, the other three wanted you benched until this is cleared up. I fought to keep you working. This is the compromise."

Her anger melted away leaving only confusion. "Why did you do that?"

"I knew if we pulled you from the team, you'd feel as if we didn't trust your skills or instincts." His eyes shimmered as they transitioned from black to silver then back.

She took a deep breath as she tried to ignore the sexual tension that suddenly rose between them. "How did you know I'd feel that way?"

Thor leaned so close his breath whispered across her ear when he spoke. His chest brushed against hers causing her nipples to tighten. Her breath caught in her lungs and she froze.

"Because, I would feel the same way." He straightened and looked into her eyes. His gaze drifted down her body, then back to her face. "We hit the streets in fifteen minutes. Be ready."

She watched him walk out of the room, and finally released her breath. For a brief moment she wondered if maybe she shouldn't take the time off and then immediately dismissed the thought. She retrieved her coffee cup and papers and then headed back to the break room for another quick cup of coffee. She had the strangest feeling it was going to be a very long and tense night.

Thor waited beside his customized 1969 Dodge Charger RT Hemi. The vehicle was decked out with all the latest gadgets for demon-hunting. Normally, he didn't allow himself any extravagance while living on another world, but Earth was different. The beauty, the people and their culture filled a hole in him. He lived a simple life here on Earth. The Charger was number two on his list of things he most wanted, and it was the one luxury he allowed himself. Considering Kendra filled the number one slot and was totally off-limits, he consoled himself by purchasing the car of his dreams. Even though he enjoyed the car, it did nothing to satisfy his cravings for her.

The door to the building opened and a few hunters walked out. Kendra broke away from the small group and headed toward him. He couldn't take his eyes off her. The woman's long-legged stride, shapely body and shoulder-length blond hair fascinated him from the first moment he met her. With her, though, it went beyond the normal lust he was used to feeling for select other women. This went deeper and stirred the beast that lived inside of him, and that had him worried. He was walking a very fine line here. Those from Torlin were forbidden to release their inner creatures for any reason outside their world, which hadn't been a problem for him until he met Kendra. Now, the beast was pulling at its chain wanting out to claim its mate. He had to get himself back under control, if not they'd be taking the Charger for an entirely different type of ride tonight.

Kendra stopped in front of him. "Does the car come with the position? All you team leaders drive the best muscle cars around."

Thor opened and held the passenger door for her. "There is nothing like this where we come from. So it's a novelty for us and we can't seem to resist the speed and power."

She laughed and her face lit up. "Well, don't feel bad. Only a crazy person would turn down a car like this."

Closing the door, he went around and climbed into the driver's seat. Kendra's scent, a mix of lavender and spice, filled the small space. It called to him like pollen to a bee. He started the car and pulled from the garage and into the last few minutes of daylight.

"Growing up, this used to be my favorite time of day. Now it's the saddest." Kendra stared out the window as the last few people on the streets headed for the safety of home or shelter.

Thor gripped the steering wheel hard. "How old were you when the first portal opened?"

"Thirteen." She watched as people ran inside. "We weren't always scared of the night, you know. There was a time when we would camp under the stars and enjoy the nighttime as much as the daylight hours. Now there are entire generations growing up who never spend a minute outside after dark."

"The portal between the two worlds should have never

been opened." Thor also knew without it he'd have never found her.

"No, it shouldn't have, but both of our governments should be held accountable. If they hadn't tampered with nature, the gateways would have remained closed forever."

He glanced over at her and his breath caught in his lungs at her sheer beauty. Turning his attention back to the road, he cleared his throat. "They should, but they won't be. Torlin officials were arrogant enough to think they could contain the demons and none would ever escape to your world. No one realized the beast would be able to travel through the openings. It had never happened before."

"It seems government officials are the same no matter what realm you live in." Kendra turned in her seat to face him. "Is it true your father is a demon?"

"Yes." Thor parked at the corner of Travis and Austin as the last of the evening light faded from the sky. In two more weeks there would be another full moon, a blue moon, and he would be fighting the demons coming through the gate and the one within. He was no longer sure which he feared most.

"What is he like?"

Her question was earnest and filled with honest curiosity, not the disdain that sounded in the voices of most people who knew the truth about him. "You have to understand, my father has feelings and morals which set him apart from the demons we track down and eliminate. He has managed to hang on to his humanity, where others don't. It is the emotional, rational part that allows him to stay in human form and not turn."

She checked her watch. "We still have thirty minutes before full sunset. Is it true your father can change back and forth whenever he wants?"

Thor reached across the small space and brushed his fingers across the back of her hand. Her skin was soft and warm. Here sat everything he wanted, everything he needed and exactly what he couldn't have.

He pulled his hand back and looked into her large, sensual eyes. "Those of us born of mixed blood live with the constant desire to transform. Most can go back and forth, but it's said each time you change you lose a portion of your humanity. Eventually, you don't have the desire or strength to change back to human form." She studied him and he wondered if she could see the beast that lived inside him.

"Have you ever changed?" Her voice was soft when she spoke.

Coldness ran through him at the question. He could lie, but if he told the truth then maybe she would stop looking at him with desire in her eyes. "Yes. After my mother was murdered, my father and I went after those responsible."

Kendra's eyes filled with compassion. "Why was she killed?"

His voice was rough when he spoke. "My father is demon while my mother was human. There were both demons and humans who felt they should never have married. It was the demons who took action against my family."

"So you became a hunter for revenge?"

"No, I had my revenge. I became a hunter so others would not have to suffer the way my father and I have."

Kendra gave him a heartbreaking smile as she took his

hand in hers. "Funny, we come from different worlds, but we both joined this organization for the same reason."

He knew all too well she signed up because her family had been killed by a group of demons and couldn't help but wonder if she hated the demon side of him. There were times he despised that side of himself and those moments seemed to be coming more frequently. He often thought he should return home, where people accepted demons more readily, but he didn't fit in there, either. Mixed bloods were as just as shunned there. He could simply ask her what she thought of him, but he'd rather face a hundred hellhounds than hear this one woman dash his dreams. "Time to get ready for work. I have the feeling it's going to be one bad night."

Chapter Three

Six hours later, Kendra was wondering if Thor's demon side gave him a sixth sense into how the night would turn out. The demons tonight seemed to be out in full force and meaner than ever. Currently there were half-a-dozen hunters fighting way too many demons on one city block. It was totally insane, Kendra thought as she blasted a demon back to the hell it'd come from. The weapon she held vibrated signaling it was out of ammunition. Damn, now all her guns were empty.

"Kendra! Behind you." Thor's voice was clear and strong over the ensuing battle.

She turned in time to see a two-headed winged Urgan launch two arrows at her. The first dart flew past her face, so close she felt the breeze. She wasn't so lucky with the second one—it tore through her pants and grazed the side of her leg.

Pain radiated up her leg as she sprinted down a dark

alley in an effort to ditch the Urgan chasing her. There was nothing to take cover behind, so she ran deeper. With her blasters empty, the only weapons she had left were antimatter grenades and her dagger. She knew there was no way she could use the dagger on the two-headed beast and survive. That left using the antimatter grenades, except now she was trapped in the dead end alley where she couldn't get out of range of the grenades' blast.

They'd been taught to use their Torlin combat coats as cover during their training. The grenade would literally disintegrate anything within a ten-yard radius. She'd witnessed a demonstration once before, and even though that person lived, she wasn't happy about trusting her coat with her life.

She pulled her dagger, but knew there was no way she could take the monster with it. With the other hand she retrieved an antimatter grenade as she ran deeper into the alleyway. From the time she flipped the switch, she'd have twenty seconds to take cover. Releasing the safety, she dropped the grenade and ran, counting off the seconds in her head.

"Kendra, where are you?" Thor's voice carried down the dark street.

She turned to see him round the corner behind the Urgan. Her heart hammered hard and fast in her chest at the thought of Thor being caught in the blast. "Stay back! I've activated an antimatter."

Before she'd finished her statement, Thor launched himself at the demon and raised his dagger. "Take cover!"

Squatting down, she wrapped the coat around her legs making sure it covered all of her and then pulled the extended hood over her head and down across her face. Last, she shoved her hands into the opposite sleeves and prayed it worked.

The blast nearly knocked her over and left her skin tingling and her nerve endings dancing as if she'd just overdosed on caffeine. As soon as the feeling passed, she stood on shaky legs and surveyed the empty alley. There was nothing, no trash, no Urgan and most importantly, no Thor. Her stomach rolled as she looked around the dark gloomy space. For a split second, she thought she might be ill, but then she pulled herself together and began to search.

"Thor!" Quickly she removed the small flashlight she carried and turned it on.

She searched the section of alley she was in, making sure not to rush so she didn't miss a thing. By the time she reached the intersection, she wanted to sit down and cry. Instead, she took a deep breath and continued the search. She walked about another twenty yards when her light caught a dark object lying on the ground. Letting the light move across the figure, she felt her breath catch in her chest as she recognized Thor's prone body. She ran to him, placing a trembling hand to the side of his face. "Please, please, please be okay."

He growled his response and relief washed over her. "Can you talk? How bad are you hurt?"

"Leave me." His voice was rougher and deeper than normal. He shifted his broad shoulders as if to rise and that's when she spotted the Urgan dart in his shoulder.

He turned to her and as she watched his eyes began to swirl with a mix of black and silver. Kendra froze and fought the urge to run. She reminded herself that this was Thor and not some street terrorizing demon.

"Don't move. I'll call Navida. She'll know what to do about the dart." She put her hand on his shoulder and gently tried to push him to the ground as she used her radio to call for help.

"Don't touch." Thor's arm shot out, and his hand caught her in the chest knocking her off balance. "Demon blood. Leave. Now. Kendra."

She landed on her butt, dropping both the radio and flashlight. The latter rolled away, cloaking them in darkness. "I'm not leaving you alone. You need help. Navida's on her way and will patch you up in no time. Now, just stay still until she gets here."

"Too. Late." Thor pushed up on all fours, arched his back and made a sound that turned her blood to ice water. "Run."

She watched, transfixed, as he climbed to his feet, growing larger by the second. His back was to her and before her eyes she watched as his already muscular shoulders broadened, he grew a good two feet in height and wings appeared on his back through his coat. He tossed his head back and gave a mighty roar, then swung around to face her.

Black-and-silver glowing eyes studied her as he moved closer. Kendra stared and for a few brief seconds wondered if she'd been dropped into the middle of a bad sci-fi movie. With his next step, Kendra snapped out of her trance and scrambled to her feet. She stood perfectly still as Thor slowly circled her. Without warning, he stopped behind her. She stiffened as she felt his hot breath on her ear followed by the soft scraping of a talon across the base of her neck. He moved around her and as he did, she got her first good look at him. The only thought that entered her mind was a winged gargoyle statue had come to life.

His chest rippled with muscles beneath his shirt and looked as hard as stone. She tilted her head back and saw strong chiseled features staring down at her. Black hair fell to his shoulders, making him look like a dark angel. Kendra forced her gaze to meet his and reminded herself that this was Thor, not one of the demons they tracked down and destroyed. "Thor. It's Kendra."

He growled deep in his chest and leaned toward her. Kendra forced herself to stay where she was. Somehow, she knew running would make things worse. From the other side of Thor, she heard fast approaching footsteps, followed by voices.

Thor heard them as well and turned to face the intruders. With wings spread and talons held high, he roared his disapproval at the group and took a step forward.

"Kendra! Where are you?" Midnight's voice echoed off the alley walls.

"Back here," she called as Thor took another step closer to the group.

"Get away from him, Kendra. We need a clear firing range," Midnight yelled.

"No." Without thought, she put herself between Thor and Midnight. "Don't hurt him."

Navida stood beside Midnight holding the medical kit. "That's not the Thor you know, Kendra. You need to move away from him."

"He's not a monster, either," she shouted back.

"It doesn't matter. He has to be neutralized before he hurts someone." Midnight raised his gun and aimed. "I'm ordering you to move, Kendra."

"Neutralized? As in dead?" Her voice broke at the thought, but she didn't move.

"No. We are going to tranquilize him, but we're running out of time. The dart must come out before too much of the poison enters his system." Navida's voice was filled with concern.

Kendra turned back to Thor. She wouldn't let them take him down like a wild dog. "Thor, the arrow in your shoulder must come out. Turn around."

Thor leaned toward her and growled over her shoulder at the others. She put her hand against his chest and felt the strong heartbeat beneath. He shifted and silver eyes glared down at her. His breath ruffled her hair. She reached up and brushed back the strands of hair that had fallen across his face.

"Kendra, you've got to move now." Midnight called from behind her with growing urgency.

"I'm sorry, Thor, but I've got to do this." She pushed against his shoulder and at the same time stepped to the side.

Reaching up, she grabbed the arrow shaft and pulled hard. Thor roared as it came free and swung around. His arm caught her in the stomach and sent her flying through the air. Kendra hit the ground as the unmistakable sound of gunfire filled the air. She rolled to her feet and ran to where Thor lay face down on the cold hard ground.

She dropped to her knees and glared up at the other two. "Did you have to treat him like some wild animal?"

Midnight stopped beside her. "It's better this way."

She placed a hand against Thor's forehead. "Is he okay?"

Navida knelt beside Thor and opened the medical kit. "We used a strong tranquilizing dart. He's asleep right now and will stay that way for the next several hours."

She watched as Navida injected Thor with a thick neon blue liquid. "What are you giving him?"

"An antitoxin to counteract the poison." Navida closed the medical kit.

Thor's entire body shuddered and a moan emanated from him. It broke Kendra's heart to see him hurting and to be unable to help. "What's wrong with him?"

"His body is reverting to human form, but it will be in very small increments because of the poison. By the time he's back to full human form, he'll be toxin-free."

His thrashing body stilled when she laid her hand against his cheek. "We need to get him off the ground."

"We'll take him back to my place," Midnight announced in his typical commanding manner.

"No. He's going to my place." Kendra looked up at Midnight, daring him to challenge her, which he did.

"Like hell," Midnight snapped. "He needs to be with one of us."

Kendra stood, putting herself on a more equal level with Midnight. Her insides felt like a bowl of Jell-O, but despite this, she held her ground and stood over Thor like a guardian angel. "He's going to my place. It's closer than yours, end of story. Now, get us some transportation."

Midnight opened his mouth to speak, but Navida beat him to the punch. "I wouldn't argue with her if I were you."

Chapter Four

Changing from human form to demon and back again was like being ripped apart and flung back together. It left one unsettled and disoriented at best. Thor lay on his side with his eyes closed. He'd started waking up slowly a while back, and knew he was in a soft warm bed that wasn't his. Even though he was back in human form, his demon senses were still running hot, making him supersensitive to light, sound and smell. He was in Kendra's bed; he could tell by the subtle scent of lavender and woman that was uniquely her. Warmth radiated from beside him. Reaching across the bed, his fingers grazed bare skin. He cracked open his eyes to see large worried ones staring back at him.

Kendra reached out and ran her fingers down his cheek and across his lips. "How are you feeling?"

"Like I've been slammed by a train and dragged behind it for a hundred miles or so." He took her hand in his and put his lips to her wrist. The feel of her skin and the subtle scent of her desire were a balm to his shattered and lost soul.

Then memories of what happened flashed through his mind like a movie in fast-forward. He looked up at her beautiful face and felt fear unfurl in his belly. "I was afraid I was going to kill you after I changed."

She laughed and it was low and sexy. "I had nothing to worry about. You never did anything threatening."

Thor frowned at her. "This isn't a game. You touched my blood as I was changing. It could have killed you."

"Navida gave me some pills to take and said I'd be fine. Stop worrying so much." She smiled at him as she tugged her hand free. "Why don't you grab a quick shower while I fix us something to eat? Erik dropped off some items for you. It's all on the bathroom counter."

Thor snagged her hand before she could stand. "This conversation isn't over."

She tugged her hand free. "I know."

He watched as Kendra walked from the room and tried to decipher the woman. It was obvious, from the fact that he was here, that she cared. Tossing back the cover, he walked into a small bathroom and was immediately assaulted by the array of bath products cluttering the space. He had maybe a dozen essential items in his bathroom and they all fit neatly into the medicine cabinet.

Here everything from Q-tips to a dozen different body lotions covered the counter space. He turned on the shower to allow the water to warm and then opened the small duffel bag. He pulled out the few items Erik had gathered for him and placed them beside the sink. He found a pink towel with lace edging under the cabinet to use and couldn't help but smile at the soft feminine luxury. He'd been drawn to the warrior side of this woman, but it was her softer side that was going to be his undoing.

He stepped into the shower and immediately the hot water pelted his skin, helping to relieve some of the aches and pains he felt. The Urgan had tossed him a good two hundred yards and he'd landed with a bone-jarring thud on the concrete. It'd hurt like hell, but not nearly as much as the memory of Kendra flying through the air. Done, he rinsed and stepped out to dry off. Thor contemplated how comfortable he was here in these surroundings and with Kendra. He wasn't sure where all of this was headed, but he knew he was going to find out where it ended.

His stomach rumbled as he entered the kitchen. "I didn't realize how hungry I was until I smelled the bacon."

Kendra smiled as she put a plate on the table. "Then have a seat."

Thor sat and dived into the food. It was nice eating a meal that wasn't served in a diner or through a fast-food window. When he finished the last bite of pancake dripping in syrup, he looked up to see Kendra studying him.

She smiled. "Guess you were hungry?"

"Sorry, I wasn't very good company just then."

She shrugged. "It's okay. After what you went through and then sleeping for most of the day, I'm not surprised."

Thor took a sip of the hot coffee and savored the way it went down. He put the cup down and looked across the table. "Why am I here and not at Navida's, or Erik's, or, heaven forbid, Midnight's?"

She lifted her chin and met his gaze. "Because I told Midnight you were coming here. He wasn't happy about it, but he finally conceded. Is there a problem with that?"

The fact that she'd insisted he be brought here thrilled him on a very primitive level. It also bothered him beyond reason that she didn't seem concerned with her own safety. "Yeah, there is. I could have hurt you in the state I was in."

Kendra shook her head. "You were so out of it, you couldn't have hurt a butterfly, much less me."

Her words did nothing to diminish the tension in him. "I changed into my demon form and that's not something to be taken lightly. I'm not in total control when in demon form. Most people wouldn't want to be around when that happens."

"Well it's a good thing I'm not like most people. You didn't scare me away then, so stop trying to do it now." Kendra pushed back her chair. "Take off your shirt."

"What?" Thor eyed her as she picked up a package of bandages and a tube of cream from the counter.

"I've got to bandage the wound." She walked behind him and tapped him on the shoulder.

He pulled the shirt over his head and flinched when her soft, warm hand touched his skin.

"Sorry, didn't mean to hurt you."

"It's nothing. Don't worry." He gritted his teeth as her fingers spread the salve across his wound. The injury wasn't close to life threatening now, but he wasn't so sure her touch wasn't. He mentally counted to ten in hopes of keeping his lust in check. She leaned in closer and the subtle scent of shampoo, body wash and woman was enough to disintegrate his willpower. He turned and captured her wrist in his hand. With a single tug she landed in his lap. She gave a startled yelp that he cut off by capturing her mouth with his.

For the briefest moment, he felt as if he was dreaming and then her arms went aroundhis neck, pressing their bodies closer. His breathing stopped and lights exploded behind his eyelids when he felt her soft, warm breasts press up against him. He let his hands skim across her back and the flare of her hips. Her breath caught and her tongue darted into his mouth capturing his in a seductive dance that threatened to send them spiraling out of control.

Thor tightened his hold on her hips, refusing to let that happen. He wasn't going to rush this, no matter how much she tried. Releasing her hips, he captured her face between his palms and slowly regained control of the kiss. She shifted in his lap, deepening the kiss, but he refused to give her back the power she wanted. Gently, tenderly he ended the kiss, pulled back and opened his eyes.

She sighed and opened her eyes. "Why did you stop?"

He reached behind her, sliding his fingers through the silken strands of blond hair. "I've waited too long for this moment to rush it."

A sly, sexy smile spread across her lips as she leaned back and placed her palms flat against his chest. "So have I."

Her hands moved down his chest to his abs and he knew if he let her go any further, they'd never make it to the bedroom. Slipping one hand behind her back, he placed the other beneath her knees and stood. "Let's go finish this in the bedroom."

She laughed and told him to hurry as she trailed a string of kisses down the side of his neck. Thor made it to the bed, turned and sat, placing her in his lap. With one arm behind her back, he captured her face with the other and slowly lowered his mouth to hers. Their lips touched and immediately Kendra tried to rush ahead, but he refused the lure and slowed them both down.

This was a moment he'd dreamed about and now that it was coming true, he was going to savor it. With the kiss and himself under control, he pulled back and watched as she raised her heavy lids. Deep turquoise eyes met his gaze, and he knew she felt the same primitive attraction he did. "Undress for me."

For a heartbeat she didn't move and he wondered if he'd crossed some invisible line, but then slowly she stood and started a very seductive dance. He barely breathed as the last item fell to the floor and she stood before him like a Torlin nymph. He let his eyes travel over her body and felt his own respond. Reaching out, he cupped her breasts, relishing the way they filled his hands and the hard nipples pushed into his palms. He rolled the hard buds between his fingers until her breathing grew rapid and her skin flushed with desire.

Her hands spread across his chest and trailed down to the front of his pants. "I want you."

Before she could do anything, he wrapped his arms around her and fell back onto the bed. Kendra laughed as they bounced and she stretched out on top of him. He then rolled, trapping her beneath his body. He watched her eyes widen as he pushed her legs apart and settled between them. Even through the layers of clothes her heat reached him and the beast inside. The animal within pulled against its restraints.

Kendra watched the internal emotions play out across his face and feared he'd pull back from her. She laid her hand against his cheek. "I'm not afraid of you."

Thor took a deep ragged breath, "You should be, because if we continue I won't stop until I have you begging."

A sensual thrill shot through her body at his words—no man had ever pushed her to the point of begging. She watched as his eyes changed from black to silver then back again. If she didn't love the man, she was sure she'd be terrified, but she knew there was no way he would ever hurt her. She was equally certain she needed to prove that to him.

Taking his face between her two hands, she looked him in the eyes. "I'm not afraid and I never beg."

Guiding his face toward her breasts, she arched toward him. "Now, please, finish what you started."

She watched as Thor lowered his head and slowly licked her nipple. Sensations shot through her body sending a rush of warmth between her legs. Then his warm wet mouth closed over her and the heat in her stomach intensified and moved lower. He feasted on one breast, then the other as his hands roamed over her body, until she was rubbing against him like a cat in heat. Need overtook logic as the spiral inside her wound tighter and the world around her narrowed to her and Thor. Pressing her hips up, she tried to get enough contact for release but he shifted, leaving her frustrated beyond words.

"No." She clutched at him trying to pull him back to her.

He looked up and his voice was rough when he spoke. "Give yourself to me completely and everything I have is yours."

He didn't give her time to answer as he lowered his mouth to hers. She expected a hot wild kiss that would push them closer to that edge, instead she got an achingly sweet kiss that brought tears to her eyes and filled her heart to overflowing.

Breaking the kiss, she looked him in the eyes. "Please, I'm begging you, make love to me."

Thor reached up and brushed the hair from her face. "Are you sure?"

"I trust you with my heart and my life. Why wouldn't I trust you with my body?"

This time when he captured her lips, there was nothing gentle or sweet about it. No, this kiss was full of heat, passion and raw sexual desire. Thor pressed her into the bed, thrusting his bulging erection against her. Kendra responded blatantly, wantonly, as she'd promised him, with no prim reservations. He answered her by thrusting his tongue into her mouth in the same tempo that his hips moved against her.

Kendra felt herself change from a woman driven by purpose to a woman guided by desire. Reaching between them, she found the button and zipper to his jeans. It took her a moment to get them undone, but then she finally managed to get her hand inside. Thor lifted his head and froze as she wrapped her hand about his hard shaft. Brazenly, she let her hand caress the length of him, wrapped her fingers around him and stroked.

He sucked in a deep breath and then blew it out with a groan as his entire body shook above hers. She delighted in the newfound power she had over this mighty Torlin warrior and finally understood that what he'd been asking for went both ways. She watched the play of emotions across his face as she worked him with her hand.

He opened his eyes and she found herself captivated by the silver-and-black swirls. She felt as if she could lose herself in them. "I need you in me."

A wicked smile spread across his lips. "Then you'll have to let go of me."

She laughed as she did as he said. He stood and she watched as he removed his pants. He didn't move as her eyes traveled over him, taking in his gorgeous male form. Her hands itched to touch him.

"Do I please you?" His voice was filled with desire.

Kendra let her eyes travel back up his body and stopped when they met his. "You more than please me, but I want a closer look."

"There will be time for that later." He moved back to the bed, stretching out over her until his erection pushed against her.

Her breath caught as he captured her lips with his and slowly entered her, inch by incredible inch. Every cell in her body felt as if it expanded with a sensual need that quickly turned into a craving. The feeling was exquisite, bringing her body to life like she'd never felt it before. At the same time, it wasn't enough; she wanted all of him. Wrapping her legs around him, she tilted her hips and tried to pull him deeper. He stopped moving altogether and ended the kiss.

The tension in her was maddening, unlike anything she'd ever experienced. Her body moved beneath his, trying to satisfy the desire that burned through her.

Thor hissed through clenched teeth. "I'm not rushing."

She rubbed her hard nipples against his chest and felt him grow harder. "I wish you would."

"I won't, but I'll give you this." He pushed all the way in.

Kendra's world shattered into a million pieces as her body awoke to a pleasure she didn't know existed. Despite that, her body knew what it wanted, no demanded, and just how to get it. Her body clenched Thor's, commanding him to follow her.

Thor held on to his control by a hair as Kendra shouted her release beneath him. He kept his eyes open and watched as gratification took her away and gave her new life. The sounds she made, the way her body moved with his and then tightened around him were now his to control, nourish and protect. Never had he felt such responsibility; never had he felt such satisfaction at giving pleasure to another.

He pulled out and drove back in with one long powerful stroke. Her eyes opened and he did it again. Her breath caught as she arched up into him. Thor felt the final threads of his control start to shred as he shifted, capturing her legs behind her knees with his arms. Moving so she was fully open to him, he began a rhythmic movement increasing the speed and force of each thrust. His self-control took a beating but he held on until her nails were biting into his hips, demanding and begging for more. Then, and only then, he released the reins to his inner beast and gave her everything he had.

Kendra smiled as she crossed the parking garage at work to Thor's car. A quick glance around assured her they were alone, so she added a little extra swing to her hips. She'd awoken earlier, wrapped in Thor's arms and couldn't help but wonder if she'd made a horrible mistake. Then he had come awake and neutralized each and every doubt running through her mind with an intense session of lovemaking in the shower. Even though that had been a couple of hours ago, she was still riding the high. Her heart skipped a beat to see how intently he watched her. The man was smart, handsome, honest, brave and loyal to a fault. She'd known all of this from working with him for so long, but it had taken spending hours with him to see a different side that ran much deeper than she would have otherwise thought. He went to the passenger door and opened it.

He pinned her between his large warm body and the cool steel of the car as she started to slip in. He dipped his head as if to kiss her, but he stopped short, so close she could almost taste him.

"I want you," he growled.

Kendra felt her face flush even as her body heated. "Already?"

"I wanted you again five minutes after I last had you." He cupped her cheek as he ran a thumb across her lips. "I'm not sure this need I have for you can ever be satisfied, but I'd like to stay here a lifetime or two and try."

Her heart skipped a couple of beats as he dipped his head. She placed a hand against his solid chest and clutched the front of his shirt as anticipation rocketed through her. As their lips touched, the bell on the elevator dinged and people started pouring out the doors. Thor stepped back so quickly that she was forced to release his shirt or be pulled over. She heard him mumble some very unkind words as she slipped into the car and he closed the door.

Neither spoke as he started the car and pulled out of the parking garage. Worry needled at her as they drove through the empty streets. Finally, unable to stand the silence any longer, she turned to him. "That was too close. We can't be caught in a compromising position."

The streetlights accentuated the hard planes of his face. "Don't worry. I talked to Midnight earlier about swapping teams with him."

She couldn't believe her ears. "Please tell me you didn't?"

Thor glanced over at her as he turned on Travis Street. "It's been done before, so there shouldn't be any problems."

Kendra turned to look out the front window as her mind tried to process this new information. Things were getting complicated quickly. It wasn't until they'd reached their destination and the car was turned off that she realized they'd made most of the trip in silence.

"What's wrong?" His voice was rough as he turned toward her.

She turned to face him. "I'm thinking we both made fools of ourselves."

He reached out and tucked a strand of hair behind her ear, reminding her there hadn't been time to secure it up like she normally did for work. "How, when we were both on our best professional behavior the entire meeting and there is no way anyone saw us in the parking garage? There is nothing that we did wrong this afternoon to raise a single eyebrow. Once Midnight trades teams with me, we have nothing to worry about."

She looked into his eyes. "Oh, we still might. The other night when you caught me in Midnight's office, I was asking for a transfer to his team."

Thor sighed. "And tonight, I asked him to change teams with me. No wonder he stared at me like I was crazy. If he did as we both requested..."

"We'd be right back in the same boat we're in."

Thor closed his eyes, and even in the dimming light, she could tell he was attempting to control his anger. Then he surprised her by tossing back his head and laughing. It took him several minutes to regain control, but when he finally looked at her, his face was filled with emotions she couldn't begin to understand.

He reached across the small space and pulled her across his lap. "I'll talk to Midnight and get it all cleared up. Next time, we need to discuss our plans first before we put them into motion."

Her breath caught in her lungs. "Next time?"

His lips brushed across hers. "Yeah, I'm planning on a lifetime with you. I hope that's okay?"

Her heart swelled at hearing Thor talk of a future together. Unable to put feelings into words, she reached up, took his face between her hands and kissed him with all the passion and love she felt. What started out frantic turned gentle, and was filled with a promise of more to come. She could have stayed there forever, if it wasn't for the annoying vibrating occurring between them. Reluctantly she pulled back, breaking the kiss. "You're buzzing."

"What?"

She tapped his coat. "Something is vibrating."

"Damn." The offensive item went off again and this time Thor pulled it from an inside pocket. "Sorry, I need to take this."

Kendra rested her cheek against his chest as he opened what looked like a very sleek cell phone, but was actually a CUCD, Cross-Universe Communication Device. Every Torlin on earth carried one. It was their only way to stay in touch with their home world.

Thor flipped open his CUCD and instantly the screen powered up and his father appeared. He held the machine in one hand and wrapped the other arm around Kendra, holding her tight, unable to shake the feeling something bad was going to happen. "Evening, Dad."

His father's angry voice filled the air. "Evening hell, its morning here and I wake up to a message from Midnight saying you'd been hit by an Urgan dart."

Thor knew he needed to take control of the conversation before his father got out of hand. "By the time I could call, I was fine. I didn't realize Midnight had left a message."

His father's voice rose. "That's no excuse, you..."

Thor spoke over his father. "Dad, there's someone here with me."

"You're usually alone when we talk at this time of day. Is it a coworker?"

He ground his teeth at the question. "Yes, I've got a coworker riding with me tonight."

Kendra made a disgruntled noise and it took great effort on Thor's part not to look at her.

"What was that noise?"

"My coworker clearing their throat." Thor grunted as a sharp elbow jabbed him in the ribs.

His father's eyes narrowed. "Who's there with you?"

Before he could say a word, Kendra spoke. "Kendra Morton."

His father's eyebrows only went up a fraction, but Thor knew his father recognized the name. The two of them had discussed the woman more than once. To Thor's relief, a smile appeared on his father's face. "Well, it's time for you to get to work. Thor, call me when you get home. I don't give a damn what time it is."

His father closed the connection before Thor could utter another word. With a shake of his head, he put the device back into his pocket.

"Is he always so direct?" Kendra asked as she moved back to the passenger side of the car.

"Only when he's worried. Honestly, he's easygoing ninety-nine percent of the time."

"But hold on to your hat when that one percent shows up."

Thor laughed. "More like, run for the hills."

Kendra smiled at him. "Guess that's a good thing to know. Now, we do have to get ready for work."

Thor reached out and took Kendra's hand in his. He held her gaze as he brought her hand to his lips. Slowly, he placed a kiss to the back of her wrist, felt her pulse quicken and knew if anything happened to her his demon would run free. "I have a bad feeling about tonight. Stay close."

Chapter Five

Kendra stood in the shadows of the New Horizon Bank Tower and sucked in much-needed air. They had barely finished putting on their gear when all hell broke loose around them. Thor stood next to her, breathing as heavily as she. This skirmish had only been going on for two hours, but it felt more like six. They had both already reached their endurance limits and that had her worried. "What is going on?"

"We are being herded away from the rest of the team. Now that they've accomplished that, they will try and divide us."

Kendra brushed her hair out of her eyes. "I figured that out about three blocks back. What I don't get is why?"

"There seems to be a traitor among those of us from Torlin. We leaders have known for a while that a couple of the gangs from Torlin are trying to stake a claim in this realm. It's now starting to seem as if they want a position within our ranks."

"By killing the two of us?"

"No, by killing you." Thor's voice was hard as steel. "Removing any of the team leads at this point would cause too many questions, but a second-in-command wouldn't be looked at twice."

"Especially if said person doesn't have family to question the events surrounding her death." The words came out rough, even to her own ears.

Thor turned to her and even in the dark she could sense his anger. Wrapping an arm around her waist, he pulled her to him. "I might not be family yet, but it doesn't mean I don't love you. If anything happens to you, I will find those responsible and rip them to pieces."

His voice was barely louder than a whisper, but each word rang with sincerity. Reaching up, she placed a palm against his chest. "You love me?"

He gave her a sly little smile. "After losing my mother, I never wanted the possibility of hurting like that again. Somehow, you got around my defenses and before I knew it—bam. I found myself head over heels in love with you."

His words left her temporarily speechless. When she finally found her voice again, a loud roar not far from them stopped her from saying what she wanted.

"Do you have any weapons left?" The kind, gentle man she'd seen too seldom was replaced by the well-honed demon-slayer.

"My dagger. I've gone through everything else." There was more noise from down the street and every nerve ending in her body wanted to run. She wasn't a person who scared easily, but right now, she was terrified, for both of them. There was no doubt in her mind that Thor would die protecting her and that frightened her beyond anything she'd ever faced.

Thor reached into his coat and pulled a small weapon from an inside pocket. He held it out to her. "Take it. There are still six live rounds in it. We are only four blocks from the back door of our office building. When I tell you to, run as fast as you can to the office. You'll be safe once you're inside."

Realization hit her like a cold, dirty dishcloth. "You aren't coming with me."

"No. I'm going to stay back and cover you."

Kendra shook her head. "No! I won't run away and leave you…"

Shouts from the street cut off her words. "Thor! Kendra! Where are you?"

Relief washed over her at the sound of her friend's, and teammate's, familiar voice. "We're in here, Campton."

"Damn." Thor stepped in front of her as Campton turned the corner and stopped several feet away. "I never thought it would be you, Campton."

"Campton?" Kendra's voice faltered even as Thor's words sank in. She'd known Noah Campton for the past three years, ever since he'd moved to this world. She considered the man a friend first, coworker second. Pain sliced through her at the betrayal. "Why?"

"Are you really that naive, Kendra?" Campton gave her a smug look. "Power, money—but mostly money. There's an entire world here that someone can control. It might as well be those I work for. You humans pay good money for protection from the demons who will one day permanently inhabit this world, and I want my cut."

She placed a hand against Thor's arm and felt the tension building in him, like the anger inside her as this turncoat's words sank in. "That's crazy. We'll never let them or the thugs you work for take over."

Thor's voice was hard as nails when he spoke. "You wouldn't, Kendra, but let a few high-ranking positions be filled by scum like him and the demons could virtually run free."

Campton growled and, in a flash, turned from human form to a beast that reminded Kendra of a hairy Minotaur on steroids. Thor pushed her away as he ran directly at Campton without changing.

Kendra raised her weapon and tried to get a clear shot at Campton. The man and beast were a blur of movement stopping her from firing for fear of hitting Thor. Campton was larger, meaner and stronger than Thor. Despite the differences, Thor was faster and used that to his advantage. Kendra moved toward them, knowing she was getting too close, but the man she loved was in trouble.

Not able to get a kill shot, Kendra changed her tactic and went for wounding the demon. Thor moved to the left, presenting her with an opening. Firing two quick shots, she hit the creature in the leg. Campton roared and swung one of his tree-trunk-size arms, landing a blow that sent Thor flying through the air. Steadying her aim, Kendra took a deep breath and slowly let it out. Pulling the trigger, she fired off two more quick rounds. The animal stopped and brushed the spots she'd hit as if it were brushing off specks of dirt. She fired her last two rounds and watched as the fiend lifted its head in what appeared to be laughter.

Green glowing eyes focused on her. Kendra pulled her knife and started running in the opposite direction. Even though she knew it was a waste of time, it was still better than simply waiting for death. She heard the creature closing in on her and knew time was running out.

Before she could turn and fight, she was tackled from behind, hard. The demon landed on her, knocking the wind from her lungs. The dagger flew from her hand and landed several feet away. With the beast on top of her and breathing down her neck, she twisted her body, slamming the heel of her hand up and into the creature's nose. Campton roared, rearing back as he did. Kendra scooted out from beneath the animal and started crawling toward her dagger. Stretching out her right hand, she managed to just touch the hilt with her fingers, but she couldn't grab hold of it. She pushed forward and was reaching for it again when cold fingers wrapped around her ankle and yanked her back.

She screamed as she frantically grabbed for her only weapon, but it was no use. Campton lifted her off the ground, swinging her around like a rag doll before slamming her to the hard ground. She fought off the pain as she kicked out, landing blow after blow, but to no avail. It was like she was kicking a brick wall. Campton pinned her to the ground, sitting across her chest, cutting off her air supply. Black spots floated before her eyes as she watched Campton lift his arms high, preparing to deliver a killing blow. Kendra felt herself drift into the darkness that was engulfing her and welcomed the nothingness in hopes that she wouldn't feel the pain of death.

Thor stood, shaking off the pounding he'd taken from Campton. The beast inside him was clawing to get out despite his effort to keep it inside. Kendra's scream was all it took for his demon to break its restraints. This time, as he changed, the uncontrollable mental confusion he hated and feared wasn't there. He was totally focused on saving the woman he loved. In two long strides, he blindsided Campton, sending them both rolling across the ground in a flurry of fists and snarling teeth.

The fight was brutal and bloody, but Thor had the advantage of a clear mind instead of the confused state that usually came with transition. He fought with the precision of a prizefighter, wearing down Campton until finally, Thor's next blow snapped Campton's head back with a sickening crack. The demon crumpled to the ground and immediately changed back to human form. Thor ran to Kendra, shifting back as he went.

Before he reached her, she stood and started toward him. "Thor!"

He gently pulled her into his arms and cupped her cheek with a shaky hand. "Are you okay?"

She smiled up at him. "Nothing that won't heal. And you?"

He grimaced, remembering the change he'd undergone. "I'm…"

Kendra wrapped a hand behind his neck and pulled him to her until their lips touched, cutting off his words with a kiss that was anything but timid. By the time she broke the kiss, he'd almost forgotten what he was going to say. "I changed."

Kendra reached out and caressed his face. "I know and you were spectacular. I don't care if you transform every night. I love you, and that will never change."

In that moment, the internal battle between beast and man he'd lived with since his teen years ended. For the first time in his life he felt complete and in control of the animal within. He had this woman to thank for that. Even if he had a thousand years, he could never begin to repay her, but he had a few ideas on how he might start.

He carefully held her in his arms, not wanting to let go. "I'll try not to change too often, but no matter which form I'm in, I'll always love you."

"I know." Kendra pulled his head down to hers, wondering how she'd gotten so lucky. "Now stop talking and kiss me."

He kissed her passionately as the rest of the world faded around them. The sound of approaching voices brought them back to the reality of where they were. With one last touch of her lips to his, she let go of him and together they turned to see Erik, Navida and Midnight watching them.

Kendra smiled. "I think our secret is out."

Erik threw his head back and laughed. "You two suck at keeping secrets. She's working with you now, Midnight, starting with your next rotation."

Midnight turned to them both. "Fine, but I expect her to be on time and no excuses for being late. And for God's sake, don't come to work wearing that silly grin. This is serious business."

Kendra laughed again. "I'll be on time, don't worry. As for the silly grin, I make no promises."

Thor turned to Navida. "You have any opinions?"

Navida gave a big sigh. "It's about time. I was beginning to think the two of you would never hook up. Now hurry up. We've still got work to do."

The three of them turned and walked away, leaving Kendra and Thor suddenly alone and her feeling very off balance. "This isn't going to be easy you know."

Thor pulled her into his arms. "Nothing worth having ever is. But together we can slay the demons that get in our way."

She wrapped her arms around his neck. "Together. I like the sound of that."

Her lips touched his and she knew, without any hesitation, that everything was going to be fine so long as they had each other. Reluctantly, she pulled away. "Well, we'd better get back to work."

Thor slipped an arm around her waist as they walked down the street. "I sure hope you can type fast when we get back to the office. I'm looking forward to going home."

"So am I." Kendra smiled as they turned to leave. She knew, in that moment, she was a very lucky woman. She'd managed to find something she thought she'd never have, her very own happy-ever-after with the man of her dreams.

* * * * *

A sneaky peek at next month...

NOCTURNE™

BEYOND DARKNESS...BEYOND DESIRE

My wish list for next month's titles...

In stores from 18th April 2014:

❑ Untamed Wolf — Linda O. Johnston

❑ Possessed by a Warrior — Sharon Ashwood

In stores from 2nd May 2014:

❑ Immortal Hunter — Kait Ballenger

Available at WHSmith, Tesco, Asda, Eason, Amazon and Apple

Just can't wait?

When five o'clock hits, what happens after hours...?

Feel the sizzle and anticipation of falling in love across the boardroom table with these seductive workplace romances!

Now available at
www.millsandboon.co.uk

 MILLS & BOON®
Book Club

Join the Mills & Boon Book Club

Want to read more **Nocturne**™ books?
We're offering you **1** more absolutely **FREE!**

We'll also treat you to these fabulous extras:

- **Exclusive offers and much more!**

- **FREE home delivery**

- **FREE books and gifts with our special rewards scheme**

Get your free books now!

**visit www.millsandboon.co.uk/bookclub
or call Customer Relations on 020 8288 2888**

SUBS/ONLINE/T1

Discover more romance at

www.millsandboon.co.uk

- ❤ WIN great prizes in our exclusive competitions
- ❤ BUY new titles before they hit the shops
- ❤ BROWSE new books and REVIEW your favourites
- ❤ SAVE on new books with the Mills & Boon® Bookclub™
- ❤ DISCOVER new authors

PLUS, to chat about your favourite reads, get the latest news and find special offers:

- Find us on facebook.com/millsandboon
- Follow us on twitter.com/millsandboonuk
- ❤ Sign up to our newsletter at millsandboon.co.uk

M&B_WEB